ONLY LADY PAMELA
would have startled aristocratic society by
becoming engaged to a man who was her total
opposite, and then refusing to change her
independent ways.

ONLY LADY PAMELA
would have taken a coach ride into danger
alone, and disguised herself as a lady's maid to
enter a manor filled with ruthless and
unscrupulous agents of the French.

ONLY LADY PAMELA
would have risked her honor and even life
itself in a bold gamble to save her beloved
younger brother from the consequences of his
extravagance and folly.

ONLY LADY PAMELA
would have defied the demands and mocked
the maneuvers of the most attractive peer in the
realm—even when despite herself she found
herself falling in love. . . .

"For all Regency Romance fans!"
—KIRKUS REVIEWS

Big Bestsellers from SIGNET

LADY
PAMELA

By
Clare Darcy

A SIGNET BOOK
NEW AMERICAN LIBRARY
TIMES MIRROR

Copyright © 1975 by Walker and Company

All the characters and events portrayed in this story are fictitious.

Library of Congress Catalog Card Number: 75-12192

This is an authorized reprint of a hardcover edition published by
Walker and Company. The hardcover edition was published simultaneously in Canada by Fitzhenry & Whiteside, Limited, Toronto.

SIGNET, SIGNET CLASSICS, MENTOR, PLUME AND MERIDIAN BOOKS
are published by The New American Library, Inc.,
1301 Avenue of the Americas, New York, New York 10019

First Signet Printing, January, 1977

3 4 5 6 7 8 9

PRINTED IN THE UNITED STATES OF AMERICA

One

Lady Pamela Frayne, descending the elegant Adam staircase of her grandfather's Berkeley Square town house on a February morning in a very fashionable light puce walking-dress of French merino, admirably becoming to her dark curls, wore a somewhat preoccupied expression upon her face. This was scarcely surprising, as she had just come from a consultation with the housekeeper, had an appointment with a famous Bruton Street *modiste* within the hour, and wished to consult her grandfather before she left the house upon the progress of his present attack of the gout.

People who saw Lady Pamela only in Society, one of the chief ornaments of which she had been since her come-out three years before, were used to consider her a dashing, extremely volatile, and even rather shatter-brained young lady, whose penchant for impulsive action could usually be counted upon to plunge her, if not into scandal, at least into interesting notoriety on the average of twice each Season. She had half a dozen times been rumoured on the brink of marriage with various members of her coterie of admirers, who ranged from the heir to one of the premier dukedoms in the kingdom to an immensely wealthy Spanish nobleman, the Marqués de Barrera. The latter gentleman's ardent pursuit of her had engaged the breathless interest of the *ton* for several months, only to end in disappointment both for him and for them when her betrothal had suddenly been announced to Adolphus, Lord Babcoke, a highly eligible and reliable peer some ten years her senior, whom she had known all her life.

The engagement was something of a surprise to everyone, including the prospective bridegroom, who, though he had been among Lady Pamela's admirers ever since she had been old enough to have admirers, had never seriously considered putting his fate to the touch until he had found himself, during a house party at Osterley Park, mysteriously alone with her in the tapestry room, benevolently observed by

1

the nymphs and Cupids represented in its famous Gobelins depicting *Les Amours des Dieux*. Perhaps heartened by this encouraging atmosphere, and by Lady Pamela's unexpectedly complaisant air, he had made his offer and been accepted, and if certain unkind mamas, the hearts of whose daughters' swains had for three Seasons past been falling down flat at Lady Pamela's feet, remarked rather spitefully that it was probably Lady Pamela who had decided to marry Lord Babcoke, rather than the other way round, it was nonetheless undeniable that the engaged pair were very fond of each other and that the match was an exceedingly suitable one.

To say the truth, as Lady Pamela's grandfather, Lord Nevans, always observed, she had a head on her shoulders when she chose to use it, in proof of which he was able to cite the fact that she had been holding the reins of his household with great skill and aplomb ever since the death of her mother two years before.

"And if she turns into one of those managing females," he was wont to conclude, "Babcoke will have only himself to blame, for though she has an odd kick to her gallop she's a sweet-goer, and needs only a light, steady hand on the reins"—which mode of expression Lord Babcoke, though a sporting peer himself, would have liked to deplore but did not dare, as Lord Nevans's hasty temper had been famous throughout England for forty years.

That that temper—despite his lordship's advanced age and present uncertain state of health—was still a force to be reckoned with was made obvious anew to Lady Pamela on this winter morning as she reached the foot of the staircase. As she did so, the door of the breakfast-parlour at the back of the hall was suddenly opened and his lordship's secretary came rapidly out—so rapidly, in fact, that Lady Pamela thought he might have been shot from a cannon except that he did not go far enough. She stopped and looked at him, between compassion and amusement.

"You poor man," she said. "Is he at it again? What is it this time? Politics? The war? Or is it only that his gout is particularly troublesome this morning?"

Young Mr. Underdown, who was the latest in a long line of secretaries whose feet Lord Nevans, to do him justice, had always seen set firmly upon the political or diplomatic ladder

2

when he let them go, mopped his brow and said he really didn't know.

"I think it's all of them, to tell the truth, Lady Pamela," he said. "*And* your brother, if you don't think it impertinent of me to say so—"

"Oh, dear!" interpolated Lady Pamela, for her younger brother and their grandfather's heir, Viscount Wynstanley, was of an age and temperament where his actions were constantly arousing disapproval in Lord Nevans's breast.

"—*and* something missing from the red Foreign Office box that was left lying on the hall table yesterday," Mr. Underdown concluded unhappily. "I daresay it is my fault. Things of that sort *should* be kept locked up."

"Fiddle!" said Lady Pamela kindly. "That is, I don't mean they shouldn't be, of course, but how you are to manage it when Grandpapa *will* keep the keys himself and send Stopford to fetch papers for him in the middle of the night when he can't sleep, and then forgets where he has put them in the morning, I cannot imagine."

Mr. Underdown, who, like every other secretary Lord Nevans had employed from the time Lady Pamela had been fifteen, had fallen in love with her elegant, tip-tilted nose, winged black brows, and dark-fringed grey eyes, which made up an enchanting ensemble that looked rather as if it had been sketched by the pen of a dashing artist, appeared gratified by her ladyship's making excuses for his negligence. But he repeated with no alteration in his careworn air that it was all his fault and he would have to make enquiries and hurried off.

"He really *is* rather a lamb, and *so* conscientious, and it is perfectly wicked of you to rake him down for something that is probably quite your own fault, Grandpapa," said Lady Pamela, entering the breakfast-parlour and advancing to kiss Lord Nevans upon the top of his massive, white-haired head.

That famous political peer, who was looking very uncomfortable with his gouty leg propped on a footstool beside the Pembroke table from which he was endeavouring to eat his breakfast, glowered at her.

"Damned young puppy!" he said. "That is, if it's Underdown you mean. And no more use to me than if he *was* one, and not weaned yet!" He looked from under his beetling white brows at Lady Pamela, who had seated herself opposite him and was selecting buttered eggs and toast from the dishes being offered her by Hadsell, the butler. When Hadsell had left the room he continued abruptly, "Where's your brother, eh? Do *you* know where he's gone?"

"Wyn?" Lady Pamela looked up in slight surprise. "Is he up and gone out at this hour? I daresay it is a prizefight then, or something of the sort, for you know nothing else will get him out of bed before noon."

"Yes, I do know," said Lord Nevans grimly. "But it wasn't a matter this time of getting him *from* his bed. He wasn't *in* it last night. *Nor*," he added, as Lady Pamela merely looked somewhat amused, though endeavouring to appear shocked to uphold the proprieties, "has he come in this morning. And there's a document missing from my despatch-box—"

"Grandpapa!" said Lady Pamela, now looking shocked in good earnest. "You *can't* think that Wyn—"

"Oh, can't I!" said Lord Nevans, his eyes kindling fiercely and his right hand coming down upon the table in a blow that made the dishes jump. "Damme, you know as well as I do, girl, that that young jackanapes is in Dun territory as deep as he can go, for all I bailed him out of the hands of the cent-percenters no longer ago than last November. And that paper has to do with Wellington's future plans; it's worth any amount he likes to name, if he's willing to see it get into French hands!"

Lady Pamela, her face expressing incredulity and indignation in equal parts, said that if anyone else had hinted such a thing about Wyn she would have his liver and lights, which caused her grandfather to say severely that she was as bad as he was, but obviously not really meaning it.

"Yes, I am," agreed Lady Pamela unexpectedly. "In fact, I am worse, because I was traitorous enough to take your meaning at once when you said that about Wyn. Grandpapa, you know he never would or could do anything *dishonourable!* He may be forever kicking up larks all over town, and getting into company with a set of people he would never dream of asking to his home, but it is the outside of enough for you to be believing that he would tamper with your official papers!"

"Then who else has done it?" Lord Nevans asked heavily. The angry flush faded from his leonine face, to be replaced by an expression of gnawing anxiety. "Underdown will have it that I have merely misplaced the memorandum, but the lock on that box has been prised, Pamela. I haven't shown it to Underdown or to anyone else; it's my hope that the shameless young cub was in his cups when he did it, and will replace the memorandum when he comes to his senses. But his not having put in an appearance this morning looks bad—very bad, indeed. You know the sort of men he has been associating with these past months. A set of rascally scrubs, rake-shames and Captain Sharps every one of them, though some, like Cedric Mansell, bear honourable names."

At the mention of the Honourable Cedric Mansell, the highly notorious second son of the Earl of Whiston, Lady Pamela's brows drew together in a sudden frown. She was not herself acquainted with the Honourable Cedric, for, in spite of his excellent personal gifts and urbane manners, he had not for some years been *persona grata* in the saloons of hostesses in the first rank of Society, and indeed was himself known to prefer the quite unmentionable haunts frequented by members of the infamous Beggars' Club. An unpleasant incident at White's involving marked cards, which had been glossed over when Lord Whiston—or, rather, Lady Whiston, who was a considerable heiress and held the purse-strings in the family—had come down handsomely with a large sum of money upon the Honourable Cedric's behalf, had been only the first of several unpalatable scandals that had attached themselves to his name. But in spite of this Lady Pamela was aware that he had a certain influence over some of the wilder of the younger men, who were flattered by the attentions of what they admiringly called an out-and-out cock of the game, up to every rig and row in town.

A few words let fall by her young brother upon the occasion of their last meeting the day before recurred uncomfortably to Lady Pamela's mind at this point. She had been descending the stairs, on her way to a rout-party at Lady Maytham's, when he had come dashing up them in his usual impetuous way, demanding the time of her as if his very life— or at least the outcome of the latest harebrained adventure in which he was involved—depended upon it.

"It is just on ten, I believe," she had replied, upon which the Viscount had said with an air of great relief that that was all right then, as his appointment was not till half after, and there was plenty of time, after all.

"Daffy Club? Or Cribb's Parlour?" Lady Pamela had

enquired teasingly, fastening the last buttons of her long French kid gloves as she spoke, for Lord Babcoke was below and she was making a praiseworthy attempt that week, knowing how he disliked being kept waiting, to be on time for all her engagements, to the extent of having escaped from the hands of her dresser, Pletcher, before that austere and fashionable female had succeeded in putting the final touches upon her toilette.

But somewhat to her surprise Lord Wynstanley, instead of laughing or impishly confessing to a much less respectable engagement for the evening, had suddenly looked serious and said no, dash it all, it was a far more important matter than that.

"I can't tell you about it now," he had said, with the portentous air that a young man of nineteen may sometimes put on to impress an elder sister, though he should know better than to try. "But Ceddie Mansell means to put me in a way to make my fortune, so you can see that it's vital I meet him tonight. If I miss him, I shall have to go down to Whiston Castle."

And he had run on up the stairs, leaving the words of distaste she had meant to utter on the subject of the Honourable Cedric and all his works unspoken upon her lips. They would not, at any rate, she was quite sure, have had the least effect upon her young brother, who was very proud of his new-found status as a boon companion to a top-of-the-trees sporting figure like Cedric Mansell. And in any event, she had reflected, if he was going to Whiston Castle there was not much harm he could get into there, for, although she was herself unacquainted with Lord and Lady Whiston, she understood from Lord Wynstanley, who occasionally visited the Earl's ancient country seat in Wiltshire with the Honourable Cedric, that his friend's papa and mama led a staid and entirely exemplary existence there.

She had therefore attached little importance to the incident at the time, thinking—if she had thought about it at all—that her brother's conviction that the Honourable Cedric would be able to put him in a position to lay his hands upon a considerable and no doubt sorely needed sum of money merely had reference to a cockfight or a badger-baiting for which his friend was about to give him a sure thing. But her grandfather's words had suddenly put the whole matter in quite a different light. She could not believe that Wyn, who had been begging Lord Nevans ever since he had been seventeen to buy him a pair of colours and allow him to join Lord Wellington's army and fight the French in the Peninsula, could have been a party to what his grandfather obviously believed was an attempt by Bonapartist agents to obtain a document of such high value to them that they would be willing to pay an extremely large sum for it. But she could well credit the fact that Cedric Mansell might be, and it was not beyond the bounds of possibility that he had either duped Wyn into helping him to obtain the memorandum, or—what was even more likely—that he had some hold over young Lord Wynstanley that had enabled him to force him by threats to deliver the document over to him. If he had been pressing Wyn over gaming debts, for example, Wyn might have been driven, in desperation, to give him the document, not realising its importance, and considering anything better than being obliged to apply once more to his grandfather to make good his losses at play.

Certainly, if the memorandum had indeed disappeared, her young brother was the only person in the house who had had both the motive and the opportunity to lay his hands upon it. Mr. Underdown she could dismiss at once as a possible suspect: he was far too young and ingenuous to have been feigning the deep concern he had expressed to her over the paper's loss. And the servants had all been in her grandfather's employ for years, to say nothing of its being highly improbable that any of them would have the least idea that this particular paper had been of any special value.

She finished her breakfast in an abstracted silence and went off upstairs to her dressing room. Here she found Pletcher engaged in laying out a dark puce pelisse and chinchilla muff for her excursion to Bruton Street, which she had by this time altogether forgotten. Of one thing she was quite certain now; she was *not* going to Bruton Street until she had got to the bottom of this matter.

"Pletcher," she said suddenly, with one of her swallow-flights of impulse that made her the despair of all sober-minded, straight-thinking people, Lord Babcoke among them, "I want to speak to Brill. Will you ask him to come here at once?"

Pletcher looked as if she were about to say that it was not

her duty to demean herself by running errands, but she had a very good place with Lady Pamela and knew it, so she contented herself with putting on a martyred look and rustled out of the room. In a few moments Brill, Lord Wynstanley's valet, appeared.

"Brill," said Lady Pamela, who never believed in beating about the bush, "where is Lord Wynstanley?"

Brill turned a face of polite and wooden composure upon her. "I could not say, my lady," he replied.

"Can't or won't?" said Lady Pamela.

Brill, who had been acquainted with both her and Lord Wynstanley ever since they had been a pair of altogether enchanting and extremely troublesome children and he a second footman, showed no surprise at this direct attack.

"Both, my lady," he responded equably. "That is to say, I have not seen his lordship since he left the house on yesterday evening, and I have no direct knowledge of where he has gone. But I may say that if I had, I should not think it proper to betray any confidence his lordship had reposed in me."

"Don't be stuffy, Brill," Lady Pamela advised him kindly. "He has gone to Whiston Castle, hasn't he?"

Brill repeated that he could not say, but admitted, upon direct cross-examination, that he had packed up a portmanteau for his lordship at an hour sometime past eleven on the previous evening.

"Good Lord!" said Lady Pamela. "Well, look here, Brill, *don't* tell Lord Nevans. I mean, it's all right about the portmanteau, but *don't* say he's gone to Whiston Castle."

"I don't know that his lordship *has* gone to Whiston Castle, my lady," Brill pointed out, a look of misgiving slowly dawning upon his face. "So I can't very well tell Lord Nevans—"

"Tell him he has gone to—to Melton, to visit Mr. Boulton," Lady Pamela said, inventing rapidly, upon which Brill, looking shocked, said it wasn't his place to tell Banbury tales to his lordship, and, besides, he had seen Mr. Boulton himself in Bond Street the day before.

"Oh, well—Sir Harry Wolford then," Lady Pamela said, nothing daunted. "Only *don't* say Whiston Castle, because it will worry him. And, Brill, I want you to have a post-chaise fetched here. I am obliged to—to go to Lady Ashlock at once. I received an express from her this morning."

Her most passionate partisan could not have claimed that

Lady Pamela was a good liar, but she was a very positive one, and had a way of looking in such limpid and innocent expectation of belief at the person to whom she had just told some outrageous faradiddle that few people had the audacity to challenge her. Brill opened his lips to speak, shut them, opened them again to say, "Yes, my lady," in accents of resigned despair, and went off.

The next person to be attacked was Pletcher.

"Pletcher," said Lady Pamela, when that estimable female had returned to her dressing room, "I want you to pack up a portmanteau and my dressing-case for me. At once. I am needed at Lady Ashlock's for a few days. An express arrived this morning."

Pletcher, well aware that Lady Pamela was on the closest of terms with her cousin, Lady Ashlock, a dashing young matron now in residence with her husband and baby at their country seat in Kent, said, scenting scandal—for there had been backstairs rumours of dissension between Lady Ashlock and her spouse on the subject of her inability to keep her expenditures within the limits of her allowance—that she hoped there was No Trouble.

"Well, yes. There is. Little Giles has the measles," said Lady Pamela, wondering if one-year-old babies had the measles and then deciding that it didn't matter, as Pletcher would not believe her story, anyway. "I am leaving at once, so pray don't delay," she went on. "Only the necessaries for a few days' stay—and I shan't need you with me, Pletcher."

"Shan't—need—me!" said Pletcher, so astounded and affronted by this extraordinary statement from a Lady of Quality that she interrupted her employer, a solecism of which she had never before been guilty in the course of an upright and fashionable life.

"No," said Lady Pamela firmly, and resigned herself to the probability that she would find, when she returned to Berkeley Square, that Pletcher, considering she had sunk herself beneath reproach by going jauntering about the country without her, had given in her notice and she would be obliged to find another abigail. "And now do hurry with the packing, for I must go at once," she concluded.

When Pletcher had departed she hurriedly filled her reticule with a plentiful supply of bank notes and gold guineas—for though it was nowhere near Quarter Day, when she customarily received the very handsome allowance Lord Nevans made her, she was always able, as chatelaine of his household, to put her hand upon additional sums without the necessity of applying to him—and then sat down at her little French writing desk to compose a note for her grandfather.

Him, she knew, she dared not face with her tale about Lady Ashlock, for he would see at once that she was cutting a sham and would have no qualms whatever about putting her through an interrogation that would be bound to end in his discovering what she meant to do and forbidding her to do it. But if Wyn was to be rescued from the consequences of his own folly she must be the one to do it, she thought, for men always went about such matters in quite the wrong way, becoming grave and official about them and ending by ruining people's lives.

Lady Pamela was extremely fond of her young brother and she had a rooted dislike to his life's being ruined, so she wrote a note to Lord Nevans, which—however much he might doubt its veracity—he could not well controvert until he had got in touch with Lady Ashlock in Kent. And by that time, Lady Pamela considered, she herself would have arrived safely back in Berkeley Square from her own journey into Wiltshire.

Brill now returned with a post-chaise and the gloomy tidings that it was coming on to snow, which news did not daunt Lady Pamela in the least. She put on her warmest muscovy sable pelisse and a pair of velvet half-boots, withstood with great firmness the representations of Brill that she had much better allow him to send down word for the post-chaise to be dismissed and his lordship's own travelling-carriage to be brought out for her journey, waved aside Pletcher's impassioned entreaties to be permitted to accompany her, and trod down the stairs to the front door.

Pletcher followed with the dressing-case and Brill with the portmanteau. Just as Lady Pamela crossed the threshold a snowflake hesitated, swirled in a strong east wind, and then gently alighted on the tip of her elegant nose. It was indeed coming on to snow.

Two

By the time Woolhampton had been reached, the snow, which had been falling steadily ever since the post-chaise had left London, was so deep and showed such a stubborn, leaden-skyed determination not to let up at all that day that the post-boys at the Angel, where a stop was made to change horses, displayed a distinct reluctance to mount the fresh team that had been put-to—a reluctance finally overcome only by the bestowal of somewhat reckless largesse from Lady Pamela's purse.

At Hungerford the roads were worse, and even gold guineas, it appeared, had now lost their power of persuasion. It would be madness, the landlord of the Bear Inn declared, to expect any vehicle to make its way through the deep-drifted roads, with darkness coming on and the snow showing not the least sign of abating. Even the Bath Mail, he was sure, would not come through that night, and Miss might well expect to be snowbound for several days. However, he added obsequiously, his eye taking in the sable pelisse and the handsome dressing-case—complete, no doubt, with a dazzling array of cut-glass bottles fitted with gold caps and adorned with diamond chips—reposing upon the seat beside Lady Pamela, if she would be pleased to step inside she would find a warm fire, a good bed, and an excellent dinner, and no cause, he was sure, to regret the chance that had made her a guest in his house.

Lady Pamela, with some impatience, said that she had no intention of stepping inside.

"My good man," she went on in her delightful voice, which made the landlord decide that he could not really dislike her, even though she *was* making him stand outside on a very cold evening, with a sharp wind whipping snow down the back of his neck, "this *is* a posting-house, I believe? Obviously, then, it is your responsibility to provide me with horses and post-boys so that I may continue on my journey. I only wish to go to Marlborough, you know," she added, as if that town were around the very next bend instead of a good ten miles away, including one of the worst stretches of road between London and Bath.

The landlord, looking harassed, said that was all very well, but she was bound to land in a ditch if she tried to get there in this weather and he wouldn't have it on his conscience to send a young lady into *that* sort of bumblebath—not he! A brief but spirited argument then ensued, from which the landlord would have emerged quite worsted had it not been for the fact that he was aware that none of his post-boys would venture himself in such a storm, so that he was obliged in spite of himself to cling to his original position.

Fortunately, before the conversation could become positively acrimonious, a diversion was caused by the arrival in the yard of a very dashing-looking coach, its crimson, blue, and white bodywork emblazoned with gold lettering proclaiming it as the *Lightning*, bound for Bath and Bristol. Its ribbons were held by a tall dragsman in a snow-covered, multicaped driving-coat, who seemed quite impervious to snow and wind, and jumped down from the box with as matter-of-fact an air as if it had been broad noon on a bright spring day instead of an arctic February dusk with snow deep upon the ground.

A pair of ostlers who had emerged from the stables at the sound of wheels—more out of curiosity, it seemed, than from any intention of performing their usual duty of figging out a fresh team and putting them to—were greeted by a shout of indignant severity from the middle-aged guard as he clambered down from his perch behind and hastened to set the steps for the passengers to descend.

"Hout! Are ye daft, then, to be standing there like a set of great loobies instead of tending to your lawful duties?" he addressed them wrathfully, in a strong Scots accent.

Meanwhile, the tall coachman, accepting a steaming glass of punch from a shivering waiter who had come running out of the inn to tender it to him, strolled up to the landlord, who was regarding him in patent astonishment.

"Surely to goodness, Mr. Carlin, you're not thinking of going on to Marlborough in this weather!" he exclaimed. "You'll never get through!"

"No!" snapped a stout gentleman in a Polish greatcoat and

a Joliffe-shallow, both so thickly covered with snow that it was obvious he had been one of the unfortunate roof-passengers on the coach that had just arrived. "He *won't* get through —and it's a wonder to me that we have arrived this far with all our limbs intact, for we were within ames-ace of capsizing half a dozen times on the way, I can tell you!"

"Wheest, man!" said the guard, whose whirlwind of activity since he had jumped down from the coach evidently had now been widened to include the practice known as "kicking the passengers," for he had removed his snow-encrusted white castor and, touching his forelock to the stout man, was soliciting a tip. "Dinna ye ken the saying that a man is no a proper coachey till he's overturned his coach at least once, or how would he ken how to right it again? But ye needna fear the Master; he's a prime whip, and if ye canna ride safe wi' him, ye'll ride safe wi' no one!"

The stout man, extracting a shilling from his pocket, bestowed it grudgingly upon the guard and then, remarking scathingly that, prime whip or not, he had no fancy to risk his neck riding with a madman who had no better sense than to spring his horses in a snowstorm, stamped on into the inn, the mullioned windows of which showed an inviting glow of candlelight in the winter dusk. The guard thereupon announced to the coachman that it appeared if they went on to Marlborough they would go empty, the other passengers having, to a man—or a woman, for there was one lady even now having a fit of the vapours to the extent that it was requiring the services of three men to lift her from the coach—having signified their intention of remaining at the Bear.

"Oh no, you will not go empty!" said Lady Pamela, suddenly putting her head out the post-chaise window through which she had been parleying with the landlord. "*I* am going on to Marlborough, and since this utterly *afflictive* man will not provide me with horses and post-boys, I shall go in your coach."

She thereupon evinced every intention of stepping down from the post-chaise into the snow, which she was prevented from doing only by the coachman, who with seeming negligence placed himself at that moment in the doorway and surveyed her calmly.

The view he was favoured with of Lady Pamela's enchanting countenance—as much as could be seen of it from beneath the fur hood of her pelisse—he appeared to find quite satisfactory, for what expression there was to be read upon his dark, handsome face, which showed, even in the growing dusk, a pair of black eyes of an almost buccaneerlike directness, was approving. Lady Pamela, however, seemed unmoved by this tacit expression of admiration, and merely remarked in a rather imperious voice, "Pray step aside, sir! Do you not understand? I wish to go to Marlborough in your coach!"

The coachman did not move. "The question is," he responded unexpectedly, pushing his shallow-crowned beaver a trifle farther back upon his cropped black locks and speaking in accents that she recognised with some astonishment as being very definitely those of a gentleman, "will you get to Marlborough in my coach? I shouldn't lay odds on it, if I were you."

"Well, of course I am not going to lay odds on it," said Lady Pamela, with an air of virtuous severity. "I never gamble! But what has *that* to say to anything? Do you mean that you won't take me? That is *quite* illegal, I am sure, so long as I pay my fare!"

"Oh, I'll take you, right enough," the coachman assured her in his matter-of-fact way. "That is, if you don't mind running the risk of ending up in a snowdrift. I can't promise that you won't, you know."

The landlord, an interested auditor of this conversation, interrupted at this point to say with a satisfied air, "There! You see, Miss! It's just as I told you; it's not safe for you to go on, even if Mr. Carlin *does* intend to try to take the *Lightning* to Marlborough. Which, if I may say so," he added, addressing the coachman severely, "is nothing more than a crack-brained start, as you'd know, Mr. Carlin, if you'd been driving on this road for longer than a pair of weeks or so! No sane man would try to take a coach down Forest Hill in this weather!"

"No, I daresay he wouldn't," the coachman equably agreed. "Not, that is, unless he had laid a wager that he would reach Bath tonight. A very red-faced man at the King's Head in Thatcham—said he was a cousin of Harry Stevenson's" (this, as even Lady Pamela knew, was a famous coachman whose skill in handling the ribbons had won the notice and admiration of the Prince Regent himself), "and

Harry couldn't do it and no more could I. Offered to put up a pair of Yellow Goblins to back his words. Naturally I accepted." He looked critically at Lady Pamela's fashionable pelisse and the little velvet half-boots peeping out from beneath it. "If I were in your place, though," he advised her, "I shouldn't go. The red-faced man was probably right, you know. I'd say it's three to one we shan't make it."

"Then why are *you* going?" demanded Lady Pamela.

But in response to this question the coachman merely smiled faintly, appearing to intimate that if one did not understand this, when he had already stated that there was a wager involved, it would really do very little good to try to explain it.

"Well, you are a strange sort of coachman!" said Lady Pamela, raising her winged black brows at him. "I wonder that your proprietors care to employ you, since you have so little regard for their property! But I shall go with you, all the same. I fancy you are merely trying to fob me off with all this talk of overturning."

She thereupon signified once more her intention of descending from the post-chaise; but the coachman, remarking that if it really was her wish to go with him there was no need for her to begin by wading through the snow, forestalled her from stepping down by picking her up bodily and carrying her over to the coach, where he deposited her inside as disinterestedly as if she had been a parcel. The guard followed with her dressing-case and portmanteau, and, having placed the former beside her on the seat and stowed the latter away in the boot, went to spur the labours of the men who were putting-to the fresh team by caustic reminders to them of the Bear's proud boast that fifty seconds was all that was needed for its ostlers to make a change of horses.

Meanwhile, the coachman stood beside the offside wheel-horse, calmly observing the ostlers' work; then, crossing to the near-side, with a few pithy comments on his new cattle, which Lady Pamela, herself schooled by a famous judge of horseflesh, could well appreciate, he cast a professional glance at harness and reins and, returning to the off-side once more, took the reins, picked up the whip, which rested in readiness on the wheelers' backs, and mounted to the box. Here he checked the tautness of the traces again and then, nodding to the ostler standing at the wheelers' heads, with a slight yielding of the reins gave the leaders the office to start. The guard at the same moment swung himself up behind and, putting his horn to his lips, loosed one long-held clear note and a cluster of upper partials into the dark, snowy air, as if in defiance of the weather.

Lady Pamela, now ensconced in solitary state in the interior of the moving coach, sat taking stock of her present situation. When she had set out from her grandfather's house that morning, her intentions had been very simple. She had meant to drive in a post-chaise to Whiston Castle, which was, she knew, near Marlborough, have a slight accident just outside its gates in that post-chaise (one could always bribe a post-boy), and seek refuge inside the Castle while repairs were being made.

Once upon the ground, she had thought, it would be possible for her, without arousing the suspicions of anyone in the house, to use her not inconsiderable influence with her brother to induce him to get the memorandum back by fair means or foul from Cedric Mansell, if he had already given it to him, or not to give it to him at all if he had not. And if Lord Nevans turned out to be quite wrong and Wyn had not taken the memorandum in the first place, there would be no harm done except for Wyn's being temporarily much incensed with her because she had suspected him of abstracting papers from his grandfather's despatch-box, and as Wyn, who was of a sunny and forgiving nature, always got over his fits of temper very quickly, there would not be much harm done in that case, either.

An accident to a stagecoach, however, appeared to present a considerably greater difficulty than one to a post-chaise, even to a mind famous throughout the *ton* for an ingenuity that was quite unimpressed by obstacles and almost awe-inspiring in its directness. Still it was just possible, Lady Pamela thought, as she frowned at the snow tumbling down from the dusky heavens outside the window, that a coachman who was not expected to be able to bring his vehicle into Marlborough that evening and who had no other passengers might be persuaded, for a consideration, to make a slight detour and go by way of Whiston Castle instead of by his ordinary route on the Bath Road. The chief difficulty here, logic argued, would be in explaining to the occupants of Whiston Castle what a Bath and Bristol coach was doing outside its gates—and suspicion, she felt, must not be cast upon her arrival or her plans would go for naught.

It was impossible, however, at the present moment for her to concoct any more promising scheme, owing to the increasingly uncertain progress of the coach, which was now lurching through drifts so deep that she found herself entirely occupied in keeping herself from sliding off the seat onto the floor. Having been warned in advance of what lay in store for her, she accepted the situation with proper resignation, only uttering a few uncomplimentary remarks upon the coachman's skill, or lack of it, that were quite undeserved, for he was keeping his horses well together under exceedingly trying conditions. It was, in fact, now snowing harder than ever, and an overturned gig lying at the side of the road presently gave mute testimony to the fate that would already have overtaken the coach had it not been for the dexterity and experience of the dragsman who held the reins.

But not even dexterity and experience are able to win the battle against Nature when it—or she—unfairly decides to throw overwhelming odds against human ingenuity, and Lady Pamela suddenly found herself careering in a very undignified manner across the seat to the opposite side of the coach and landing in a tangle of furs against the far window. Her dressing-case, which had arrived there before her, banged painfully against her ribs as she did so.

"Confound it!" said Lady Pamela, righting herself indignantly.

She crawled up the seat to the window beside which she had been sitting—for the one against which she had landed was quite smothered now in a snowdrift—and found herself staring up into the amused eyes of the coachman, already standing outside and wrenching the door open for her.

"You look like a cat crawling out of a well, and almost as bedraggled," he informed her, extending his hand to her. "Don't look so fierce; I told you we might come a cropper, you know."

"Yes, I do know—and it is, after all, quite what I intended—only not *here!*" Lady Pamela said, climbing out into the road with Carlin's assistance and attempting to smooth her ruffled apparel into some semblance of propriety. "I *do* think it is odiously inconsiderate of you to have had an accident in this place, where it will do me not a particle of good, instead

17

of outside Whiston Castle! But I daresay," she went on, recovering her temper almost immediately and looking about her at the dark, windy, drifted landscape, "that it is not *entirely* your fault. After all, you could not have known what I wished to do, and I must say that I don't see how you have managed to keep the road this far. What are we to do now?" she enquired, with such complete confidence in his providing her with an instant solution to the problems caused by the overturning of the coach that the amused expression upon Carlin's dark face lit into positive laughter.

Lady Pamela's brows went up. "Well, I *don't* see anything to laugh about!" she said. "We shall freeze to death if we stay here! Is there an inn, or at least a house, anywhere near?"

The coachman, composing his countenance, said there was an inn of sorts not far distant where they might find shelter—"also," he added, "of sorts. You would have done far better, you know, to have stopped at the Bear in Hungerford."

"People who say, 'I told you so,'" said Lady Pamela with great hauteur, "are even more odious than people who overturn other people in snowdrifts."

"Yes, I know," said Carlin sympathetically. "But I shall redeem myself by not asking you to explain to me why you desire to have an accident outside Whiston Castle until after I have got you to a place more suitable for conversation than this."

And he thereupon plunged through the snow to assist the guard in freeing the horses from the overturned coach.

"What a *very* odd coachman he is, to be sure!" thought Lady Pamela, staring after him and determining to put some questions of her own once they should have reached shelter. "He must be a gentleman who has come down in the world, though from the looks of him one would think it far more probable that he would have taken to a career as a highwayman rather than as a coachman to mend his fortunes!"

She then called to him to say that, since at least one of the horses appeared to be uninjured, she was sure it would be possible for her to ride it if he would engage to lift her upon its back and lead it, and added imperatively that on no account were her dressing-case and portmanteau to be left behind. This caused the guard to mutter something in strong

Scots about *women*, which fortunately the wind blew away, and in a short time Lady Pamela, perched upon the broad back of one of the lead horses like a damsel in a mediaeval tapestry going on a pilgrimage, with her portmanteau and dressing-case strapped upon its mate's, was being led by Carlin through the drifted snow, while the guard struggled behind, leading the remaining horses.

Three

The Swan and Bell was one of those very small, very ancient, very inconvenient inns that would certainly have been open to extend hospitality to Lady Pamela had she actually been a medieval damsel, contemporary with Chaucer, seeking shelter upon a pilgrimage. It had an undulating thatched roof over wattle-and-cob walls, stone-flagged floors, and rooms so low-pitched that she was certain her tall coachman must be in imminent danger of concussion whenever he attempted to pass beneath one of the door-lintels.

As a haven from the storm, however, it was a great deal better than a cow-byre, which was the only other structure they had passed on the way, and Lady Pamela, making the best of the matter, accepted with equanimity the fact that there was no private parlour and that the small, lattice-windowed, dimity-hung bedchamber to which she was shown was almost entirely taken up by a very large and lumpy-appearing bed.

Her best bedchamber, the landlady, awed almost to tears by the sables and the dressing-case, nervously explained, was occupied at the moment by a young woman who had been brought into her house not an hour before after an accident to a gig in which her leg had been broken—"if you'll pardon the expression, my lady," she added in an access of prudishness, as if she had suddenly been stricken with the idea that real Ladies were above having legs like ordinary people and floated upon the earth on nothing but wispy draperies and the tips of Denmark satin sandals, or, in the present case, velvet half-boots.

Lady Pamela, however, accepted the term without any visible signs of shock, much to Mrs. Parslow's relief, and asked what was being done for the unfortunate young woman.

"Well, my lady," confided Mrs. Parslow, again suppressing tears, whether of gratification over being in conversation with a real Lady or sympathy over her guest's plight she herself could not have said, "you might rightly say nothing at all, beyond making her as comfortable as I can, poor thing, for there's nobody to send for the doctor unless it was my own boy Ned, and he's only twelve and small for his age, being as Parslow went off to Marlborough this morning with the pig and not hide nor hair have I seen of him since. And the young fellow that was driving the gig no better than Ned, which has sprained his ankle, or so he *says*, though if you want *my* opinion he's that terrified of the storm he'd nap his bib if I sent him out in it."

Lady Pamela, who was quite accustomed to managing things, said that was all right then, for she had brought two strapping fellows with her, one of whom might go off to fetch a surgeon at once—upon which Carlin, an appreciative auditor of this conversation, said that for his own part he preferred being asked.

"Well, I never!" gasped Mrs. Parslow, torn between shock at this lack of respect for the higher orders and her natural reverence for the coachman's profession, for such representatives of that calling who found their way to the Swan and Bell always received the due they expected in the way of obsequious service and an admiring retinue of ostlers, small boys, and hangers-on dogging their footsteps.

But Lady Pamela, to her relief, did not take umbrage, only saying, "Fiddle!"—which made the tall coachman laugh. He then, having enquired of Mrs. Parslow where the doctor was to be found, took himself off.

Lady Pamela, left alone in her little bedchamber, where a very cheerful fire was burning, took off her snow-wetted clothes, did her hair, and put on a high-waisted frock of cherry-coloured merino with a narrow skirt trimmed with embroidered braid. Unaccustomed as she was to performing such services for herself, she was rather proud of the effect when she had finished, and thought that even Pletcher could not have disapproved of it, except in principle.

That Pletcher had been quite right upon another point, however—that of the unsuitability of her travelling without her maid—she had already been made aware. Even Mrs. Parslow, though unused to catering for the Quality, had been unable to conceal her surprise at her unattended state, and that the odiously bold-mannered coachman was also nourishing a good deal of curiosity about her she was by now perfectly conscious.

However, as she was equally curious about him she felt it was no more than fair exchange. And having an idea at the back of her head that a man of his rather unusual qualities might come to be useful in some as yet unspecified way to a young lady under the possible necessity of matching wits with one or more unscrupulous gentlemen, she considered that if he would satisfy *her* curiosity she would satisfy *his*, and then see if an arrangement might not be worked out.

At about the time she had got this far in thinking things out, there was a tap at the door and Mrs. Parslow put in an anxious face.

"Excuse me, my lady," she said, "but it's a bit of crimped cod and a curd pudding and some calf's fry, unless you'd like the boiled tongue with turnips instead"—by which Lady Pamela understood that she was being invited to partake of such dinner as the Swan and Bell afforded.

Declining the boiled tongue and turnips, she draped a handsome Norwich silk shawl to fall negligently over her arms at the elbows and followed Mrs. Parslow down the narrow stairs, the latter lamenting all the way the lack of a private parlour in which her distinguished guest could be served in suitable solitude and state.

"Not that there's anybody in the coffee room just now," she said, as she stood aside to allow Lady Pamela to enter that snug apartment, its crimson-hung windows glowing in the light of a well-made-up fire. "But if Mr. Carlin was to call for his dinner now, I *couldn't* ask him to eat it in the kitchen, my lady!"

Lady Pamela said of course she could not, and looked with approval at the shining brasses of the fender and the snowy cloth spread invitingly upon the table, at which she at once seated herself, for she was quite famished after her journey.

While a frightened little maid brought in a well-laden tray from the kitchen, a noise of footsteps and voices outside in the passage betokened the arrival of the doctor, and a moment later the door of the coffee room was opened and the guard looked in. Upon seeing her, he apologised and would have withdrawn, but she called to him without ceremony to come in.

"Have you been to fetch the doctor?" she enquired, seeing

his snow-covered boots and clothing. "You had best come in and warm yourself at the fire. I fancy there is not another so good in the house."

The guard thanked her, and stood by the large stone fireplace warming his hands and occasionally regarding her with a scrupulous appearance of not doing so. On the whole, he seemed friendly in spite of his ferocious black brows, and appeared to have got over his disapproval of her insistence upon having her portmanteau and dressing-case rescued from the coach along with herself, so that she thought it safe to enter into conversation with him.

"Is the storm growing any worse?" she asked.

The guard said no worse and no better, adding after a moment that they wouldn't get the *Lightning* on the road again *that* day or the next, and then looked with speculative interest at her dinner.

"You had better go and ask Mrs. Parslow for something," Lady Pamela said, correctly interpreting the look. "There is a boiled tongue and turnips, I believe. But don't go yet," she added, at once regretting having placed temptation in his way, as she had not yet broached the subject she wished to discuss with him. "Where is Carlin? Did he go with you to fetch the doctor? And what is *your* name?" she went on, adding question to question in a manner that even Lord Babcoke, who considered her in all other respects a very good sort of girl, was sometimes wont to deplore.

The guard, however, who had had a good Scottish mother and was therefore used to inquisitiveness, took the questions quite in stride and, answering them in reverse order, said Quinting, and what call had the Master to be going out in that weather when one could do the job, and if he had finished seeing to the horses he might be upstairs washing up.

"Yes, he seems quite particular about his appearance—I mean for a coachman," Lady Pamela said. "*Not* that he wears several waistcoats, one more perfectly dreadful than the other, and a coat with so many capes that it makes him look like a deformed mountain, and mother-of-pearl buttons as big as platters, the way they *do*. But he *does* look clean."

Quinting glowered, and muttered something about why wouldn't the Master be clean?

"I don't know," said Lady Pamela frankly. "He *is* a gentleman, isn't he? I daresay he has suffered reverses and come down in the world. Was it gaming?"

The guard gave her a harassed glance and then began to look obstinate as only a Scotsman can. But if it was his idea to escape further inquisition by pretending sudden deafness—an art developed to a high degree by uncooperative gardeners and ladies' maids seeking to evade their lawful duties—he soon found that he had met his match, or indeed his mistress, in Lady Pamela. That elegant young lady was quite used to dealing, with a shattering directness quite belying her fashionably fragile appearance, with recalcitrant underlings, and in the space of ten minutes she had dragged out of Quinting a good deal of information concerning Carlin with which it was evident he did not much care to part.

Yes, he admitted reluctantly, Mr. Carlin was a Scotsman, like himself.

Had been in the army, perhaps? He seemed to have something of the air of a military man.

Yes, that he had.

What regiment? (Quinting was obstinately silent.) *What regiment?*

Quinting, in obvious despair at the persistence of women, grudgingly named the prestigious 3rd Dragoon Guards, and Lady Pamela's brows rose skeptically.

"Yes, I daresay he *would* tell you something of the sort," she said. "More likely a Line regiment—"

"That it was not!" said Quinting indignantly.

"But how do you *know* that?" enquired Lady Pamela, her skepticism unabated, which had the effect of driving Quinting into a frenzy of circumstantial assertions and evasions, leading to the clear impression that he could answer if he would, as far as giving information about Carlin's army career was concerned, but that his lips were sealed.

"Good heavens!" said Lady Pamela, her curiosity now thoroughly aroused. "Do you mean to say he was cashiered?"

"No!" roared Quinting, regarding her with such an air of righteous wrath that Lady Pamela, feeling something like Mary Queen of Scots before John Knox, hastily retreated and said she hadn't meant to imply that there was necessarily anything disgraceful in Carlin's past.

"Disgraceful!" said Quinting scornfully. "And him mentioned in despatches time and again by his lordship

24

himself!"—by which Lady Pamela quite correctly understood him to mean that the tall coachman, before coming down in the world and taking to the road, had received the commendations of Lord Wellington for bravery and efficiency in carrying out his military duties in the Peninsula.

"But then," she could not prevent herself from arguing logically in reply, "why should he have wished to leave the army?"—upon which Quinting muttered something darkly about family reasons that made her wonder quite groundlessly about an entanglement with the Colonel's wife or something of the sort—not too far-fetched a supposition, it appeared to her, in view of the coachman's personal endowments and obvious easy address with the opposite sex, though it was just as possible that Quinting did not have the least idea what he was talking about and the real reason for Carlin's having left the army had to do with gaming debts that he had been unable to pay.

At any rate, this conversation gave impetus to the vague idea she had already formulated in the back of her mind about enlisting Carlin's aid in her pursuit of the missing document, and when he himself came into the coffee room a few minutes later, looking remarkably cheerful for a man whose coach lay at the moment overturned in the snow, she surveyed with interest and approval his alert, intelligent (and incidentally remarkably handsome) features, his athletic figure, and his general air of being perfectly competent to cope with any problem that might be presented to him.

He himself appeared to have his attention fixed chiefly upon the very good dinner Lady Pamela was eating, which he regarded with an expression of interest almost equalling that which Quinting had displayed, and, the small maid scuttling into the room just then bearing the forgotten curd pudding, he enquired of her whether there was any more where that came from.

"Oh yes, sir!" said the maid, in a terror-stricken whisper. "In a moment, sir!"

And she thereupon vanished, Quinting seizing his opportunity to make good his escape as well. The coachman drew up a chair to the table and looked enquiringly at Lady Pamela.

"I hope you have no objection?" he asked politely. "I looked into the kitchen just now, but it is a very small room, smelling strongly of onions, and as it seemed more than a little overcrowded already——"

"Oh, do sit down, by all means," said Lady Pamela affably. "It may be boiled tongue and turnips instead of calf's fry, I believe, but you may have some of this curd pudding, if you like."

Carlin said he was hungry enough to eat a boiled ox entire, to say nothing of its tongue, and accepted the curd pudding with suitable gratitude. The little maid then came into the room with more calf's fry, a large tankard of ale, and half a large goose-and-turkey pie, on which the coachman fell with avidity.

"You don't seem at all put about by the accident to your coach," Lady Pamela observed, remarking his hearty appetite. "Won't the proprietors be very much displeased at your having taken it upon the road when it was so very probable that you must come to grief?"

Carlin, neatly turning the tables upon her, said that he fancied no more than her relations would be at her having taken the equal risk of travelling in such weather.

"Yes, but relations cannot *discharge* one," Lady Pamela pointed out, "and your proprietors can. Still, as you are such an excellent whip, I daresay you will be able to find another situation quickly if they do." She added speculatively, "I expect you would be very much pressed for money if you did not?"

"Oh, I should not find myself quite under the hatches," Carlin assured her. "Why?"

"Why?" repeated Lady Pamela, rather blankly.

"Yes, why?" said Carlin. "You may as well cut line, you know, because it's perfectly obvious that you want something of me. You have been looking at me ever since I walked into this room like a highwayman at a prospective victim. What is it, my money or my life?"

"Well, actually," said Lady Pamela, regarding him with evident respect for his perceptiveness, "neither. But I *did* think you might be of some help to me, especially if you feel you may be discharged from your position and would like to earn—oh, shall we say, twenty guineas, for example?"

Carlin looked first amused and then severe. "Look here," he said, "you can't go about offering chance-met strangers large sums of money in hedge-taverns without running the risk of very unpleasant consequences. You're far too young and pretty to be knocked on the head and robbed, which is the least of what may happen to you if you're not more careful."

"Gammon!" said Lady Pamela. "I am one-and-twenty, and *quite* accustomed to looking after myself. And, though I believe I am generally accounted to be pretty, my nose is not at all classical."

"I like it that way," remarked Carlin, which piece of gross impertinence Lady Pamela decided to overlook.

"As a matter of fact," she went on, "it is the greatest coincidence that you have likened me to a highwayman, for I have been thinking ever since I met you that that is exactly what you remind *me* of. I suppose you have not—?" She paused delicately.

Carlin assured her gravely that he had not yet been driven to those straits, upon which Lady Pamela looked regretful.

"Now *don't* tell me," said Carlin, "that you wish to engage my services in holding up a coach."

"Well, not precisely," Lady Pamela acknowledged. "But if one wished possibly to—to steal something back that was one's own property, or at least one's relation's—"

Carlin pushed back his chair. "Good God!" he said. "You had better tell me the whole of it. Just what is it that you are up to? But no!" He held up his hand. "Before we begin, are you really Lady Pamela Frayne, as the landlady assures me you told her you were, or is that, too, a part of the plot and you are actually the Princess Charlotte in disguise?"

"I *don't* think," said Lady Pamela, somewhat affronted, "that you are taking this seriously, Carlin—if that really is *your* name, which I am much inclined to doubt. This is a matter of the utmost gravity; in fact, the fate of the country may hang upon it!" She hesitated, wondering momentarily if she was quite mad to be taking this stranger into her confidence, even if he *had* served with distinction in the 3rd Dragoon Guards; but there was something in his manner that overcame her doubts. He *did* appear so very capable of dealing with the sort of situation it seemed possible she might be confronted with at Whiston Castle, and, after all, one *had* heard of gentlemen who had gambled away their fortunes at White's or Watier's and had taken to the coachman's life as being one eminently suited to their sporting talents, although she personally had never met any of them. "I daresay you have heard of Lord Nevans?" she went on to Carlin, taking the plunge.

"The very prominent member of His Majesty's Government? To be sure. But what—?"

"He is my grandfather," said Lady Pamela, the whole story tumbling out helter-skelter, now that she had begun. "And he *is* growing rather old, and has *never* been properly careful of things, Mr. Underdown, his secretary, says; only of course Mr. Underdown does not know all about this as yet, and no more would I, if Grandpapa had not been in such high fidgets over Wyn's disappearing at the same time as the memorandum that he flew into one of his takings and told me the whole before he knew what he was about. Wyn is my brother, Viscount Wynstanley," she explained. "So you see I *must* find him, *and* the memorandum—"

"Wait!" begged Carlin. "You will have to go back a bit, because I don't see in the least. But it sounds to me, on the face of it, as if you were taking something into your hands that doesn't belong there in the least, and if I were you I should return home at once and let your grandfather handle the matter. I am certain he will make a much better job of it than you will."

Lady Pamela said coldly that her grandfather was in the gout and couldn't leave the house, and besides, how could he—Carlin—possibly know what sort of job she would make of it when he knew practically nothing at all about her?

"When Cissie Pelfrey was engaged to a perfectly odious man and couldn't get *un*engaged from him because her father and mother doted on him, I was the one who told her what to do and it succeeded beautifully," she said. "And I *do* think you may be useful to me now, although I don't as yet know exactly how, because if Cedric Mansell—he is the man I think may have gotten the memorandum from Wyn—does not *quite* like giving it back to him, you look as if you might be able to—to persuade him to do so. Wyn is very young, you see, only nineteen, and though he does go occasionally to Jackson's Boxing Saloon, I am afraid he does not take it seriously enough, so that Lord Babcoke says he is sometimes *glaringly abroad*, if you know what that means. Lord Babcoke is the man I am going to marry," she added, upon which Carlin enquired if his lordship knew that.

"Of course he knows it! He asked me to," said Lady Pamela indignantly.

"Well, don't fly up into the boughs," Carlin advised her. "I only thought it might be another of your plans, and if it was, I'd say it had a much better chance to come off than the one you are engaged in just now, no matter who Lord Babcoke is. But I wonder," he added thoughtfully, "if he knows exactly what he is taking on."

Lady Pamela said loftily that that was none of *his* affair, and then, becoming practical, proceeded to enlighten him as to what had been her scheme for gaining admittance to Whiston Castle under plausible circumstances, and what she hoped to accomplish when she got there.

"But now the snow has ruined everything," she concluded. "I *did* think of bribing you to take your stagecoach to Whiston Castle and overturn *it* there, but I can see that there might be difficulties about that. I mean, it *is* out of the proper way for a Bath and Bristol coach—"

Carlin asked in a very logical manner if she had ever thought of simply driving up to the gates of Whiston Castle, announcing herself, and asking to be admitted.

"Oh no, that wouldn't do at all," said Lady Pamela decidedly. "Wyn would be quite put out, and I shouldn't blame him, besides its being bound to put everyone on their guard."

"Put *who* on their guard?" demanded Carlin, but Lady Pamela only said she was sure it ought to be *whom*, and would he really do it, then?

"Do what?" asked Carlin.

Lady Pamela sighed. "You don't *look* stupid," she said, "but I daresay appearances are deceiving. Very well. I'll put it to you one time more. *Will* you drive me to Whiston Castle, and undertake to help me when I get there?"

"No," said Carlin unequivocably.

Lady Pamela rose from the table and, with what in a young woman of lesser degree would certainly have been called a flounce, walked out of the coffee room and up the stairs to her bedchamber.

Four

❦

When Lady Pamela came down to breakfast on the following morning she found that the snow had stopped, the sun had come out upon a cold and glittering world, and Carlin and Quinting, accompanied by the young man who had overturned the gig and Mrs. Parslow's son Ned, had gone to see what could be done about putting the *Lightning* and the gig on their wheels again.

Being unable to formulate any plan for leaving the Swan and Bell in their absence, and being the sort of person who, like Shakespeare's Hotspur, is apt to say, "Fie upon this quiet life! I want work," when not confronted with battles or at least minor crises to solve, Lady Pamela, when she had finished her breakfast, went to enquire of Mrs. Parslow how the young woman who had had her leg broken in the accident to the gig was doing. Informed that she was doing as well as might be expected, except for being "quite in the mopes," Lady Pamela went upstairs, fetched a bottle of lavender water from her dressing-case, and, knocking at the door of the best bedchamber, went inside to take matters in hand with her usual energy.

She found the sufferer propped up in bed looking very wan and woebegone, but quite willing to confide her troubles to her once she had arranged her pillows in a more comfortable fashion and had bathed her forehead with the lavender water. Her name, she said, was Maria Clover, and she came from Hungerford, where she had been employed as abigail to an elderly lady of quality who had died suddenly a fortnight since. By a fortunate circumstance, however, the elderly lady's niece had possessed a distant relation, a countess, whose daughter, just turned seventeen and about to make her come-out in London, was in need of a maid, and this position had been offered to Miss Clover, as possessing a reliable and sober character and having given satisfaction over a period of two full years to a lady whom Miss Clover herself had no scruples in describing as "a regular old brimstone."

"But she *was* used to deck herself out in the very latest style," she grudgingly admitted, "and to go to Bath every winter and to London for the Season, so that a person did have a chance to see a little Life, my lady"—which innocent phrase, Lady Pamela shrewdly suspected, observing Miss Clover's black curls and very pretty face, undoubtedly covered a good deal of backstairs flirtation with willing under-butlers and gentlemen's gentlemen. "Only I *was* so looking forward," continued Miss Clover dolefully, "to having a *young* lady to do for. I've never seen Lady Sabrina, but Lady Overfield—she was my *old* lady—was used to say she was a regular picture, and as lively as a grig, so that her mother had a hard time of it to keep her in hand. And now here am I, laid up with this horrid broken leg, and of course Lady Whiston will be obliged to get someone else for her daughter."

Lady Pamela, who had been giving this narrative something less than her full attention, her mind being occupied with various schemes for getting herself to Whiston Castle as soon as possible, suddenly sat up with a jerk.

"Lady *who?*" she ejaculated.

Miss Clover stared at her. "Lady Whiston," she repeated. "She is Lady Sabrina's mother, you see—"

"You don't mean—" breathed Lady Pamela, "you *can't* mean—Lady Whiston of Whiston Castle?"

"But I can. I do," said Miss Clover, her eyes growing round in her pretty face.

"By Jupiter!" said Lady Pamela, reverently and quite improperly. "I *am* in luck! My dear girl, how would you like to earn—shall we say, ten guineas?—for doing nothing but lying here in this bed?"

Some two hours later, when Carlin, along with Quinting, Ned Parslow, and the young man who had been driving the gig, returned to the Swan and Bell, he found Lady Pamela in the deserted coffee room, almost bursting with her impatience to talk to him. Having summarily dismissed the other members of the party to the kitchen (where, it may happily be reported, a blazing fire and hot rum toddies were waiting to welcome them), she dragged Carlin into the coffee room and closed the door.

"You can't think what a piece of luck I have had!" she said, regarding him so triumphantly that Carlin, although a man not noted for prudence, at once began to look wary. "You know that young woman upstairs who has broken her leg?"

"Yes," said Carlin. "Look here, did I hear someone mention rum toddies?"

"They can wait," said Lady Pamela impatiently. "Her name is Maria Clover—"

"No, they can't," objected Carlin. "It's as cold as—well, it is deuced cold out there, and I want warming."

"If that isn't just like a man!" said Lady Pamela scornfully. "Very well! You shall have a rum toddy, then!"

She went to the door and sent an imperative call out to the kitchen, whence in a few moments there emerged the little maid, bearing a tumbler of something hot and aromatic, which she tendered to Carlin. He accepted it with thanks, whereupon she scuttled back to the kitchen again and Lady Pamela shut the door of the coffee room behind her.

"Now," she said, "*will* you listen to me? That girl is engaged to go to Whiston Castle as maid to Lady Whiston's daughter—"

A look of comprehension, not unmixed with amusement and a certain awe, crossed Carlin's face on the instant.

"Good God!" he ejaculated. "Don't go on. You wouldn't— you couldn't—"

"Oh yes, I can, and I shall!" said Lady Pamela. She looked at him with some approval. "I must say you are very quick on the uptake," she said. "The idea occurred to *me* the moment I heard the girl say she was going to Whiston Castle, but I never expected you to be so clever."

"It's not cleverness, it's madness!" said Carlin with conviction. "How in the devil's name do you think you can succeed in passing yourself off as a servant? That imperious manner of yours would betray you in five minutes."

"It might," agreed Lady Pamela with aplomb, "if I intended to masquerade as anything but a fashionable lady's maid. It is quite obvious that you know nothing at all of those superior creatures. My own dresser has a manner that would freeze a duchess, and refused to take the situation at all unless I provided her with an underling to do the brushing, pressing, cleaning, and other such menial tasks. *And*," she added, as she saw Carlin's eyes going over her elegant cherry-coloured frock, which even to masculine eyes shrieked of fashionable *modistes* and no expense spared, "Miss Clover and I are quite of a height, and she is almost as slender as I am as well, so there will be not the least difficulty about clothes."

Carlin shook his head. "I don't believe it," he said flatly. "Do you mean to tell me that it is your intention to go to Whiston Castle in that wretched girl's clothes and try to pass yourself off as a lady's maid? You may not know the Whistons—I hope I may give you credit for not being such a peagoose as to engage in this harebrained scheme if you did— but what the *devil* do you think your brother will say when he claps eyes on you?"

"Well, I have been thinking of that," said Lady Pamela seriously, "and in the first place, you know, he may not even be there any longer by the time I arrive. And in the second place, Wyn is *not* such a clothhead as to give me away. He would simply wait until he could get me alone and then ask me quite privately what kind of rig I was running."

"He sounds as bad as you," said Carlin uncomplimentarily.

"Oh, he is much worse!" Lady Pamela assured him with pride. "But that is neither here nor there. The thing is that I want you to help me, because though I shall of course go to Whiston Castle quite as Miss Clover would have done, in that young man's gig, so that there will be no difficulty now about *that*, there is no telling what sort of situation I shall find when I get there, as far as the memorandum is concerned, and so it seems quite possible that I shall need some help in getting it back. So I thought, since you know about horses, you might contrive to be taken on as a groom at Whiston Castle, and then if I need you, you will be there."

Carlin put the empty tumbler down upon the sideboard with what seemed to Lady Pamela quite unnecessary emphasis.

"No!" he said. "I thought we went all through this yesterday, Lady Pamela."

"Well, we did," acknowledged Lady Pamela. "But sometimes when people have an opportunity to think things over, they change their minds."

"Well, I haven't changed mine," said Carlin flatly.

Lady Pamela looked scornful. "Oh, very well, then," she said, "if you are so poor-spirited as that." A thoughtful expression suddenly descended upon her face. "Perhaps Quinting—" she began tentatively.

Carlin grinned. "You are welcome to try," he said. "Care to lay a wager on the result?"

"I have already told you that I never gamble," said Lady Pamela coldly. "One gamester in the family is quite enough. *Not* that I blame Wyn," she added, anxious not to be misunderstood, "for he cannot help it. It is in the Blood"—upon which Carlin asked what about *her* blood?

"I have cured myself of it," said Lady Pamela proudly. "It happened when I was ten, and lost a pony I particularly liked to an odious cousin I didn't like at all. But I believe," she went on, the thoughtful look returning to her face, "yes, I *do* believe I am about to have a relapse. Carlin, I shall lay you fifty guineas to one that you cannot succeed in introducing yourself into the household at Whiston Castle. What have you to say to that?"

And she gazed at him so triumphantly that Carlin, for his part, looked as if he would have liked very much to shake her, which made her, though ordinarily quite brave, take a prudent step or two backward out of his reach.

But he controlled himself, and only said in an exasperated tone that he considered that as taking an unfair advantage.

"Yes, it is," said Lady Pamela, "but one can't bother about being fair when it is something as important as this. Will you take the wager?"

Carlin said he would think about it.

"You are afraid you will lose, I expect," said Lady Pamela encouragingly, "but I do think you should give it a try. One never really knows how clever one can be at inventing things until one makes the attempt. For example, I left word with my grandfather that I was going to my cousin, Lady Ashlock, because I knew it would worry him if he thought I had gone after Wyn."

Carlin said disrespectfully that just because she was an unprincipled liar there was no reason she should believe that everyone else was, and he would have to think about the *Lightning*. Lady Pamela enquired if it was much damaged.

"No," he said. "But neither of the wheelers is fit to go, and I shall have to go to Marlborough for horses, which I shall probably be able to do tomorrow. The wind is changing and unless I am much mistaken we shall have a thaw tonight."

"Oh, famous!" said Lady Pamela. "Then I shall be able to get on to Whiston, too"—for she had been much exercised over the delay to her plans caused by the snow, and only the thought that the weather must have caused an equal delay in any plans Cedric Mansell might have for getting the memorandum out of the country had kept her in reasonable patience throughout the day.

Being unable now to obtain any more definite assurances from Carlin that he would take up the wager she had offered him, she went upstairs once more to Miss Clover's room to perfect her plans for her coming sortie into Whiston Castle. She found her, despite her broken leg, in such a state of euphoria over the thought of exchanging her own modestly fashionable wardrobe for a sable pelisse, a dressing-case worth at least fifty guineas, and ten guineas more in coin of the realm, all at the price of a situation that she was unable to take up at any rate, that it was difficult to pin her down to giving the information concerning her recent situation with Lady Overfield, which Lady Pamela considered she should be familiar with in order to be able to take her place without suspicion at Whiston Castle. But this information was eventually extracted from her, together with certain useful details concerning Etiquette Belowstairs, of which Lady Pamela, in spite of having lived all her life among servants and doing a very good job of managing her grandfather's establishments in town and country, had had no very clear idea.

As Lady Sabrina Mansell's maid, Miss Clover informed her, she would rank in precedence after the butler, the housekeeper, the groom of the chambers, Lord Whiston's valet, and Lady Whiston's abigail, with which select group of individuals, along with the personal attendants of any other guests or members of the family in residence at the Castle, she would be expected to foregather before dinner in the Housekeeper's Room.

"The Honourable Cedric Mansell's valet will no doubt take you in to dinner, my lady, if he is in residence," Miss Clover went on, warming to her subject, "as I understand Lord Whiston's eldest son is abroad at present. I daresay it might make it simpler for you, as to how you are to act with the butler and the housekeeper, if I was to say you might think of him as the Prince Regent and her as the Queen. What is the matter?" she interrupted her lecture to enquire, as Lady

Pamela, seized with a fit of the giggles, suddenly lost her battle to preserve her countenance.

"N-nothing," said Lady Pamela unsteadily. "I am sorry. Do go on. I was only thinking that, as the Prince is so little inclined to stand upon ceremony among his friends, I might better think of the butler as—as the Archbishop of Canterbury?"

Miss Clover, considering this, said that it might be an excellent idea. She then went on to inform her that it would be felt to be proper for her, when among her fellow servants, to refer to her own young lady as Sabrina, just as the Honourable Cedric's man would refer to his gentleman as Cedric, but that, out of deference to one's colleagues, it was customary to refer to *their* gentlemen and ladies by their titles.

"And I think, my lady," she said, "that you will find everything done quite *comme il faut*, as we say, at Whiston Castle. I had an auntie there in service a few years back who has since gone to her reward, poor soul, and she told me there was no mixing of the classes *there*, with housemaids and footmen getting above themselves and having their after-dinner wine in the Housekeeper's Room with the upper staff, or the head still-room maid trying to take precedence over the head housemaid."

Lady Pamela, her head reeling at these disclosures, said it might be as well if Miss Clover gave her further details as to what the proper etiquette was in regard to belowstairs meals.

"Upper and lower staff, dinner in the Hall, but upper staff leaves after the meat course to eat their pudding and drink their wine in the Housekeeper's Room," said Miss Clover crisply and rather severely, as if surprised by Lady Pamela's ignorance in such matters. "After they leave, the first footman takes the butler's place at the head of the table and the head housemaid the housekeeper's—unless there is a female cook," she added, with ineffable contempt for such establishments as did not engage a proper French chef. "*She* ranks above the head housemaid. The footmen, under-butler, coachmen, and pantry-boys take all their meals in the Hall, but housemaids take breakfast in the housemaids' sitting room and still-room maids take theirs in the still-room—"

"Wait—pray!" begged Lady Pamela, who was beginning to get quite out of her depth and felt something like a Chinaman or an Indian suddenly thrown in with countesses and duchesses and wondering which of them he was expected to take in to dinner and if he would be excommunicated if he walked out of the room before someone more important than he. "I think you had best tell me only what *I* must do, and not about the others," she said. "You see, I *do* quite know what I shall have to do for Lady Sabrina, for I am acquainted with all that my own maid does for me, but when I am away from her belowstairs it will all be quite new for me, so I don't think you should confuse me with talking about housemaids and still-room maids."

"Oh, no! You will have very little to do with *them*, my lady!" said Miss Clover, with all the contempt of a pre-Revolutionary French duchess for the *sans-culottes*.

And, though she was herself convinced that Lady Pamela was quite mad, having had only a very sketchy explanation from her as to her reasons for desiring to masquerade as a lady's maid at Whiston Castle, and expecting that at any moment her relations would appear and put her under restraint, carrying off the sable pelisse, the magnificent dressing-case, and the ten guineas as well, she went on very kindly explaining to her the intricacies of life belowstairs, halting only when Mrs. Parslow appeared in the doorway with a dish of Restorative Pork Jelly for her.

Five

❦

A thaw, as Carlin had predicted, set in overnight, and early on the following afternoon Lady Pamela, attired in the neat grey frock and demure kerseymere pelisse in which Miss Clover had arrived at the Swan and Bell, was able to make her escape from that hostelry and set off for Whiston Castle.

This was not accomplished without a certain amount of difficulty, for the young man who had been engaged to drive Miss Clover to the Castle, not being of a particularly powerful intellect, could not at first grasp the reason for its being necessary for him to venture his vehicle upon roads that resembled quagmires rather than thoroughfares, and to address Lady Pamela as Miss Clover, who he knew very well was lying in Mrs. Parslow's best bedchamber with a broken leg. But a golden guinea slipped into his hand acted as a notable stimulus to his mental processes, so that he eventually consented to look upon matters in the proper spirit, allowing Lady Pamela to drive him out of the yard of the Swan and Bell without protest, for that young lady had decided, after one look at the way he handled the reins, that they would both be much safer if she took the ribbons.

She had had a most unsatisfactory parting word with Carlin, who also left the Swan and Bell that afternoon. He had still refused to make any commitments to her regarding Whiston Castle, and she was obliged to believe that whatever difficulties she might encounter there she would have to deal with without his assistance. Of course if she found Wyn there, all would be well, but if Wyn had already departed, having been induced to leave the memorandum in the Honourable Cedric's hands, she could not view the future so optimistically.

As there was no possibility of making definite plans before she reached Whiston Castle, however, she very sensibly did not fret over the matter, and devoted herself instead to seeing to it that the gig did not repeat its misfortunes of a few days before and end up on its side in a ditch.

When they neared Whiston Castle she allowed the inexpert young man to take the reins again, and was driven by him through a pair of great iron gates and along a winding drive that led through open parkland, flourishing shrubberies, and smooth lawns to the massive grey stone pile of the Castle itself. This imposing monument to the pride of a mediaeval ancestor had been gently going downhill, as far as upkeep was concerned, ever since the start of the eighteenth century, the recent Earls of Whiston having been a vague and inefficient lot, quite unlike the swashbuckling Mansell who had built the family fortunes. But the marriage of the present Earl to an immensely rich heiress, the daughter of a brewer-king, had turned matters and prevented the Castle from finally slipping out of the hands of the Mansell family altogether. It may be recorded, however, that the present Earl, who was kept upon very short financial rations by his wife and obliged to live the year round upon his ancestral estates because Lady Whiston did not care for London, sometimes wished that it had.

Lady Pamela had little opportunity to admire the magnificent rounded towers of the Castle's south, or entrance, front, because, in her rôle of Maria Clover, this was naturally not her destination. She was driven instead by a side route to an archway leading to a cobblestoned yard at the rear of the house, where she was deposited before a large door and allowed to wait for several minutes before the door was opened to her by a very young scullery maid.

"I am Miss Clover. Lady Sabrina's new maid," Lady Pamela added, her self-confidence deserting her momentarily as the little maid dropped her a frightened curtsey, exactly as she would have done if Lady Pamela had announced herself by her true title. But then she remembered Miss Clover's lecture on the rules of precedence belowstairs, and realised that she was only being given her due as Lady Sabrina's personal attendant by the lower orders of the Whiston Castle staff.

The scullery maid conducted her, with many breathless apologies for having kept her waiting, along a stone-flagged corridor to a door at its end, where she tapped and was bidden by a rather terrifying bass voice to come in. Lady Pamela, who had been given the impression that she was being led into the housekeeper's presence, was for a moment slightly confused, but upon entering the room she found herself indeed confronting a female, a very stout one in black bombazine, with such a large and overflowing double chin that it appeared to carry her face down almost into her bosom.

The scullery maid, basely deserting her charge at the sight of what Lady Pamela reminded herself was to her the equivalent of Royalty, said something incoherent and bolted off down the corridor, and Lady Pamela, considering a curtsey called for by the baleful glance being directed at her out of the small eyes above the double chin, dropped a respectful one and stood waiting for Royalty's permission to speak.

"I take it," said Royalty in Its rumbling voice, apparently mollified by this evidence of a proper attitude, "that you are Lady Sabrina's new lady?"

Lady Pamela said that she was, adding that her name was Maria Clover.

"I," said Royalty, condescending to extend a pudgy hand, "am Mrs. Biddlecombe. The Housekeeper. Welcome to Whiston Castle, Miss Clover." And she then took all the bloom off her condescension by adding in the measured tones of a judge pronouncing sentence upon a criminal in the dock, "You. Are. Late."

"Yes, I know," said Lady Pamela. "I am so sorry, but it was the snow. The gig overturned and I was obliged to spend two nights in a horrid little inn."

To her great relief Mrs. Biddlecombe, instead of going on with the sentence, relented and said the Sacrifices they were called upon to make for the sake of the Upper Orders were Something Cruel, to which sentiments Lady Pamela sychophantically gave her assent.

"You will take a glass of port with me, Miss Clover, before we go upstairs to Lady Whiston," said Mrs. Biddlecombe, moving ponderously to a very well-stocked sideboard and decanting a rich liquid into two glasses.

Lady Pamela, who detested port, resigned herself and accepted one of the glasses with what she hoped would be taken as a smile of delight at the honour being done her.

"You will find, Miss Clover," said Mrs. Biddlecombe, who apparently quite approved of Lady Pamela's leaving the conversation chiefly to her, "many changes here, I have no doubt, from your previous situation. We have, you might say,

Great Plans for our little Sabrina. Very shortly we shall be taking her to London to visit the Fashionable Shops, which will be quite a Treat for her, not being used to City Life. Lady W., you see, does not favour the Metropolis. The necessity for our little Sabrina to make her come-out there this spring is all that drags her away from the Joys of Whiston Castle."

Lady Pamela, looking about at the room in which she sat, its walls, ceiling, and fireplace seeming bowed with the strain of supporting the huge bulk of the Castle above it, but very snug indeed with its blazing fire on the hearth and its windows showing the depth of the four-foot-thick walls in which they were set, thought that for the belowstairs party, at least, Whiston Castle did seem a quite satisfactory sort of domicile, which one would not be eager to leave for the crowded discomfort of the servants' attics of a London town house. But that was neither here nor there as far as she was concerned, and after expressing a suitable polite interest in Lady Sabrina's come-out she got down to the main point at once and enquired if the family were all in residence at the Castle.

Royalty, looking none too well pleased by this introduction of a subject not of Its own choosing, said in a rather repressive voice that they were not.

"Our eldest son, Viscount Weare, is abroad at present," Mrs. Biddlecombe condescended to explain. "The Honourable Cedric, our second son, came down from London on the Wednesday but left this morning, not being inclined to spend much time at the Castle. Owing to Quarrels," she added elliptically. "I fear the Honourable Cedric is Not All He Should Be."

Lady Pamela, her spirits suffering a considerable depression at the news that the bird she had gone to such pains to pursue had already flown, enquired if there were any guests then in the house.

Mrs. Biddlecombe said regretfully that they were quite thin of company at present.

"There is only Mr. Broadbank, the gentleman who came by appointment to meet the Honourable Cedric here on the Wednesday," she said. "And why the Honourable C. didn't take him away with him this morning I cannot say, I'm sure, for nobody else in the Castle ever so much as set eyes on him before. Mr. Mingle, our Butler, says he told Lord W. he was interested in studying the arkytecture of the Castle. Arkytecture my eye," said Royalty, suddenly becoming alarmingly colloquial and looking balefully at Lady Pamela. "If it's studying arkytecture to be poking your nose into all sorts of places where it's got no business to be, then he's studying it, right enough. Otherwise not. And that man of his is just as bad. One of them foreigners he is—a nasty, cribbage-faced little snirp with eyes like gooseberries."

Having concluded this graphic description, Mrs. Biddlecombe ponderously rose and informed the supposed Miss Clover that she would now take her upstairs and present her to Lady Whiston, leaving Lady Pamela to follow her from the room in a highly unsettled state of mind. It was quite clear to her by this time that neither Wyn nor Cedric Mansell was at the Castle, and that, moreover, Wyn had never been there; but now she had been presented with another problem in the person of the mysterious student of architecture, Mr. Broadbank, with his foreign manservant. Was it possible, she thought, that he too was a part of the puzzle she was trying to unravel? If Wyn had succeeded in passing the memorandum to Cedric in London, and Cedric had then come to Whiston Castle to turn it over to a foreign agent . . .

But if he had already given the memorandum into Mr. Broadbank's hands, why then was Mr. Broadbank remaining at the Castle? This was a question to which Lady Pamela felt that she would much like to have the answer, and as she followed the regal figure of Mrs. Biddlecombe along the corridor and up a very tight and inconvenient circular stone staircase (in which she felt some concern that her guide might become wedged, causing her to speculate for a moment as to whether fifteenth-century people were never fat and so made no provision for extra human width in their building), her mind was busy with Mr. Broadbank.

There is an old phrase beginning, *Speak of the devil*, and in this case merely thinking of him appeared to have the same effect. As Mrs. Biddlecombe pushed open a green baize door at the top of the staircase and Lady Pamela followed her into what she at once perceived to be the Great Hall of the Castle, she found herself confronted by an elderly gentleman of such overpowering proportions that for a moment it seemed to her reeling mind that she was gazing upon the masculine twin of her conductress.

In an instant, however, she perceived her error. In sheer bulk Mr. Broadbank (for such, a ventriloquial whisper from Mrs. Biddlecombe informed her, was the gentleman who had so abruptly appeared before them) was undoubtedly a match for the housekeeper. But where her eye was baleful, his was benevolent, and where it appeared that laughter upon Mrs. Biddlecombe's lips could occur only as the result of a kind of upheaval of nature, Mr. Broadbank's face seemed to be wreathed in a perpetual smile, ready to expand at any instant into a good-natured chuckle. Yet a certain watchful and enigmatic expression in the small eyes set in that benevolent face for some reason made Lady Pamela regard this entire jolly ensemble as being far more sinister than Mrs. Biddlecombe's open hostility to the human race.

Mrs. Biddlecombe dropped a curtsey; Lady Pamela, almost forgetting herself momentarily in her interested survey of Mr. Broadbank, hurriedly did likewise.

"And who is this pretty miss?" asked Mr. Broadbank in avuncular tones, quite as if, Mrs. Biddlecombe observed later in strong disapproval, he was One of the Family.

Mrs. Biddlecombe said dampingly that it was Lady Sabrina's new abigail, and gave Mr. Broadbank a glance that dared him so much as to lay a finger upon one of the suits of armour ranged stiffly about the walls of the severe. barrel-vaulted Hall or to repose himself upon one of the highly uncomfortable carved chairs offering the only alternative to the stone window-seat facing the cavernous fireplace. She then toiled on up the great staircase leading to the floor above.

Here, in a modern sitting room done in the latest fashion, all yellow damask and elegantly gilded furniture. which came as a most unexpected surprise after the mediaeval severity of the lower portions of the Castle, they found Lady Whiston, in a half dress of amber figured silk, seated at an escritoire with a heap of papers upon it, which she appeared to be dealing with in a masterful and peremptory fashion.

Lady Whiston was a plump, fair woman with an autocratic manner, who did not stop talking from the time Lady Pamela entered the room until she left it. She looked Lady Pamela up and down. informed her that she would find she had a good place at the Castle if she was prompt and willing, and adept at doing a head, said that as the matter of wages had

43

already been settled they need not discuss that, and dismissed her to go to Lady Sabrina. As Lady Pamela left the room she almost walked into a small, anxious-looking gentleman apparently about to seek admittance to it, and heard him uttering a nervously deprecatory greeting as he went in behind her.

"Lord Whiston," said Mrs. Biddlecombe, as she conducted Lady Pamela to Lady Sabrina's room, and she added, "Poor Man," in a tone that told Lady Pamela more about Lord Whiston than an hour's dissertation could have done.

Lady Pamela, who at this point badly wanted time to think out what her next step would be, was not granted that time, even though she was released from the overpowering presence of Mrs. Biddlecombe as soon as the latter had made her known to Lady Sabrina Mansell. Indeed, in Lady Sabrina's presence no one ever had time to think of anything, for she was a vivacious little blonde, quite as voluble as her mother though in a much less objectionable way. She at once flew at Lady Pamela with a host of questions about the London amusements and fashionable shops to which she was shortly to be introduced.

"You see, I have never been *anywhere*, Clover," she informed her, as she curled up expectantly in a bergère armchair beside the modern tent-bed in her very pretty bedchamber. "I don't count Bath, because it is so dreadfully fusty, at least when we have gone there, which was during the Season, when everyone who isn't at least *ninety* years old is in London. But Mama says you were in London last Season with Lady Overfield, and will be able to do my hair *à la Meduse*, and tell me what sort of bonnets everyone is wearing, and how the Prince looks, and the Princess Charlotte—"

Lady Pamela, looking into the pretty, eager face upturned so expectantly to hers, at once characteristically decided that here was someone who needed taking in hand. Temporarily abandoning her concern over the memorandum, she said very firmly *not* the Medusa.

"Too, too *demi-monde*," she said, and then, remembering her menial status, added, "my lady. *A l'Anglaise*, I think, for a young lady about to make her come-out. I expect your hair falls naturally into those lovely curls and does not need to be papered?"

Sabrina looked rebellious for a moment. She had obviously

had it in mind to appear at Almack's wearing her hair in a maddeningly seductive manner, with her petticoat dampened to make her gown cling revealingly to her charming little figure; but she soon found herself seated willy-nilly in a chair before her dressing-table mirror while Lady Pamela's deft fingers gave her a simple, natural, and most becoming coiffure, of which even Pletcher could have been proud.

"Oh, it is perfectly *splendid!*" cried Sabrina, when Lady Pamela had handed her her glass so that she could properly admire it from every angle. "I *do* look *quite* grown up now! Only what a pity that there is no one in the house to see it except that horrid Mr. Broadbank Ceddie brought here! Or at least he didn't bring him but he came to see Ceddie, and now he won't go away!"

"Won't go away?" repeated Lady Pamela, her ears at once on the prick. "That seems very odd, my lady! Is it the extremely stout gentleman I met on my way upstairs?"

"Yes," said Sabrina, with a very *un*grown-up giggle. "Isn't he a perfect Bartholomew baby? But for all he looks so innocent, there is something very queer about him, *I* think. In the first place, though he pretends that he and Ceddie—that is my brother Cedric, you know—are great friends, I heard them having words last night, and he told Ceddie in the most *sinister* way that what he was doing was extremely dangerous, and that if he wouldn't take the price that was being offered him, he wouldn't be responsible for the consequences. I told Mama about it, but she only said it was all a hum and Ceddie had some very odd friends. But she *is* annoyed that Mr. Broadbank won't go away now, because she doesn't in the least know what to do with him; only he says she needn't do anything, because all he wishes to do is to study the architecture of the Castle—"

Sabrina prattled on, divagating presently from the subject of Mr. Broadbank to return to her favourite topic of her forthcoming visit to London; but Lady Pamela attended to her with only half an ear. She was thinking furiously, putting together Mr. Broadbank's quarrel with the Honourable Cedric and his strange desire to remain at the Castle, now that Cedric had departed. If it was indeed the missing memorandum that Cedric had in his possession and that Mr. Broadbank was endeavouring to obtain from him, she thought it would seem far more probable that Mr. Broadbank, unable or unwilling to meet the price Cedric was asking for it, would choose to follow him, instead of remaining at the Castle, and perhaps try foul means of obtaining it where fair ones had failed.

Except, her thoughts ran on, *except* if Mr. Broadbank had reason to believe that Cedric had prudently decided not to keep upon his person or in his immediate possession a document of such dangerous importance, and had instead left it behind in some place of safekeeping at the Castle. That would explain Mr. Broadbank's refusal to leave, as well as his sudden passion for architecture, which allowed him to poke about into odd corners of the Castle. . . .

Lady Pamela made up her mind. Wyn or no Wyn, Cedric or no Cedric, if Mr. Broadbank remained at the Castle, so would she, and she too would try her hand at finding where Cedric had hidden the memorandum.

Six

Once she had arrived at this conclusion, her chief difficulty was how to find an opportunity to initiate her search for the memorandum. Sabrina indeed consented to part with her presently long enough for her to be shown to her room in the servants' quarters, where she was agreeably surprised to find that the underling assigned to do the menial tasks of brushing, pressing, and mending that Pletcher so scorned was quite as diligent in unpacking her (or rather Miss Clover's) possessions as any servant who had ever waited upon her in her higher estate.

But Sabrina, having taken a violent fancy to her, besides being anxious to go with her into the matter of the additions to her wardrobe that were to be purchased in London, claimed her again almost immediately. It was not, in fact, until she had sent that young lady down to dinner in a very pretty frock of blue sarsnet, with her fair curls faultlessly arranged in the admired new style, that she was free to institute her first investigation of the Castle.

Where to begin was a problem she had been puzzling over all the while she had been poring with Sabrina over the pages of *La Belle Assemblée* and guiding her errant taste away from such unsuitable costumes as a dashing evening toilette of diaphanous spider gauze, lavishly adorned with silver fringe, and a travelling dress of purple satin, worn with a daring bonnet *à la Hussar*. The Honourable Cedric's bedchamber appeared a logical first choice, but as it was situated (as she had been able to learn by adroit questioning of Sabrina) directly across the passage from Lord Whiston's chamber, and Hort, his lordship's valet, was annoyingly popping in and out like a jack-in-the-box on various errands connected with preparing his noble master for his appearance in the dining room, she decided that she must postpone her search of this promising hunting ground until later.

She was therefore obligated to content herself instead with

a rapid survey of the Castle's first floor. This consisted of the Great Hall and a pair of large withdrawing rooms, all furnished with such Spartan severity that unless the Honourable Cedric had somehow managed to insert the memorandum inside one of the suits of armour gloomily ranging the walls of the Great Hall she could not conceive where he might have concealed it there.

She was thoughtfully examining the huge stone fireplace, which seemed to have nothing at all feasible to offer, when the hall-boy came in to inform her that dinner would be in half an hour, as soon as His Nibs, by which term Lady Pamela understood him to mean Mingle, the butler, was able to leave the dining room abovestairs and take his place at the head of the table. Apparently being a lad with no proper sense of reverence for his superiors, he then looked her over approvingly and said she was a regular dasher, wasn't she?— which compliment Lady Pamela, in her rôle as Clover, accepted with a toss of the head and an admonition to him to keep his sauce to himself.

Rather well satisfied with herself, she then went off to her own chamber to make such alterations in her toilette as she judged proper for the occasion, and shortly afterwards repaired to the Housekeeper's Room, where she found the rest of the company already gathered.

In the course of three London Seasons, Lady Pamela had gained a considerable amount of social experience, but she had to admit to some nervousness at the idea of facing a roomful of very superior upper servants as an equal, and rather wished that Carlin were there to assist her, for being a gentleman who had descended to becoming a coachman he might have been able to give her some valuable hints as to how she was to conduct herself. But since he was not, she fell back upon Miss Clover's instructions and was very deferential to Mrs. Biddlecombe and the butler, a tall, severe man who would have made an excellent bishop, and very patronising about Lady Sabrina.

"She seems a nice little thing," she said in an offhand voice, upon being asked her opinion of her, and this on the whole made a good impression. For though Sabrina was a universal favourite with the staff, and predictions were made to Lady Pamela that she would have all the Pinks of the Ton dangling at her shoestrings when she went up to London, and go off in her first Season as sure as check, it nevertheless appeared to be felt that one ought not to go too far in encouraging the pretensions of the Upper Orders by indiscriminate praise of them.

As the Honourable Cedric was not in residence and his valet was therefore unavailable to partner Lady Pamela, she went in to dinner on the arm of Mr. Broadbank's man, Droz. This suited her very well, though being an elegantly tall young lady and Droz very short, she found herself feeling quite a Maypole beside him. Mrs. Biddlecombe's description had prepared her for his rather odd appearance, but he had a courtly air towards the female sex that would have suited an ambassador, and aside from displaying a somewhat primitive technique at table with a knife and fork could have filled that position with great credit.

Lady Pamela, determined to make the most of her position beside him at dinner, inaugurated the conversation by enquiring from what part of the country his employer came.

"I beg your pardon," said Droz, looking at her out of his mistrustful gooseberry eyes. "A thousand pardons. I do not speak very well the English."

Lady Pamela rapidly considered admitting to a knowledge of French but decided against it. Miss Clover had indeed used the term *comme il faut* in her conversation with her at the Swan and Bell, but it was obvious that this phrase, and perhaps *à la mode*, was the extent of her acquaintance with that language. So she smiled encouragingly instead and said she was sure he spoke English very well.

"From Sussex, isn't he?" she asked, choosing a county at random, and went on, shamelessly plagiarising from Miss Clover. "I had an auntie there in service a few years back who has since gone to her reward, poor soul, and I am sure that was the name of the gentleman she worked for."

Droz, looking alarmed, said no, Mr. Broadbank did not come from Sussex.

"Well, where then?" Lady Pamela asked, with her usual directness.

Droz said evasively that his employer lived a great deal abroad, and then, seeing Lady Pamela about to bear down upon him with another question, hastily added in Portugal.

"Dear me," said Lady Pamela. "Why does he do that?"

Fortunately for Droz, Mingle here took a hand in the con-

versation by providing the information that that was where
port came from, adding judiciously that, if anybody wanted
his opinion, Lady W. kept his lordship on such a monkey's
allowance, when it came to the wine he was able to bring
into the house, that the cellars would be empty before long.

"Is she a squeeze-crab, then?" Lady Pamela enquired, her
interest momentarily diverted from Droz.

Mingle looked for a moment as if he might be going to
resent her putting herself forward by speaking before she was
spoken to, but, being inclined to an appreciation of female
beauty, he decided to overlook the solecism she had been
guilty of and replied in a stately manner that her ladyship
would tip over the dibs in style any time it was a matter of
something for herself or little Sabrina, but that she was a fair
purse-leech where his lordship was concerned.

"There's nothing he'd like better," he said, "than to pop up
to London now and again and look in at White's or Boodle's,
or be off to Newmarket for the races; but will Lady W. come
up with the pitch and pay for a nice little jaunt like that?"

A commiserating murmur from the table at large gave the
answer.

"But I should think," said Lady Pamela interestedly, recall-
ing Lady Whiston's extremely fashionable dress and manner,
"that Lady W. would care for London herself—?"

"Not *her*," said Mrs. Biddlecombe, in deep scorn. "She was
Nobody at All before she married his lordship, and we all
know what *that* means when it comes to being Somebody in
London. Lady Jersey's dresser's sister told Mr. Mingle's
cousin, him that was head groom for Lord Branch, that they
called her the Brewer's Daughter when she first went up there
with his lordship. Trying to push herself in everywhere, and
his lordship that mortified he didn't know where to look. His
old father made him marry her because of the money, they
say, and a worse piece of work he never did in his life. The
poor gentleman hasn't drawn an easy breath, I'll be bound,
since he got himself leg-shackled to her."

Lady Pamela, though much interested in these intimate
revelations of Life at Whiston Castle, recollected at this moment that she was neglecting Droz, and went back to her
conversation with him.

"I have been told," she said to him chattily, "that Mr.

Broadbank is interested in arkytecture. Are you interested in arkytecture, Mr. Droz?"

Droz hastily disclaimed any interest in or knowledge of the subject.

"Does he make drawings?" Lady Pamela perseveringly enquired. "In my last place but one, there was a gentleman who visited all the Great Houses and made simply reams and reams of them."

Droz, fixing her with a harassed eye, said firmly that Mr. Broadbank made no drawings.

"No," Mrs. Biddlecombe's bass voice cut in unexpectedly. "He don't! He spends his time poking into places where he's got no business to be—such as cabinets in the gun room. And what I want to know is, how long is he going to stay about here doing that? No offence to present company, of course," she added, looking terrifyingly at Droz out of her small eyes.

Droz said he didn't know, at which admission of ignorance everyone at the table regarded him in pitying contempt and Lord Whiston's valet said he'd like to see the day when he didn't know old Percy's plans before old Percy knew them himself. Lady Pamela, gathering that old Percy was Lord Whiston, gazed at him respectfully, and Droz looked crushed.

But crushed or not, no information could be dragged from him concerning his employer, even though both Mingle and Mrs. Biddlecombe joined in the inquisition. When driven to the wall, he fell back upon his imperfect knowledge of English, maintaining his air of abject bewilderment all the while. But Lady Pamela, surprising a darkling glance from the gooseberry eyes and a vengeful mutter of—"*Sacré tas d'imbéciles!*"—as they rose from the table to return to the Housekeeper's Room for their pudding and wine, thought that he was not quite so innocent as he wished to appear. As a matter of fact, he was almost as sinister, she decided, as his master, besides being—despite his name, which sounded Middle European—by his accent undoubtedly French.

The chief difficulty in having no one with whom to discuss one's plans in a crisis is that there is nobody to warn one to proceed with caution. Certainly, had Carlin been at the Castle and available for consultation, he would have advised Lady Pamela not to show her hand to her opponents by letting them see she was aware of what they were up to.

But Carlin was not there, and Lady Pamela, rushing her

fences as she would never have been guilty of doing on the hunting field, said to Droz as they were having a glass of the second-best Madeira together, "Oh, Mr. Droz, I hear that your Mr. Broadbank and the Honourable Cedric had the most frightful quarrel last night. Do tell me what it was about. I don't think even Mrs. Biddlecombe knows, and I would so love to know something she doesn't so that I could boast about it to her."

This was the sort of appeal that, coming from Lady Pamela, had been known to cause subalterns shamelessly to betray the peccadilloes of their superior officers and rising young diplomats to babble official secrets; but valets, she now discovered, were made of sterner stuff. Droz, taking alarm on the instant, gave her a reproachful glance and said that Mr. Broadbank was a very nize gentleman, who never quarrelled.

"Well, he quarrelled with the Honourable Cedric," said Lady Pamela obstinately, with an "in for a penny, in for a pound" feeling. "I *do* know that."

"How?" demanded Droz, looking at her intensely. "You were not here yesterday, Miss Clover, I do not think—*hein?*"

"No, I wasn't here," said Lady Pamela. "Someone told me."

"Then that someone will perhaps tell you also what this quarrel I do not believe in was about," said Droz, turning a gaze of such fixed intensity upon her now that Lady Pamela felt her disguise coming apart beneath it and waited with an uncomfortably breathless feeling for everyone to discover that she was not Maria Clover.

So firmly fixed did this apprehension become in her mind that when Droz, turning the tables on her, suddenly began questioning her about her own antecedents and past situations, she pleaded fatigue and fled to her bedchamber to escape, where she remained until summoned to assist Sabrina to retire.

She found that volatile young lady yawning but in even higher spirits than she had been in during the afternoon. A note, she informed Lady Pamela, had most unexpectedly been brought by hand from Marlborough just after dinner, and on the morrow they were to have a welcome guest at the Castle.

"It is Lord Dalven, a friend of my cousin, Sir Harry Allensworth, from Scotland," she said. "He has sent Mama a very civil note saying that, as he is in this part of the country, he would like to call and pay his respects, and Mama means to ask him to stay for a few days if he is able. Harry is in the Peninsula now, you know, with Lord Wellington's army, and Lord Dalven says he was with him there, and often heard Harry speak of us. Harry is a very *dashing* person, you see, and as Lord Dalven says he is his most intimate friend, I should think he must be dashing, too—don't you? So do you think the French cambric tomorrow or the new sprig gown? Oh, no! That makes me look so *young!*"

Lady Pamela, whose interest in Scottish cousins and their noble friends, dashing or not, was at the moment quite non-existent, said the French cambric would be very nice, and tried to turn the conversation to the quarrel Sabrina had overheard between Mr. Broadbank and her brother Cedric. But she might have saved her breath, for with a dashing young man in the offing Mr. Broadbank was nothing and less than nothing to Sabrina. Lady Pamela was obliged to leave her at last, having learned not a whit more of Mr. Broadbank, and return to her own bedchamber in the servants' quarters.

In this apartment, however, she had no intention of remaining. As soon as the household should have settled down for the night she would, she was determined, embark upon her interrupted explorations, and this time there would be nothing to prevent her from carrying out a thorough search of the Honourable Cedric's bedchamber.

Having provided herself with a candle, she accordingly stole out of her room just as the stable clock was chiming one and made her way along the passage to the circular staircase and up its draughty, winding steps. Not being a fanciful young woman, the thought of the inevitable Castle ghost—in the case of Whiston, that of a lady in grey, of whose existence she had kindly been informed during dinner by Mrs. Biddlecombe—did not trouble her. She proceeded boldly into the Great Hall, ignoring the leaping shadows the unsteady flame of her candle cast along its walls, and went on up the stairs to the floor above. Here, moving swiftly along the passage, she reached the door of the Honourable Cedric's bedchamber and had just laid her hand upon the door-latch when a gleam of light that certainly did not emanate from the candle she held in her hand caught her eye. It came from the other end of the corridor and was proceeding steadily towards her.

Lady Pamela did not hesitate. In an instant she had extinguished her candle and whisked herself inside the Honourable Cedric's bedchamber. There could be no danger of anyone's finding her there, she assured herself, albeit a trifle breathlessly. No matter whose footsteps they were that she could hear approaching quietly down the passage, their owner could have no reason to enter the Honourable Cedric's unoccupied room.

The footsteps reached the door; the door opened, and candlelight fell into the room. Lady Pamela was betrayed into a squeak of alarm, and stepped swiftly behind the bed-curtains. The intruder, apparently also alarmed, raised the candle so that it illuminated his pale, round face and gooseberry eyes, and at the same time displayed a pistol in his other hand.

"Who is there?" said the unmistakable Gallic tones of Droz. "Answer, or I shoot!"

"Dear me!" said Lady Pamela, emerging from behind the bed-curtains. "Is it you, Mr. Droz? I made certain it was burglars! Oh, how you have frightened me!"

And, sinking into a chair, she gave an excellent imitation of a young woman about to be overcome by a fit of the vapours, begging him to assure her that there were no housebreakers in the vicinity and that he would protect her in case there were.

Droz stood regarding her, looking nonplussed and of a divided mind.

"My dear mademoiselle—My dear Miss Clover—" he said, from the chivalrous part of that mind, attempting to soothe her; but then the other part, the practical one, got the upper hand. "What are you doing here?" he demanded.

Lady Pamela, unable to think of a suitable answer, temporised. "What are *you* doing here?" she countered.

Droz, acknowledging a hit, looked nonplussed again. Then inspiration struck.

"I came in because I saw you come in," he said. "I thought you were a—how do you say it?—a *cambrioleur*—"

"A burglar?" said Lady Pamela. "Is it part of your duties as Mr. Broadbank's gentleman, Mr. Droz, to search for burglars in the houses where you stay? *With* a pistol," she added, looking thoughtfully at that useful article.

Droz, visibly driven back against the wall, rattled in gamely once more and said that Mr. Broadbank had rung for him and as he was nervous of strange houses in the dark he had taken the pistol with him.

"And Lady Sabrina rang for *me*," said Lady Pamela, swift to turn a clever stroke of her opponent's to her own advantage. She stood up. "So if you will assure me that there are no burglars, I shall go to her now," she said. "Pray light my candle for me before you go."

They stood there regarding each other, neither, it seemed, willing to leave the other in possession of the field. Lady Pamela was quite certain that Droz's purpose in prowling about the Castle at night was the same as hers, and had no intention of tamely going off and permitting him to search the Honourable Cedric's room at his leisure; nor, she saw, had Droz any intention of allowing her to do so.

A compromise was reached without words. Droz rekindled Lady Pamela's candle from his own and, standing aside, allowed her to precede him out of the room, whereupon she paused just beyond the threshold to make sure that he had followed her. Checkmated, he closed the door. Only then did she start off down the passage in the direction of Sabrina's bedchamber. Upon reaching it, she glanced back and saw that Droz, standing before the door of Mr. Broadbank's room, was doing likewise. Then they simultaneously turned the doorknobs of their respective employers' chambers and went inside.

How Mr. Broadbank received this unexpected nocturnal intrusion Lady Pamela had no way of knowing, but to her profound relief Sabrina remained fast asleep, dreaming, no doubt, of Lord Dalven and the joys of receiving the attentions of a buck of the first head that might be hers on the morrow. Lady Pamela, unable to stir for fear of wakening her or to leave the room until a sufficient period of time had elapsed for it to be presumed that she had attended to the orders that were the alleged reason for her having been called to Sabrina's room at this odd hour, began to feel very cold and sleepy, suppressed a sneeze, and thought longingly of her bed. No doubt it was her duty to try to devise some method by which she could return to the Honourable Cedric's bedchamber that night and search it without the danger of further interruption, but she could not think of one at the moment.

The unfortunate thing was that there were two of them—Mr. Broadbank and Droz—and only one of her, which gave them, she considered, an unfair advantage. If Wyn were there—And where was Wyn, and how was she to set about finding him while she was detained here at Whiston Castle by her search for the memorandum? If only that odious Carlin had consented to help her!

Ten minutes later, considering that she had waited long enough, she cautiously opened the door and stepped out into the hall. At the same moment, farther down the passage, Mr. Broadbank's door opened and Droz emerged. He came down the passage towards her.

"Ah—Mademoiselle Clover!" he said politely. "May I escort you to your room?"

"Yes, certainly, Mr. Droz," she replied equally politely, but with mayhem in her heart.

They walked sedately along the passage together and down the stairs. Mr. Broadbank, thought Lady Pamela wrathfully, could not have a clearer field now to search the Honourable Cedric's bedchamber. She could only hope that Cedric's cleverness in hiding the memorandum had been superior to Mr. Broadbank's cleverness in looking for it, and was comforted by the thought that, from what she had heard of Cedric, it probably was.

So, as there seemed nothing else to do that night, with Droz undoubtedly willing to sit up watching her door until dawn like a terrier at a rat hole, she went back to her room and to bed. It had been a long day, she reflected, and perhaps in the morning she would have new ideas and new plans.

Seven

❧

But in the morning she found herself kept so well occupied by Sabrina and Lady Whiston that she had scarcely time to think of the memorandum, far less do anything about it. Apparently Lady Whiston's energetic handling of estate matters—in which, Lady Pamela had been given to understand, she rode roughshod over her lord's tenantry, interfering in the most intimate details of their domestic lives, from the acquisition of a new broody to the marriage of their daughters—did not cease at her own doorstep, and the appearance at Whiston Castle of a presumably unmarried peer was obviously not to be neglected by her as an opportunity to meddle. She was in and out of her daughter's room several times while Lady Pamela was attempting to dress her hair and attire her in the charming frock of French cambric that Sabrina had chosen for the occasion, until Lady Pamela, teased almost past endurance by her constant—"This will not do!"—and—"You must change that, Clover!"—at last gave her a tart answer and received in return a sharp set-down for her impertinence.

"You must mend your manners, my girl, if you intend to remain in *my* employ!" said Lady Whiston, looking at her with an expression of extreme disapproval upon her face. "I wonder that Lady Overfield should have endured such impudence from a servant!"

Lady Pamela, seething, made no reply, but proceeded to dress Sabrina's hair as she had been bidden and to attire her in the new sprig gown, resolving at the same time to be kinder to Pletcher in the future. But this could only be called a work of supererogation, for that haughty female had no qualms about giving as good as she got, and usually did.

At last Lady Pamela was able to see her young mistress go off downstairs looking to her mama's satisfaction, and she was about to settle down to do some really serious thinking about her own problems when, to her annoyance, a footman came upstairs to tell her that Lady Whiston had decided she would like Lady Sabrina's new Norwich silk shawl with the sprig gown, and would Clover bring it down at once. With an exasperated sigh, Lady Pamela searched out the shawl, and was descending the stairs with it when a well-remembered masculine drawl from below suddenly fell upon her ears.

"Will you tell Lady Whiston that Lord Dalven has called?" said Carlin's voice, and Lady Pamela, proceeding on down the stairs in a kind of fascinated and horrified trance, saw Carlin himself, looking very smart in a drab driving-coat and gleaming top-boots, composedly handing his fawn-coloured beaver and York tan driving gloves to Mingle.

For a moment Lady Pamela, who had never fainted in her life, was quite certain that she was about to do so, for the walls swam about her and a kind of mist rose before her eyes. These phenomena were followed by a moment's quite horrible doubt of her own sanity. She had been thinking of Carlin, she told herself, and now she had superimposed his features upon the no doubt quite different face of the man who had just announced himself as Lord Dalven. She squeezed her eyes shut and then opened them again, hoping against hope that the apparition would have disappeared and leave her gazing rationally into the face of a complete stranger.

But at that moment the apparition, glancing up and beholding her transfixed upon the stairs, the shawl clasped in her arms, gave her the merest shadow of a wink, which left no doubt whatever in her mind as to the identity of its perpetrator.

"It *is* Carlin!" she thought, her head whirling. "But—as Lord Dalven? No, it is impossible!"

Mingle, who had disposed of the supposed Lord Dalven's hat and gloves, now trod at a stately pace into the east withdrawing room to announce the caller, and Carlin and Lady Pamela were momentarily left alone in the Hall. Lady Pamela ran quickly down the remaining steps, while Carlin advanced to meet her in a more leisurely manner, a quizzical half-smile upon his dark face.

"Well, Lady Pamela?" he enquired blandly, as they met. "Are you prepared to pay me my fifty guineas? I have won our wager, I think."

For a moment Lady Pamela, who was never at a loss for words, stood uncharacteristically entirely speechless.

"But—but what have you done with Lord Dalven?" she demanded when she had found her tongue.

"Well, I have not murdered him, as you appear to think," Carlin assured her soothingly. "As a matter of fact, I expect he is still in the Peninsula. But if he is not, it makes no great odds. He is not likely to turn up here, I think."

"Yes, but—but—" sputtered Lady Pamela, finding it impossible to marshal her unruly thoughts, which were divided between admiration of an audacity exceeding the limits even of her own most daring flights and shock at the deception about to be practised upon the unsuspecting Whistons.

The sound of Mingle's footsteps returning in measured progress to the Hall was heard.

"Later," Carlin's voice cut her off firmly, and he turned his back upon her and began examining with the aid of his quizzing-glass a remarkably fine suit of eleventh-century Norman armour, complete with conical iron helm, coif, and hauberk of linked chain-mail.

Mingle, approaching him magisterially, said that the ladies were in the withdrawing room, if his lordship would be pleased to follow him. Carlin, accepting with aplomb this respectful form of address, did so, and Lady Pamela suddenly awoke from her bemused state, bethought herself of the Norwich silk shawl she was carrying, and started after him. She reached the door of the withdrawing room in time to see him being greeted with the greatest effusiveness by Lady Whiston.

"My dear Lord Dalven, such an unexpected pleasure to see you here! You can't think how *charmed* I was to receive your note, and my little Sabrina has been cast *quite* into transports over the thought of meeting one of her cousin's friends! Oh! This *is* Sabrina. Sabrina, come and make your curtsey to Lord Dalven. She is to make her come-out this Season, you know; I *do* hope we shall see you at our ball! Do you go to London? You have been in the Peninsula, I understand. *So* dangerous—but I see you have escaped quite unscathed. Clover, what in the world are you doing here? Oh—the shawl! Let me have it, and then you may go."

Carlin, taking advantage of this momentary diversion of Lady Whiston's attention from him, had possessed himself of Sabrina's hand and was greeting her with practised gallantry.

Really, thought Lady Pamela, blinking in astonishment, for a coachman he did it amazingly well! But one had to remember that, after all, he *had* been born a gentleman. She was almost perishing with curiosity to stay and hear what would happen next, but there was no possible excuse for her to remain in the room any longer, now that the shawl had been delivered, so she reluctantly withdrew, almost colliding with Lord Whiston in the doorway as she did so.

The Earl advanced upon Carlin, his hands outstretched.

"Well, well, my boy—this is indeed a pleasant surprise!" Lady Pamela heard him exclaiming as she left the room.

"If I were a proper sort of female, I should have palpitations, or a fit of the vapours, after *that* encounter!" she told herself with some asperity, as she climbed the stairs to Sabrina's room once more. "That abominable man, not giving me the least hint of what he was planning! And how can he hope to stay here and impose on the entire family with this Canterbury tale that he is Dalven! Thank heavens, he *does* seem to know the man, but still he is taking the most appalling risks!"

Encountering Droz in the upstairs hall, she gave him a cool good morning and went on into Sabrina's room, her mind once more going back to its speculations as to whether he or Mr. Broadbank had returned to the Honourable Cedric's bedchamber and searched it during the night just past. If they had, she did not believe they had found what they were looking for, at any rate, for Droz seemed quite as mistrustful and watchful of her as he had appeared the night before, and she had heard no hint that Mr. Broadbank intended to leave the house. It was with some satisfaction—in spite of the shock that Carlin's appearance had given her—that she reflected that she too would now have an ally in her quest for the missing document, for it never occurred to her that, once having succeeded in introducing himself into the Castle, Carlin would persist in his refusal to help her.

It soon appeared, however, that—laudable as his intentions along this line might be—he would have some difficulty in putting them into practice. Lady Whiston, it seemed, had taken to her bosom this exceedingly ineligible (if only she had known it! Lady Pamela thought) friend of her nephew's, whom she appeared to consider as at least good practice material in the campaign she was about to open to secure a suitable husband for her daughter. And Sabrina herself, of a romantic age and temperament and with an exceedingly limited experience with men, showed alarming signs of being about to fall in love with him before she had been in his company above two hours.

"He is so very handsome! Don't you think him handsome, Clover?" she demanded dreamily, regarding her reflexion in the mirror with unseeing eyes as Lady Pamela's deft, elegant fingers tidied her curls before she went down to luncheon.

Lady Pamela, who was no more blind to broad shoulders, an athletic figure, and strong, well-chiselled features than the rest of her sex, said judiciously that she dared say he was, but added somewhat dampingly, remembering a favourite tag of her old nurse's, that handsome was as handsome did.

"Oh, yes!" said Sabrina enthusiastically. "And Lord Dalven *is!* Or do I mean he *does?* He has told us the most *interesting* things about the Peninsula, and being in Lord Wellington's army and fighting the French, and though he will not say so directly, one can see that he is frightfully brave and—and chivalrous—"

"Chivalrous! Good God!" said Lady Pamela indignantly, remembering Carlin's cavalier rejection of her pleas for assistance at the Swan and Bell. "My poor deluded child—"

"I am *not* deluded! And what can *you* possibly know of him?" Sabrina demanded, firing up on the instant. "You have scarcely laid eyes upon him!" She relapsed into dreaminess once more. "Only think, Clover!—he has promised to come to my ball in London, and has already engaged me for two dances! I said he might have three, but Mama said it wouldn't be proper and he quite agreed with her—though I don't think myself that he really cares a pin about the proprieties. Oh, Clover, you can't think how exciting it will be to have him here for two whole days, for he says he can spare us that much time before he must go on to London!"

"God give me patience!" said Lady Pamela to herself, mentally resolving to give Carlin a severe rakedown at the first opportunity she had of conversing with him. His impudence really passed all bounds, she thought, for, not content with gulling the entire household with this outrageous imposture, he must needs begin casting out lures to a bread-and-butter miss the moment he clapped eyes on her.

But perhaps he had been so strongly attracted to her as she

was to him, the uncomfortable thought suddenly obtruded—and why it should have been uncomfortable Lady Pamela could not have said, except that one's brains had quite understandably become somewhat addled from the shock of seeing a coachman standing in the Great Hall pretending to be a Scottish peer.

At any rate, she was determined to have a conversation with Carlin very soon, and would no doubt have been betrayed into doing something decidedly risky and improper in a lady's maid to attain her resolve had not Carlin forestalled her by communicating with her himself. This he did by the simple expedient of sending Charles, the second footman, to her with a note requesting her to meet him that evening after dinner in the walled garden behind the Castle. If anything else had been needed to make her quite furious with him, this did the trick. Of course that horrid, grinning footman must think that Lord Dalven, having cast his ogles on a prime bit of game, as he, Charles, would put it, was seeking an assignation with her!

"Well?" said Charles, watching her with a meaning smirk as she perused the note and glanced up at him, her countenance suddenly quite flushed. "What answer am I to take back?"

"None at all!" snapped Lady Pamela.

And she walked off, fuming to herself.

But in spite of continuing to fume all afternoon she was in the walled garden at the appointed time, thanking heaven that at least a day of mild weather had made it possible for her to do so without catching pneumonia.

She had scarcely entered it when Carlin also appeared, smoking one of the cigars that the officers of Wellington's army had learned to enjoy in the Peninsula, but that most hostesses still refused to permit inside their saloons or drawing rooms.

"Good evening," he said and, indicating the cigar, enquired politely, "Do you object to this?"

"Object to *that!*" said Lady Pamela, with strong feeling. "As if that weren't the least of what you have given me to object to! What do you mean, you abominable man, by sending me that note? Didn't you *know* what Charles would think?"

"Is Charles the footman?" asked Carlin, reluctantly casting the cigar away. "No, what *did* he think?"

"I," said Lady Pamela, with extreme propriety, "have too much delicacy to put it into words!"

Carlin grinned. "Clumsy of me, I admit, but I couldn't think of any other way to get in touch with you," he acknowledged. "Have I made you the Scarlet Woman of the Servants' Hall?"

"Well—not quite," said Lady Pamela, suddenly overcome by an irrepressible gurgle of laughter. "But I was obliged to take the most severe measures with myself at dinner or I should have had a fit of the giggles! Carlin, do you know that servants have *no* morals whatever when it comes to the Upper Orders? I am the envy of every female on the staff from Mrs. Biddlecombe down, and the housemaids are in positive awe of me for having managed to draw your notice so quickly. One of them told me in a reverential tone that she thought you a *lovely man*, only so dark that you quite frightened her, and said she thought the way your hair curled was *ever so nice!*"

"Who," said Carlin with an appreciative grin, "is being abominable now?"

"Well, you quite deserve it," Lady Pamela pointed out, "for serving me such a backhanded turn as to appear here out of the blue as Dalven. I think you must be quite mad! What if by some horrible mischance he should turn up here himself?"

"He won't," said Carlin reassuringly. "I am very well acquainted with Lord Dalven, and I can promise you that nothing is more unlikely than that he should suddenly appear at Whiston Castle. But tell me now," he went on, dismissing the subject, "how you are getting on with your own masquerade. Have you solved the problem of your brother's disappearance? He certainly does not appear to be here, as you believed he would be."

"No, he is not," Lady Pamela acknowledged, her brow wrinkling. "And I am convinced now that, if he did give the memorandum to Cedric Mansell, he must have done so in London. Where he can have gone himself has me in the greatest puzzle! But the memorandum itself is here; I am quite certain of *that*."

And she gave Carlin a brief account of her adventures since she had arrived at the Castle.

When she had finished her story she saw that he was wearing a rather enigmatic expression upon his face, which at once brought her to the attack.

"Don't you believe me?" she demanded. "Or *do* you believe me but are so poor-spirited that you don't wish to help me, and so you will pretend you think it is all a faradiddle? If that is so—"

"Don't fly up into the boughs," Carlin advised her. "Now that I have been such a shuttlehead as to involve myself in this affair, I shall certainly see it through, though I should know better than to do so. Now then, you say you are quite certain that the memorandum is here and that Broadbank has not found it yet, and on that point I am inclined to agree with you. I met Broadbank at dinner—apparently he spent the rest of the day over his 'architectural' investigations—and your assessment of his character seems perfectly accurate to me. A smooth-speaking, jovial rogue, but a rogue all the same—and getting any information out of him as to what his real business is here is a lost cause. He is far too clever to let anything slip that he does not fully intend you to know about him."

"Yes, I should think so," said Lady Pamela, pleased and relieved that Carlin at last appeared to realise the seriousness of the situation, "though of course I have had no chance to talk to him myself. But what are we to do, then? If *he* cannot find the memorandum, I don't quite see how we shall have better luck, for I should think he must have had a great deal more practice at stealing things from other people than either of us has had. Unless—"

She cocked a questioning eyebrow at Carlin, who said to her calmly, "Don't be offensive, my girl. A coachman's is an honest trade. You may take it from me that I have had no more experience than you at purloining papers that do not belong to me."

Lady Pamela, deciding to swallow the "my girl" in view of the fact that Carlin at last seemed disposed to help her, said in that case what were they to do?

"Wait," said Carlin.

"Wait!" expostulated Lady Pamela. "If *that* is the best thing you can think of to do—!"

Carlin looked at her with a certain cool gleam in his dark eyes that she had not seen there before, and that for some reason caused the rather heated protest she had begun to die on her lips.

"There is one thing I believe we had best have perfectly clear, Lady Pamela," he said. "You want my help, and I am prepared to give it to you, but upon one condition. My decisions are my own. I shall not be guided by your—if I may say so—somewhat birdwitted ideas as to how to go about the business."

"*My* birdwitted ideas!" Lady Pamela's eyes sparkled. "And what about yours, Carlin? A common coachman going about posing as a peer of the realm! I daresay that must be a—a criminal offence!"

"I daresay it might be," said Carlin placidly. "Would you like to lay information against me?"

Lady Pamela bit her lip. "No, of course not!" she said. "I know you are only doing it to help me. But you ought not to make me lose my temper. I say horrid things when I do!"

"Never mind. I forgive you," said Carlin soothingly.

Lady Pamela threw him a darkling glance. "I haven't asked you to forgive me!"

"That is quite all right. I shall do so nevertheless. I am feeling magnanimous this evening."

Lady Pamela, mastering her indignation with a strong effort, was about to make a spirited response when she became aware that there was a smile lurking at the corners of her opponent's lips.

"What an odious man you are!" she said feelingly. "I believe you are making game of me again! Are you never serious?"

"No, I have found that it seldom pays," acknowledged Carlin.

"Well, I should think that sort of attitude would land you in the briars sooner or later," said Lady Pamela severely. "And speaking of that—I wish you will tell me what in the world you are about with Lady Sabrina!"

Carlin, apparently taken somewhat by surprise by this attack, said that as far as he knew he had been about nothing at all.

"Don't quibble," said Lady Pamela. "Are you trying to make her fall in love with you?"

"God forbid!"

"Is that the truth?" said Lady Pamela, looking at him critically. "Because if it is, I think I should warn you that she is. Falling in love with you, I mean. Could you contrive to be a little disagreeable to her, perhaps? Or no—that wouldn't do, I daresay. Girls expect romantic heroes to be disagreeable."

"Little devil!" said Carlin, upon which Lady Pamela, quite unimpressed, again gave her enchanting gurgle of laughter.

"She says she thinks you have a secret sorrow," she said, with such a strong light of mischief in her eyes that Carlin said that if he were that unfortunate fellow whose name he had forgotten, who was engaged to marry her, he would turn her over his knee and teach her manners. To this Lady Pamela replied with emphasis that Lord Babcoke would scorn to do anything so ungentlemanly, to which Carlin's rejoinder was, "The more fool he," and after that conversation rather lapsed for a time while they regarded each other with a mutual lack of sympathy.

It was Carlin who eventually recalled them to the realities of their situation by making the totally unexpected suggestion that she give in her notice as Lady Sabrina's abigail that very evening and go back to London, since he was firmly established in the Castle now and could go on with the task of finding the missing memorandum without any further assistance from her. Lady Pamela looked at him in astonishment.

"I shall certainly do nothing of the sort!" she exclaimed. "This is *my* problem, not yours, Carlin."

"But you have made it mine," Carlin pointed out, "by taking me into your confidence. Besides, I have a strong feeling that I shall go on much better without you."

"You can have all the feelings you like, but I am not going," said Lady Pamela. "And if you are thinking," she went on dangerously, "of giving me away to Lady Whiston, let me remind you that two can play at that game!"

Carlin shrugged. "Very well," he said. "But I think I must warn you that this is *not* a game, Lady Pamela. If everything you have told me is correct, it would appear that you and your brother have been involved with a pretty set of hedge-birds, with whom neither of you can have the least notion how to cope—"

"Fiddle!" said Lady Pamela loftily. "In Society one has to

cope every day with persons who are quite as poisonous in their own way as Mr. Broadbank and that creature Droz, and I assure you that I have been doing very well at it. What are we to do now?"

"As I said before, wait," replied Carlin. She seemed about to respond once more with warm disapproval to this suggestion, but he forestalled her. "No, don't rip up at me again!" he said. "Unless I am much mistaken, Cedric Mansell, now that he has given his prospective customers time to search for the memorandum and realise that they cannot find it, will be turning up here again very shortly to hear their next bid for his merchandise. We shall then be in an excellent position to determine what goes on between them, and if Broadbank purchases the memorandum and attempts to leave here with it, I imagine I shall be able to persuade him that it is not in his best interests, after all."

Lady Pamela looked approvingly at her tall coachman's muscular figure and broad shoulders.

"Yes, that is why I wanted you to help me," she said. "After all, not being a man, one can't do quite *everything* oneself! And now," she added, "I think I had best go in. Shall I meet you here again tomorrow evening at the same time, in case we have no opportunity to speak to each other during the day?"

"By all means," Carlin agreed, his face grave but his eyes alight with amusement. "That is, if you feel your reputation can survive these repeated meetings—"

"Well, actually, it can't," said Lady Pamela frankly. "But it can't be helped, so I shall come. I hope Miss Clover never learns how dreadfully I am abusing her character! Still, she *has* got my dressing-case and my sables, and as no one will ever believe she came by them without parting with her virtue, I daresay it does not signify." She looked up at him composedly. "And now good night, Carlin—and one last word. *Do* try to be more careful about Lady Sabrina. It is *most* tiresome to be obliged to listen to her constantly going into raptures over you!"

Eight

If Lady Pamela had been inclined to view with considerable
impatience Carlin's plan of tamely waiting upon events before making any new move, she was obliged to admit upon
the following morning, which was Sunday, that he had been
right and she had been wrong. This admission was caused by
the reappearance of Sabrina in her bedchamber after church
looking very cross, with the news that her brother Cedric had
just arrived and was monopolising Lord Dalven in the library.

"Oh, dear!" thought Lady Pamela, not knowing whether to
be dismayed or pleased, for on the one hand she was certain
to be able to get on with the business of the memorandum
now that the Honourable Cedric had returned, but on the
other she found herself being slightly nervous as to whether
Carlin's impersonation of Lord Dalven would take Cedric in
as satisfactorily as it had Lord and Lady Whiston and Sabrina. Horrid visions of his being haled off to Newgate,
charged with *lèse majesté* or whatever it was when the Lower
Orders pretended to be the Upper, rose in her mind, and so
lacking in sympathy was she for Sabrina's wish to have her
hair done in a Sappho, apparently inspired by the idea that
this would lure Lord Dalven away from Cedric, that she
called her a goose, which led to her being given her notice by
that incensed young damsel and then reemployed in the space
of less than five minutes.

A servant's life, Lady Pamela considered, undoubtedly had
its drawbacks!

One of the chief of these, she felt, was her lack of opportunity to observe what was going on between the Honourable
Cedric and Mr. Broadbank. She hoped that Carlin, situated
so much more conveniently than she was in this regard,
would be able to make up for what she was unable to do herself, but a hurried word exchanged between them in the up-

stairs passage just after luncheon informed her that he had as yet nothing to report.

"They haven't had a chance to be alone together yet," he said. "Whiston's a nice old boy, but he gets devilish bored down here in the country all year long and he clings to company like a limpet."

"Well, you must simply contrive to draw him off, then," Lady Pamela said impatiently. "And then Cedric and Mr. Broadbank will talk about the memorandum to each other and you can listen."

Carlin said that was all very well, but if she could explain how he could keep Lord Whiston entertained and simultaneously eavesdrop on Mr. Broadbank and Cedric he would be obliged to her; and at that moment Hort, Lord Whiston's valet, appeared at the end of the corridor, so that this brief and unsatisfactory conversation perforce came to an end.

Lady Pamela, feeling very cross and frustrated, then went back to Sabrina's room to instruct her underling about mending a small tear in the flounce of the tamboured muslin gown in which Sabrina intended to dazzle Lord Dalven at dinner that evening. She left her there engaged in this task, and started off herself down the stairs to the Great Hall. As she turned the angle of the staircase, however, she was greeted by a sight that made her come to a sudden halt—that of Mr. Broadbank standing in conversation at the far end of that cavernous apartment with a tall, rather florid-faced younger man. The Honourable Cedric, without a doubt, she thought, and her spirits rose abruptly. Carlin *had* managed to draw Lord Whiston off, then, and if she could only manage somehow to get close enough to hear the conversation now going on between Mr. Broadbank and Cedric it might very probably give her the best of clues as to what the situation was in regard to the memorandum.

She had little opportunity to reflect on how to accomplish this laudable but rather impractical end, however, for as she stood there, scarcely visible from the Hall below behind the uncompromisingly heavy stone banister, she saw both gentlemen turn and begin to move in the direction of the east withdrawing room, the door of which opened almost directly beneath her. Providentially, she saw, the row of armoured figures ranged along the wall might provide a screen of sorts for any movements she made in that direction, added to which there was the comforting fact that the dull winter light left the great apartment in the kind of murky gloom that it would have required a score of flaming mediaeval torches and cressets to dispel. Without stopping to think further than this, she nipped down the stairs and into the withdrawing room.

Once inside, she stood looking about her quickly for some suitable place of concealment. The withdrawing room, though retaining much of the mediaeval austerity of the other apartments on the lower floors of the Castle, had fortunately been "modernised" during the eighteenth century to the extent that its furnishings were not made entirely of wood or stone, and Lady Pamela, her eyes fastening upon a large table, draped quite to the floor with a heavy cover of puce-coloured velvet, which stood in the center of the room—apparently for the sole purpose of displaying a pair of enormous and revolting Chinese vases—made a dash for it and got herself beneath the cover and among the legs. She fetched up hard against one of them with her forehead, and restrained an agonised cry with great fortitude, owing to hearing footsteps just then entering the room.

It was exceedingly dark and, she discovered, rather dusty under the heavy cloth, for which she quite unfairly set down a black mark against Mrs. Biddlecombe, who, if she had told the second housemaid once that just because you can't *see* a thing, my girl, is no reason for not dusting it, had told her so a dozen times. Lady Pamela could see nothing from her hiding place, but she could hear very distinctly everything that was going on in the room, and the first sound that came to her ears, after the tread of heavy masculine boots entering the room, was that of the door being firmly closed.

Well, I am for it now, she thought, settling herself as comfortably as she could beneath the table, which in the pitch blackness seemed to have as many legs as a centipede, and wondering what she would find to say for herself if Mr. Broadbank or Cedric should suddenly decide to lift the table cover and peer beneath it. It was not very probable that they would do so, of course, provided they were not engaged in the perpetration of some crime, but she was not at all certain that they were not so engaged, and criminals, to her knowledge, which was based chiefly upon a perusal of the highly coloured literature dealing with the activities of highwaymen to which Lord Wynstanley had been addicted in tenderer years, were a notoriously suspicious lot.

To her great relief, however, neither Mr. Broadbank nor the Honourable Cedric approached the table, both being entirely immersed, it seemed, in the conversation they had begun in the Hall. The first words she could distinguish came in Mr. Broadbank's deep, oleaginous, and now highly injured voice.

"But, my dear fellow," it protested, "I assure you I *haven't* got it! Really, it is quite profitless for you to drag me in here and insist, as you put it, upon having things out. There is nothing to have out, I give you my word! I have never laid eyes on the memorandum, and you do me the greatest injustice, I must protest, to suggest that I have it in my possession!"

"Do I?" Lady Pamela had been prepared to dislike the Honourable Cedric Mansell, and at the sound of the clipped, sneering tones she at once decided that she had been quite right. "No, by God, I don't believe I do!" the voice went on. "The only injustice I've done you, Broadbank, is in believing you weren't quite so clever a rogue as to be able to bubble me! But you are underestimating *me* if you think you can put the change on me. You may have the paper, but—"

"My dear Mr. Mansell, do consider for a moment!" Mr. Broadbank's voice interrupted him. "If I *had* succeeded in laying my hands upon the document, do you think it likely I should have remained here in this house, waiting for you to arrive and make just such an accusation as you are making now? Not very likely, eh?"

The Honourable Cedric's voice grudgingly admitted after a moment that it was not.

"But if *you* haven't got it," he demanded, "then who the devil has? There isn't another soul in the house who knows anything of the business except your man Droz. Do you think he—?"

"Droz? No, no!" Mr. Broadbank's voice reassured him. "Not the least likelihood of that! He is completely loyal to me—been in my employ for years. If he had the document in his possession, I should certainly know of it." A pause ensued, and then Mr. Broadbank's voice went on thoughtfully, "But I wonder—"

"You wonder what?" asked Cedric sharply, as the voice paused again. "You suspect someone else, is that it?"

Mr. Broadbank's voice said soothingly that the Honourable Cedric had quite mistaken the matter and he suspected no one, but it was obvious that Cedric was not to be put off by this denial and he remarked after a moment in an unsatisfied way that it was a queer thing this fellow Dalven turning up at the Castle just now.

"Says he's a friend of my cousin, Harry Allensworth, who's a hell-born babe if ever there was one," he said. "I'd say by the looks of him this fellow's the same. But it beats me how he could have got wind of the business—"

Mr. Broadbank's voice said he was sure Lord Dalven had nothing to do with it, and that he seemed far more interested, by what gossip had to say, in the charming little ladybird who was Lady Sabrina's new abigail, upon which the Honourable Cedric remarked that he hadn't seen the girl yet, adding a coarse comment that made Lady Pamela stiffen indignantly in her hiding place. He then went back to the missing document. It was obvious to Lady Pamela that he was of two minds about believing Mr. Broadbank's assertion that he had not discovered it and made off with it, and she herself had no idea what view to take of the matter. Perhaps Mr. Broadbank was speaking the truth, but on the other hand it seemed possible that if he had indeed found the document he might consider that the best way to avoid pursuit and retribution by the Honourable Cedric would be to remain calmly at the Castle, deny all knowledge of the memorandum's whereabouts, and then go off with it at his leisure when he had convinced Cedric that he did not have it.

The two gentlemen, at any rate, seemed quite as incapable as she was herself of reaching any satisfactory conclusion on the matter, and after a good deal of brangling back and forth, leading nowhere, Mr. Broadbank left the room. Unfortunately, the Honourable Cedric, apparently considering the withdrawing room a suitable place in which to carry out the cogitations made necessary by this conversation, did not do likewise, so that for a full half hour Lady Pamela was obliged to remain in her uncomfortable retreat, cursing all castles the while, which were invariably built with such hard, cold, and damp stone floors as to make sitting upon them a form of mediaeval torture.

At length, however, the Honourable Cedric too departed, and after a suitable interval Lady Pamela was able to lift the velvet cover and crawl rather stiffly from her hiding place.

Of course her first thought now was to share this puzzling new information with Carlin and consult with him as to what it might mean. If some third person, other than Mr. Broadbank or Cedric, was in possession of the memorandum, their search for it would have to take an entirely new course; only what that course should be she had not the least notion.

That someone else had ideas on the subject, however, she was soon to learn, for, making a foray a little later into the Great Hall, where she had no business to be, on the off-chance that she might run across Carlin there, she was seized upon by Mr. Broadbank, who entered it from another door just as she pushed open the green baize door from the servants' quarters.

"One moment, my dear!" he said, as she dropped a hasty curtsey and was about to walk past him to the staircase. "Don't scurry off! If I am not mistaken, you and I have a matter of some mutual interest to discuss. A matter," he went on, laying a plump, well-cared-for hand detainingly upon her arm as Lady Pamela, staring at him in distaste, seemed about to move off, "connected with a nocturnal visit you made the other night to Mr. Cedric Mansell's bedchamber—"

For one mad moment Lady Pamela entertained the notion that Mr. Broadbank, having heard the Castle rumours of her rendezvous with the supposed Lord Dalven and believing her visit to the Honourable Cedric's chamber also to have been connected in some way with an affair she was carrying on with *that* gentleman, was about to enter into an elderly pursuit of her favours himself. But a glance into Mr. Broadbank's cautiously jovial face at once dispelled this idea. It was not lechery she saw in those small blue eyes, but cunning. Mr. Broadbank, she perceived, was working on a plan. A plan which, she suddenly realised, probably involved the presumption that *she* was in possession of the memorandum, having succeeded in discovering its hiding place in the Honourable Cedric's bedchamber where he and Droz had failed.

His next words confirmed this suspicion.

"My dear Miss Clover," he said to her, speaking with an elephantine attempt at lightness, "let us say, for the sake of argument, that you discovered a certain article in Mr. Mansell's chamber the other night. Let us also say that you are prepared to sell that article to—er—any interested party. Let us further say—still for the sake of argument, you understand—"

"But I *don't* understand!" Lady Pamela interrupted him, putting on the most convincing show of virtuous innocence of which she was capable. "I only went into Mr. Mansell's chamber because I heard Mr. Droz coming down the passage and thought he was a housebreaker—and really, if Mr. Droz told you anything else," she went on, here introducing the clipped tones and haughty manner of an offended Pletcher, accused by the housekeeper of breaking a pink lustre teapot of which she, the housekeeper, was particularly fond, "all I can say is that he's a Nasty Liar. I'm sure I wouldn't so demean myself—"

"Tut-tut!" said Mr. Broadbank, waving this spirited defence aside. "No need to put on a show for *me*, my dear. I can assure you, you won't get into trouble by confiding in me. On the contrary, I am prepared to be exceedingly grateful to you. Shall we say, grateful to the tune of five hundred pounds?"

Lady Pamela, considering rapidly what the real Maria Clover would say to this munificent offer, blinked. "Well, I never!" she gasped. "Five hundred pounds! For what, sir?"

"For the article, my dear," said Mr. Broadbank. "The document. The paper." His small blue eyes gleamed. "You *have* got it, haven't you?"

Lady Pamela regretfully shook her head. "No, I haven't," she said. "What kind of paper is it?"

Mr. Broadbank looked frustrated. "Not high enough, eh?" he said. "I daresay you think Mansell may pay you more. But let me tell you, my dear, that you will be ill-advised indeed to put your trust in any promises *he* makes you. *He* has been under the hatches for years. *He* wouldn't have the faintest notion where to put his hands on five hundred pounds or even half that sum."

"Well, he hasn't offered it to me," said Lady Pamela, tossing her head and looking severely at Mr. Broadbank, with the air of taking these latest remarks of his as a clear aspersion upon her virtue. *"Nor* he wouldn't dare to, I shouldn't think. I don't know what all this talk about papers is, but if you're trying anything on with me, sir, I can tell you that I'm a respectable girl and it'll do you no good at all."

Mr. Broadbank eyed her malevolently, and seemed almost at the point of exchanging persuasion for threats when the appearance of Carlin and Lord Whiston in the Hall put an abrupt end to the conversation.

"Oh, there you are, my dear fellow!" the Earl happily addressed Mr. Broadbank. Obviously he did not share his wife's irritation over the unreasonable prolongation of his guest's stay at the Castle; to Lord Whiston, it seemed, the sight of any human face not connected with his restricted daily round was a welcome one. "Too bad you weren't with us just now. Dalven has been giving me a most interesting account of the battle of Ciudad Rodrigo—the storming of the main breach, Mackinnon blown to pieces by a mine, assault of the lesser breach by the Light Bobs—stirring scenes, my dear fellow, stirring scenes! And afterwards, unfortunately, a great deal of insubordination, I believe—rapine and plunder, that sort of thing. Yes, yes, most regrettable, but understandable. I am told that some of our brave fellows actually drowned in casks of brandy. Drunk, quite drunk, you understand," said the Earl, with the wistful air of a man who had had a single glass of claret with his luncheon and could look forward only to a very inferior port with his dinner.

Mr. Broadbank, masking his irritation at the interruption, began a suitable reply, and Lady Pamela hurried away.

Her head was by this time in a whirl, but one thing was very clear. Mr. Broadbank definitely did not have the memorandum in his possession, or he would not have been trying just now to buy it from her. It was still possible, of course, that the Honourable Cedric himself had the document and, for reasons of his own, was pretending otherwise to Mr. Broadbank. Or he might even already have disposed of it to some other interested person who had been willing to pay him more for it than Mr. Broadbank; but on the whole Lady Pamela did not think so. For why, in that case, should he have returned to the Castle and Mr. Broadbank?

She was on tenterhooks for the evening to come, and her rendezvous with Carlin.

Nine

She had no further sight of either the Honourable Cedric or Mr. Broadbank during the afternoon, and even Droz did not appear in the Servants' Hall for dinner that evening, being, as Mrs. Biddlecombe informed the assembled company in her impressive bass tones, Somewhat Indisposed.

This left the company free to loose their tongues and imaginations upon the character and conduct both of Droz and his employer, much to Lady Pamela's instruction, for she soon discovered that tittle-tattle among the *ton*, though justly famed for its wit and acidity, was as nursery prattle compared with gossip in the Servants' Hall. Mr. Broadbank and his minion were held up to ridicule and condemnation, their characters blackened, and slurs cast upon their antecedents, and all without the slightest recourse made to mundane fact, for as far as the Servants' Hall knew they might have dropped from the moon, and have every intention of returning there as soon as their business at the Castle—whatever that was—had been concluded.

Considerably impressed by this ingenuity in raising such a magnificent structure of suspicion and innuendo upon no foundation at all, Lady Pamela returned to her own chamber at the conclusion of the meal to fetch a pelisse in which to depart for her rendezvous with Carlin. But she had scarcely stepped inside the room and lit the candle standing upon the table when her eyes opened very wide and an exclamation leapt to her lips.

"What on *earth*—*!*" she ejaculated.

The room was in the wildest disorder. Clothing was tumbled about on the bed and on the floor; drawers had been pulled out and their contents emptied in indiscriminate haste; even the bed-curtains had been pulled down.

"Droz!" thought Lady Pamela. "Of course! When Mr. Broadbank discovered he couldn't *buy* the memorandum from me, he sent him to try to steal it! That is why he was 'indisposed' and didn't appear at dinner."

She looked around in vexation at the disorderly room, but there was no time to do anything about it now: she would have to hurry off to the garden or she would miss Carlin. She picked up her pelisse from the floor, put it on, and walked down the passage to the door leading to the stable-yard, and so through it to the walled garden behind.

It was a dark, overcast night, without a moon, and she might have been pardoned if, after the shocking discovery that her bedchamber had been ransacked, she had felt somewhat nervous of entering the even darker shadows of the walled garden. Not being of a nervous disposition, however, she felt nothing of the sort, which was a mistake, as she soon discovered. For scarcely had she stepped inside the archway leading into the garden than an indistinct figure suddenly loomed before her, raised one arm, and showed every intention of bringing down upon her head the object that it held in its hand.

Lady Pamela, in spite of being taken quite unawares, had no idea of submitting tamely to such treatment, and, executing a sort of rapid dance step that would have been much admired at Almack's, succeeded in averting disaster to the extent that the intended blow merely descended almost harmlessly upon the side of her head. The next moment, however, she found herself seized in a wiry grip and flung roughly against the wall; a pair of hands fastened themselves in a most unpleasant manner about her neck, and tightened there in an alarming fashion. She struggled violently, but her attacker, though not large, was stronger than she, and she was beginning to have a very disagreeable feeling that she was losing consciousness when her attacker abruptly uttered a pained "Ouf!"—and unexpectedly loosed his grip.

"Good girl!" said Lady Pamela to herself in high exhilaration and approval. "You did it! Yes, but what did I do?" she asked herself in some puzzlement, and it suddenly occurred to her that she was feeling rather dizzy and had really much better sit down.

"Are you all right?" Carlin's voice sounded importunately in her ear.

"I think," Lady Pamela said with dignity, "that I must sit

down for a while. That is, if you will stop holding me in this ridiculous fashion."

It felt very agreeable, however, with one's head still swimming nastily, to have a pair of strong arms about one; in point of fact, she discovered, it was really not necessary to sit down, after all.

"What happened?" she asked, reclining her head comfortably against Carlin's excellently cut coat of blue superfine.

"I arrived just in time to find that scoundrel Droz trying to choke the life out of you," Carlin said grimly. "Are you up to telling me why?"

"Oh, yes," said Lady Pamela obligingly, feeling much better but seeing no reason, in her slightly dazed state, to alter her position. "He thinks I have the memorandum."

"He thinks *you—?*" Carlin said incredulously.

"Yes. You see, they appear to have lost it—Cedric and Mr. Broadbank, I mean."

Carlin said firmly, "I had best take you back to the house. You're not yourself—"

"I *am* myself!" said Lady Pamela indignantly, raising her head from his chest. "And I know exactly what I am saying! I overheard them talking to each other about it, and they both say they have not got it. And then Mr. Broadbank tried to buy it from me, and when I said I would not sell it—I mean that I *could* not, because I had not got it—he didn't believe me, and sent Droz to search my bedchamber while I was at dinner."

It required some minutes of further explanation, during which Lady Pamela, gradually becoming aware of the impropriety of her situation, removed herself with some hauteur from the support of Carlin's arms, before she was able to make clear to him exactly what had occurred since she had spoken to him in the upstairs passage earlier that day.

"Well, that settles it," he said then, decisively. "I shall have to get you away from here. I daresay all that fellow Droz intended was to knock you unconscious so he could discover if you were carrying the memorandum on your person, but he might have been carried away and used enough force to kill you."

"But he *didn't* kill me," Lady Pamela pointed out logically. "I feel a bit queer, and it is not at all agreeable, of course, to have someone trying to throttle you, but I can't go away now, without finding out who *has* got the memorandum. Do you think it is Cedric? I must say, he didn't *sound* as if it was. He sounded very angry, and suspicious of Mr. Broadbank, and I think it is likely—unless he is a *very* good actor—that he really *does* think that Mr. Broadbank found out where he had hidden it here at the Castle and took it. Which of course he did not, or he would not have tried to buy it from me. But if neither of them has got it, who has?"

"I haven't the least notion," said Carlin. "But I shall do my best to find out, after you have left."

"Cedric seems to think you may have something to do with it," said Lady Pamela, ignoring the latter half of this remark. "Not that he suspects you are not Lord Dalven, but he said that his cousin, Sir Harry Allensworth, was a hell-born babe and that you had the look of being one, too. *Is* Sir Harry a hell-born babe?"

"Yes," said Carlin without hesitation. "Now listen to me, my girl; I have had enough of this. You are leaving here—is that understood?"

Lady Pamela looked rebellious. "No," she said. "It isn't understood at all. It appears to me that if Cedric thinks *you* have the memorandum, you are in quite as much danger as I am, and *you* are not going away."

"What we ought to do, if we had the least degree of sense," said Carlin, "is to call in the authorities and put the whole matter into their hands. Obviously that is where it belongs."

Lady Pamela stiffened. "If you do that, Carlin," she said ominously, "I shall—I don't know what I shall do, but I shall make you sorry! Don't you know that if the authorities *are* called in and it was Wyn who gave Cedric the memorandum, he will be disgraced forever, to say nothing of being drawn and quartered, or whatever it is they do to traitors?"

Carlin, looking unmoved, said he thought not since the sixteenth century or thereabouts, and besides it would serve him right if he really had taken the document.

"He is only a boy!" said Lady Pamela indignantly. "And he was probably foxed as well; I am sure he hadn't the least notion of what he was doing. What—who is that?" she interrupted herself to enquire a trifle nervously, as her ears caught a noise that sounded uncommonly like footsteps approaching the garden. "Do you think it is Droz coming back? He has a pistol, you know. I am quite sure, because I saw it the other night."

But long before she had finished uttering these rather breathless words, Carlin was taking action on his own. Stationing himself beside the archway, he flattened himself against the wall and stood waiting, on the alert. The footsteps came closer and a dark figure walked through the archway. In an instant Carlin was upon it. The intruder found an arm of steel about his throat, and his right arm twisted behind his back and held by an equally ruthless grip. Lady Pamela, lost in admiration of these successful tactics and feeling quite valiant now in the presence of her erstwhile attacker, approached boldly.

"If you will go on holding him, I shall see if he has his pistol," she said. And then her voice suddenly died away and a look of utter astonishment crossed her face. "Oh!" she exclaimed faintly. "It isn't Droz! It's—it's *Wyn!* Oh! Let him go!" Her voice gained strength again and she flew at Carlin, pulling at the arm that was still tightened like a steel band about the intruder's throat. "Let him *go,* you great brute! You will throttle him!"

Carlin, rather justifiably incensed and pardonably confused by this sudden attack upon him by the young lady he was doing his best to protect, loosened his grip upon the intruder and said with more forcefulness than civility, "What the devil do you mean? Your brother? It can't be!"

"Yes, it is—it is!" insisted Lady Pamela, throwing her own arms enthusiastically around the intruder's neck. He staggered backwards under this new assault, uttering a protest in a somewhat croaking voice.

"No, really, Pam! Give a fellow a chance!"

"But—but, Wyn, what are you doing here? It can't be you—but it *is!* How in the world did you know where I was?"

Viscount Wynstanley, a tall, slender young man in a magnificent fifteen-caped driving-coat, raised his hands to his injured cravat, attempting to repair the damage done to it by Carlin's cavalier attack upon it.

"Well, it wasn't easy to find you, I can tell you that!" he said. He broke off, looking with some bitterness towards Carlin. "Who is this fellow?" he demanded. "And why the deuce did he come flying out at me like a—a dashed highwayman?"

"Oh, it is only Carlin," said Lady Pamela impatiently. "He

was a coachman, only then we had an accident and I made him a wager that he could not manage to get into Whiston Castle and help me, so now he is pretending to be Lord Dalven."

The Viscount looked bewildered. Carlin, who appeared to have recovered his good humour, looked at him with a faint, sympathetic grin.

"Your sister's explanations have a way of leaving one rather more confused than one was before she began to speak," he said. "If you really are Wynstanley—"

"Well, of course he is!" said Lady Pamela indignantly.

"—I shall give you an account of her doings," continued Carlin imperturbably. "But first I think it would be as well if you were to explain to *us* exactly how you came to turn up here."

"Yes, do!" urged Lady Pamela. "Because I cannot think how in the world you could have known that I was here!"

The Viscount, still occupied with his injured cravat, said with some asperity that he had had the very deuce of a time tracking her down, but that she might have known she couldn't run off like that without raising the devil of a dust.

"If you expected Grandpapa to be taken in by that brummish tale about your having had a sudden fancy to go off to the Ashlocks' in a post-chaise—well, he wasn't," he said bluntly. "When I turned up at Berkeley Square that evening I found him in a rare tweak, fretting like a fly in a tar-box, and the long and short of it is, I decided to have a go at finding out what you were up to. Not hard to trace the chaise you'd gone off in: Brill told me he'd ordered it from the Bear in Piccadilly, and the post-boys weren't likely to forget a passenger like *you*. Followed your trail to Hungerford, and then found you'd gone off in a stagecoach bound for Marlborough. It took a bit of doing to find out what you'd done next, for it was plain you'd never arrived at Marlborough, and I had to make enquiries at every dashed hedge-tavern from Hungerford to Marlborough until I finally hit on the Clover woman at the Swan and Bell, and she spilled the whole tale to me."

"Well, I do think that was very clever of you," said Lady Pamela, fair-mindedly but a trifle anxiously. "Only, you see, *I* am known as Maria Clover here, so I hope you did not tell the Whistons that I am not—I mean, who I really am—"

"Didn't tell them anything," said Lord Wynstanley. "Deuce take it, Pam, whatever kind of rig it is you're running, you don't think I'd cry rope on you, do you? Went round to the stables—I know this place pretty well, you see; been here before with Ceddie—and told the head coachman I was looking for Maria Clover. He seemed to know dashed well where I could find you, too!" he concluded, looking belligerently at Carlin, who laughed and said to Lady Pamela, "I told you you would be the Scarlet Woman of the Servants' Hall." And, to the Viscount, "There's no need for you to look like bull-beef, you silly young chub! I am as much a victim of your sister's peculiar passion for setting the world's affairs to rights as you are."

And he proceeded to give Lord Wynstanley a very succinct and logical account of the events that had led up to that young nobleman's finding him in the garden with Lady Pamela. But even this seemed to accomplish little in the way of lessening Lord Wynstanley's bewilderment, although it did add to it, apparently, a strong sense of injury.

"You thought *I* had the memorandum!" he exclaimed, looking wrathfully at his sister. "Well, if that don't beat the Dutch! A pretty notion of me you must have, to think I go about prigging papers from Grandpapa's despatch-box and selling them to the French!"

"Then you didn't take it?" Lady Pamela asked, her face brightening.

"Of course I didn't take it!" said the Viscount heatedly. "I tell you, I don't know a dashed thing about the plaguey paper; I can't think how you ever came to believe that I did!"

"But you *said* you had some sort of business dealing with Cedric Mansell that was going to make your fortune," Lady Pamela defended herself. "And then you simply disappeared without a word—"

"Good God!" exploded the Viscount. "Do I have to tell you every time I want to go to a cockfight? Or Grandpapa either, as far as that goes!"

"A cockfight!"

"Yes, a cockfight! And it had nothing at all to do with Ceddie Mansell! That was another matter altogether. You see, there's this new young fighter he has in training—"

There was a smothered sound from Carlin. Lady Pamela rounded on him severely.

"I see nothing whatever to laugh about!" she said.

"Don't you? My dear good girl, here you have put yourself to the devil's own amount of trouble, been overturned in a coach, snowbound, hired yourself out as a lady's maid, and even stood in danger of being strangled—and all because your brother went off to see a cockfight!"

"Well, as far as I can see, it makes no difference whether he went to a cockfight or not," said Lady Pamela quellingly. She turned to her brother. "You *did* see Cedric before you left London that evening, didn't you?" she demanded.

"Yes, but not to give him the memorandum!"

"I know that *now,*" said Lady Pamela. "But will the authorities believe that was not your reason? After all, you *did* need money, you *did* see Cedric that night, and *someone* gave him the memorandum. They will be certain to think it was you unless we can prove somehow that you did not—or unless we can get the memorandum back and they never find out that it has been missing at all!"

The Viscount, who Carlin had noted was a very personable, open-faced young man, not resembling his sister in the least except in a certain air of insouciant recklessness, looked less insouciant and said there might be something in that, by Jupiter.

"Yes, I think there is," agreed Carlin dispassionately. "Occasionally—very occasionally—the creature *does* have glimmerings of reason. You are certainly the prime suspect, Wynstanley, unless you have information pointing to someone else?"

The Viscount said unhappily that he had not.

"So you see we cannot tell the authorities what we know," said Lady Pamela, pressing her advantage. "In the first place, there is Wyn, and in the second place, we don't really *know* anything at all, except that Mr. Broadbank has not got the memorandum and Cedric probably has not got it, either. What are we going to do next?"

Carlin said he could tell her what she was going to do, which was to go back to London before she did one rash thing too many and someone really did murder her.

"I think the best thing will be for Maria Clover to disappear without notice, tonight," he said. "It is rather too dangerous for you to go back to the Castle, for Droz and Broadbank will certainly try again to discover if you are carrying the memorandum on your person." Lady Pamela began to utter a protest, but Carlin, ignoring her, turned to Lord Wynstanley. "You drove here, I expect?" he said. "Then you can escort your sister to London with perfect propriety—"

"In these clothes?" said Lady Pamela scornfully. "And without a scrap of luggage, no night-gear—?"

"You may put up tonight at the Swan and Bell," said Carlin, unmoved. "I imagine you will have no difficulty in persuading Miss Clover to disgorge enough of your wardrobe to allow you to return to London without damaging your reputation. What you will have done to hers by eloping in her character from Whiston Castle with a Tulip of the Ton is another matter. But we shall not allow that to trouble us just now."

Young Lord Wynstanley, who looked as if he were not quite certain whether Carlin's acknowledgement of his claims to membership in the dandy set was meant as a compliment or not, said somewhat truculently that he agreed with Carlin about the necessity of getting his sister out of the way of possible harm, but that he considered it his place, not Carlin's, to stay on at the Castle and deal with matters there.

"I see," said Carlin, with perfect equanimity. "You would prefer Lady Pamela to elope with me."

"No, of course not!" Lord Wynstanley said. He eyed Carlin with considerable disfavour. "Never said anything of the sort! Got a notion there's something dashed smoky about this business of your following m'sister here, at any rate, meeting her in gardens—"

"Oh, Wyn, for goodness' sake, don't begin spouting propriety—you, of all people!" begged Lady Pamela. "Too, too totally out of character, my dear!"

"Well, deuce take it, you're my sister!" said the Viscount, stung. "Can't have you larking about the country with coachmen!"

"No, indeed!" said Carlin soothingly. "Quite the proper spirit to show, my lord, if I may say so. Where did you leave your phaeton—curricle—whatever it is? Not in the stable-yard, I hope?"

The Viscount said it was a curricle and it was in the lane behind the Castle.

"Good!" said Carlin. "Then may I suggest that you lose no time in escorting your sister to it? It is not beyond the bounds of possibility, you know, that Droz may return, *with* his pistol, in which case we may all be at some disadvantage. I promise you I shall do everything in my power to discover if the memorandum is here at the Castle."

Lady Pamela was heard to state in a very distinct voice that she was not going anywhere at all.

"In that case," said Carlin, "I shall carry you—with Lord Wynstanley's permission, of course—to his curricle and put you up into it. Lord Wynstanley?"

The Viscount, who had never in his life succeeded in making his sister do anything she did not wish to, looked at Carlin with considerable respect.

"Never thought of doing that myself," he acknowledged. "But if she's of a mind to, she might set up the devil of a screech, you know."

"Nonsense!" said Carlin encouragingly. "I am sure she has far too much conduct to behave with such impropriety!"

Lady Pamela, observing the gleam in his eye, said dangerously that he knew very well that she would behave as improperly as she pleased.

"Yes, I do know," said Carlin. "And I am quite resigned, therefore, to the screeching. Wynstanley, if you are ready—"

Lady Pamela, capitulating hastily as he took a step towards her, said that if people were bullies one couldn't help it and she would go.

"Thank you!" said Carlin, looking so relieved that Lady Pamela almost told him indignantly that she wasn't as heavy as *that*, but thought better of it. "I'll be in touch with you," he went on, to Lord Wynstanley. "If you want my opinion, though, the odds are that Broadbank won't hang about here when he finds his bird has flown, especially since he may very readily discover from the coachman the identity of the young man she went off with. My advice is, deny everything. You've never been in Wiltshire, either of you; you've never heard of Maria Clover. Do your hair differently," he said to Lady Pamela, "paint your face, lie like a trooper. You women know how to do the trick."

Lady Pamela said pointedly that as a liar she was no better than other people she knew, who pretended to be earls ("Nothing of the sort: Dalven is a mere baron," Carlin corrected her) when they were actually coachmen. But as Lord Wynstanley now had her by the arm and was escorting her rather hurriedly, in case she changed her mind, towards the archway, she was unable to continue the conversation and presently found herself, in a very dissatisfied mood, being handed up into the Viscount's curricle and driven off in the direction of the Swan and Bell.

Ten

The drive to the Swan and Bell was accomplished without noteworthy incident, except for a brief altercation between Lord Wynstanley and Lady Pamela on the subject of the latter's having allowed herself to be drawn into an appearance of such intimacy with Carlin that her brother had found her name being bandied about in a most unseemly manner at Whiston Castle.

Lady Pamela said that it wasn't *her* name, it was Maria Clover's, and she didn't think Miss Clover would mind as long as it was being bandied with a lord's.

"That makes no odds!" said the Viscount, who was feeling rather careworn for the first time in his life and did not much like the sensation. "The thing is—dash it, Pam, you ought to think of Babcoke! Puts him in the very deuce of a position! Betrothed haring about the country with a coachman, meeting him in gardens—Fellow seems to have been a gentleman once, but still, Babcoke couldn't call him out."

"Good heavens, I should hope not!" said Lady Pamela, much incensed. "As if there were the slightest need for such a thing! Wyn, if you breathe a word of this whole affair to Adolphus, I shall have your liver and lights! Not that you will do so, at any rate," she added practically, "because if you did you would be obliged to tell him about the memorandum, and you can't do that."

"You don't think," suggested Lord Wynstanley, who had been racking his brains as to what to do next and felt sadly in need of advice from some quarter, "that you *ought* to tell him? I mean to say, he might have some ideas as to what we should do."

"Good God, no!" said Lady Pamela. "He would only say, 'Do just as you like, my dear,' and think he had settled the matter to everyone's satisfaction. You know how he dislikes being put on end."

The Viscount, who had long been acquainted with his prospective brother-in-law's easygoing disposition, said in a dis-satisfied way that that was all very well, but what *were* they going to do, then?

"Well, I have been thinking," said Lady Pamela, "and it seems to me that it is quite certain that as soon as Mr. Broad-bank finds I have left the Castle he will try to follow me, be-cause he thinks I have the memorandum. And then Cedric will follow *him*, because he either thinks that Mr. Broadbank has the memorandum or perhaps he still has it himself and wants to sell it to Mr. Broadbank as soon as he can make him pay the proper price. So there we shall all be in London, and it will be quite the same as if we had stayed at the Castle, only better, for I shall be able to be myself instead of Maria Clover, and that will make things far easier."

Lord Wynstanley, looking unconvinced, said that as far as he was concerned he thought it would make things harder, because Mr. Broadbank might recognise her.

"My dear boy," said Lady Pamela superbly, "of course he will recognise me. That will be part of the fun. If I can't face down a fat scoundrel on my own home grounds, I shall deserve to be outwitted by him. But I shan't be, I promise you."

The Viscount grinned suddenly and said no, by Jupiter, he didn't think she would be, and then, throwing off his unwont-ed sobriety and becoming his natural carefree self, said more optimistically that he dared say they would come about in the end.

"Of course we shall," said Lady Pamela. "We always do."

Their arrival at the Swan and Bell at this moment perforce brought their conversation to an end, Lady Pamela being obliged to cope with the lively curiosity both of the real Maria Clover and of Mrs. Parslow, the latter of whom told Parslow that night in their conjugal bed that it was as good as a play and she would give a pair of Yellow Boys to know the rights of it all, but that there was a man in it she would take her Bible oath.

"There'll always be men when That One's around," she said in inelegant reference to Lady Pamela. which as a tribute to that young lady's charms was quite deserved but would have made her justifiably indignant in this case, where her motives were entirely altruistic and even patriotic.

The next morning, having ransomed such portions of her

wardrobe from Miss Clover as might enable her to appear
suitably in her proper character in London, she set off with
Lord Wynstanley for the metropolis. The affair of the
memorandum, and what might be happening concerning it at
Whiston Castle, formed the chief topic of their conversation
during the journey, and it was decided between them that
Lord Wynstanley, immediately upon depositing his sister in
Berkeley Square, would return to Wiltshire and get in touch
with Carlin at the Castle, to determine what his next move
should be. This was part of a plot of Lady Pamela's, for she
had little reliance upon her young brother's discretion, and,
being convinced that the action must now move to London,
was very willing to see him out of the way for the time being,
and so encouraged him quite unscrupulously in this plan.

Meanwhile, there was her grandfather to be coped with,
who was likely to be in a mood of high suspicion and demanding to know all manner of unprofitable things about
where she had been and what she had been doing. But about
this, it developed, she need not have troubled herself, for
when she arrived in Berkeley Square she found that Lord
Nevans had taken to his bed with a violent attack of
dyspepsia, and was in no case to worry about anything but
his own discomfort.

"It was the curried crab he had at dinner yesterday, I believe," said Mr. Underdown, who was looking more harried
than ever, or would have done if the mere sight of Lady
Pamela had not made him look dazzled and quite foolishly
adoring instead. "I did tell Mrs. Meggers she ought not to
give in to him and order it, but she was afraid not to, after
he had expressed a wish for it."

"Yes, I know. He terrorises over all of you, and it is really
too, too cowardly of you to allow him to do it," said Lady
Pamela severely. "You don't see him terrorising over *me*, do
you?"

"No, my lady," said Mr. Underdown, who found himself
wishing, in a way quite foreign to his hard-working, conscientious nature, that someone would only try to, so that he could
fly immediately to her rescue and kill him.

But Lord Babcoke, who, outside of her grandfather,
seemed to be in the best position to do so, was far too indo-
lent and good-humoured to attempt anything of the sort, and
the best Mr. Underdown had been able to do up to this time

had been to give Brill a sharp set-down when that old and trusted retainer had uttered the opinion that Lord Babcoke had best be prepared to live under the cat's foot if he married Lady Pamela, because she was far too hot at hand for him or any man of his kidney to handle.

Much to Lady Pamela's vexation—for, though really very fond of his lordship, she had more important matters on her mind just then—Lord Babcoke himself turned up in Berkeley Square within a very short time of her arrival there, just after she had come downstairs from a very brief visit with her grandfather.

"Thought you'd be back today," he greeted her, bestowing a chastely affectionate salute upon her cheek and thus allowing her a closer view of a really masterful example of a cravat tied in the Mathematical style, for though not precisely a member of the dandy set, he could hold his own in the matter of a cravat with any Brummel or Alvanley.

"Did you?" said Lady Pamela, slightly puzzled. "Why?"

She motioned her betrothed to a chair, and he sat down, explaining in his bored, pleasant drawl, "My great-aunt Augusta's dress-party, dear girl! Tonight, you know. She was rather in a fidget when she heard you'd gone off to Kent: well, you know what great-aunts are! Thought you might have forgotten. Assured her you wouldn't, but she's a terrible woman; never believes any good of anyone." He added solicitously, "You're looking a bit hagged, ain't you? I expect it was the measles—"

"The measles?" Lady Pamela looked blank.

"Why, yes. Wasn't that why you went to Kent?" Lord Babcoke asked innocently. "Peggy Ashlock's brat had the measles? Though why she should send for *you* has me at a stand. *You* don't know anything about babies *or* measles. But Peggy always was a cork-brained widgeon."

Lady Pamela said mechanically how too utterly true, while her mind, which seemed to have become Maria Clover's mind in actual fact, so far removed had it been for almost a week from the intricacies of life in the *ton*, struggled recalcitrantly with dates and facts.

"But it isn't Monday!" she said at last. "Lady St. Abbs' party is on Monday, and it *can't* be Monday."

"Can't it?" said Lord Babcoke, looking skeptical. "I rather think you're wrong there, old girl. Must be Monday. Lunched with Chuffy White today, and I always lunch with Chuffy on Monday. Besides, I ran into Great-aunt Augusta in Bond Street this morning. *She* thinks it's Monday, too. Told me not to be late."

Lady Pamela, who knew Lady St. Abbs very well, was tempted to say that if *she* thought it was Monday it would have to be Monday even if it was Tuesday, but being on the whole a kindhearted girl and knowing in addition that Lord Babcoke had a great deal of family pride in his great-aunt, as being the worst-tempered woman in England, she refrained.

"But I have been travelling all day!" she objected, taking a new tack and looking piteously at her betrothed. *"Couldn't* I cry off?"

"Well, I rather think not, you know," said Lord Babcoke judiciously, not wishing to be hardhearted, but having seen Lady Pamela upon innumerable occasions put in a long day in the hunting field and then dance all night, he knew that she was almost incapable of fatigue. "She'd be certain to take it in snuff and make a new will tomorrow cutting me off with a shilling, and that will be deuced awkward when we're married, you know. Never pretended to you that I was swimming in lard; rather necessary to keep in the old dragon's good books."

"Yes, I know," said Lady Pamela resignedly. "Very well, I shall go. But *don't* let her get me alone, Adolphus, and tell me horrid things about what you were like when you were a little boy, because the last time she did that I told her I wanted *all* our children to be *exactly* like you, and she was dreadfully put out with me."

"Did you, by Jove!" said Lord Babcoke, looking gratified and preening himself slightly in a self-complacent male way.

"Yes, but only because I wanted to give her a set-down," said Lady Pamela, and then laughed at her betrothed's crestfallen face and ran upstairs to put herself into Pletcher's hands.

But rather remarkably—for she was, beneath all her recklessness, a sensible young woman, quite willing to look facts in the face—the thought of having a procession of children, all looking and acting and talking exactly like Lord Babcoke, depressed her so much that she made Pletcher bring out a quite daring new gown of the most diaphanous blossom-pink muslin that fell off both shoulders at the slightest provocation, which she had been saving for some occasion when it would be necessary for her to assert her leadership in fashion among the younger members of the *ton*.

Pletcher, who had earlier endured a severe snub from her young mistress when she had commented in a pointed fashion upon the absence of her dressing-case and certain items of her wardrobe, then revenged herself by observing primly that it was not for her to say, but everyone knew Lady St. Abbs disliked the new fashions and she was sure the pomona-green sarsnet made Lady Pamela look so sweetly pretty and would please her ladyship much better. Upon which Lady Pamela said quite terribly that she would not only wear the blossom-pink muslin but would dampen her petticoats as well—a fashion she had hitherto not adopted out of deference to her grandfather and Lord Babcoke, who were both of the opinion that the extremely revealing display of the wearer's charms it brought about was more suitable to ladies of the *demi-monde* than of the *ton*.

The result was that even Lord Babcoke, ordinarily not the most observant of men where his betrothed's appearance was concerned, exhibited a rather startled expression upon his face as he saw her descending the elegant Adam staircase that evening.

"I—*say!*" he remonstrated mildly. "Hadn't you—? I mean, ought you—? That is to say, you know Great-aunt Augusta—"

"I," said Lady Pamela, looking Lord Babcoke straight in the eye, "do not tell Lady St. Abbs that people who wear purple turbans with garnet velvet gowns and emeralds make me feel quite violently ill. Which they do! So I do not see by what right you expect me to dress to please *her*."

Lord Babcoke said feebly that she was a very old lady.

"You mean a very rich one," said Lady Pamela inexorably. "Very well. If you don't care to take me in this gown, Adolphus, I shall remain at home."

But this was a threat against which Lord Babcoke was not proof, and, choosing the lesser of two evils, he put her evening mantle about her shoulders and escorted her out to his waiting carriage.

As it was only the beginning of March, London was still rather thin of company, but the Countess of St. Abbs' position in Society was such that the best of what was to be had, she got. Being the childless and immensely rich relict of a hapless earl whom she had bullied into his grave so many years before that everyone had forgotten he had ever existed, and being connected by birth or marriage with half the noble families of England and Scotland, she took shameless advantage of her position to dragoon the best people into attending her immensely dull routs and evening-parties, where one was quite likely to be offered ratafia instead of champagne, or be expected to sit for hours listening to the latest of her ladyship's musical discoveries singing Gluck or Handel rather off-key or performing in a very mediocre fashion upon the harp.

Upon the present occasion the *pièce de résistance* was to be a cantatrice whom her ladyship was obstinately endeavouring to foist upon Society as a rival of Catalani, though the only resemblance that connoisseurs could detect between the two was the fact that both were very fond of asking exorbitant fees for their services. As Lord Babcoke and his betrothed were exemplarily early, the musical portion of the evening had not yet begun when they arrived; in point of fact, as Lady Pamela later resentfully remarked, they themselves were at once singled out to provide the entertainment for any guests within earshot of the great carved chair where Lady St. Abbs, wearing the St. Abbs emeralds in total disregard of a purple turban and a puce gown, sat receiving.

"Ha! Babcoke!" was her greeting to her great-nephew as he dutifully kissed her clawlike hand. "About time you put in an appearance! Told you to be here early, didn't I?" Her eyes then lit upon Lady Pamela and the blossom-pink gown and she said, "Ha!" again, but with a good deal more emphasis and not, as everyone who heard her understood, as an expression of either mirth or greeting.

"How do you do, Lady St. Abbs?" said Lady Pamela, advancing with all her usual grace and aplomb and causing two very young Tulips of the Ton, who had been coerced by their mamas into attendance and had come determined to express utter boredom from start to finish, to forget to do so and fall in love with her on the spot. "How very nice to see you and I do *adore* your gown."

This, of course, immediately took the wind out of the Countess's sails and she found herself obliged to say

"Humph!" very ungraciously by way of acknowledging the compliment. Any lady with even the most elementary sense of politeness would then obviously have found it impossible to embark upon an attack upon the complimenter's gown, but Lady Pamela knew enough of Lady St. Abbs not to count upon this forbearance on her part and, bestowing a dazzling smile upon her, passed on at once to join a group of her admirers.

"Flibbertigibbet!" snapped Lady St. Abbs, baulked of her prey and rounding upon Lord Babcoke in revenge. "You must be all about in your head, Babcoke, to be thinkin' of marryin' that girl! What does she mean by it, tell me, walkin' into my house dressed like a—a female out of a bagnio?"

Lord Babcoke, loyalty to his betrothed overcoming prudence, said he doubted very much if his great-aunt knew what females wore in bagnios, and that he could assure her, at any rate, that Lady Pamela's gown was in the highest kick of fashion, besides being, to his mind, exceptionally becoming.

"Becoming!" said Lady St. Abbs, with a malignant cackle. "Yes, I daresay, but is it *decent?*"—a statement so provocative to a prospective husband's feelings that the fascinated onlookers at this little scene held their breath for Lord Babcoke's response, and could have killed the butler when his magisterial tones were heard announcing, "Lord Dalven!"

A tall, very self-possessed gentleman in a coat of Bath superfine fitting so exquisitely over his broad shoulders, a cravat arranged in such intricately elegant folds, that Lord Babcoke, a connoisseur in such matters, felt a pang of envy, advanced and bowed over the Countess's hand.

"My dear Lady St. Abbs," he said, with a cool impudence that made every lady within earshot at once forget Lord Babcoke and his difficulties and determine to do something to cause the newcomer to speak to her in exactly that way, "you won't have me thrown out, I hope, even though you have not invited me to come here tonight. I arrived in London only today, and it seemed to me that neither you nor my poor grandmama would forgive me if I did not come at once to pay my respects. You and she were bosom-bows while she lived, I believe."

To the considerable surprise of the onlookers, who had

seen Lady St. Abbs deal with impudence before in a terrifying fashion, the only rebuke she bestowed upon the intruder was a sharp rap upon the knuckles with her fan, while her wrinkled face curved almost into a smile.

"Dalven!" she said. "Well, well! So you are Maria's grandson! Your father was like her, but you're of a different cut." Her eyes took in his tall, excellent figure approvingly. "I like a man to have height," she said. "Only good thing about my nephew Babcoke: he's tall. D'you know Babcoke?"

The newcomer said he had not that pleasure, and, having had Lord Babcoke pointed out to him by the fan, exchanged bows with that gentleman.

"You may sit beside me durin' the concert, Dalven," said Lady St. Abbs, indicating a large and hideous French *canapé* covered with crimson brocade that stood adjacent to her chair. "I want to hear all about East Lothian—haven't been there for forty years, not since the year before St. Abbs died. You weren't born yet. Babcoke," she added without pausing for breath, "where's that young woman of yours? Tell her to put this on."

And with some difficulty she extricated from the cocoon of scarves and shawls in which she was wrapped a heavy pelerine of a peculiarly revolting dark puce colour.

Lord Babcoke, caught between his great-aunt's order and what he knew his betrothed's response to it would be, said with great courage, "What for?"

"Decency, for one thing," said Lady St. Abbs. "And in the second place, she will probably catch a chill if she doesn't. Dampened petticoats in March! Come, come, Babcoke! Signora Vermelli is about to begin."

She held out the shawl to Lord Babcoke, who looked around rather wildly for succour.

"Allow me," said the gentleman who had had himself announced as Lord Dalven, and he took the shawl out of the Countess's hands and brought it across the room to where Lady Pamela was standing in animated conversation with Lord Alvanley of the Bow-window set.

"Good evening, Lady Pamela," he said politely. "Lady St. Abbs thought you must be cold and very kindly sent me to bring you this shawl. May I put it on you?"

Lady Pamela, turning about sharply at the sound of a

well-remembered drawl, dropped her reticule and uttered a startled *"Oh!"* as she found herself gazing up, with a quite demented feeling that this really could not be happening to her, into the dark, faintly smiling face of Carlin.

Eleven

Not having observed his entrance into the room, she had been taken completely unawares by his sudden appearance before her—a fact of which Carlin at once took unfair advantage by placing Lady St. Abbs' pelerine about her shoulders and leading her back to the *canapé* upon which the old Countess had indicated he was to sit.

"I think you will be quite comfortable here, Lady Pamela," he said, as he guided her still dazed and unresisting steps to this hideously *un*comfortable article of furniture.

She sat down automatically and he placed himself beside her with a bland air of taking his position there so much for granted that Lord Babcoke, who was ordinarily quite uncritical of how much attention his betrothed received from other members of the male sex, and was even able to accept with equanimity the expression of hungry devotion with which that most ardent of her admirers, the Marquès de Barrera, continued to regard her in spite of her engagement, decided to be jealous and sat down with rather unnecessary emphasis in a chair on her other side.

Lady St. Abbs was looking sharply at Lady Pamela. "Humph!" she said, managing to convey in this brief ejaculation a comprehensive suspicion of the human race. "I see you two have met before."

Lady Pamela, who, as she had heard neither the butler's announcement of Lord Dalven nor the conversation between Carlin and Lady St. Abbs, had not the faintest notion under what name her reprehensible acquaintance had chosen to insinuate himself into the Countess's house, hastily said *No*, at the same moment that Carlin said *Yes*.

Carlin looked at her reproachfully. "Surely you haven't forgotten, Lady Pamela!" he said.

Lady Pamela, looking daggers at him, said she was sorry but she had, while Lady St. Abbs, with her black eyes now boring into them so penetratingly that it seemed quite possible they would go straight through them and make holes in the mahogany back of the *canapé*, remarked to Carlin that she had understood him to say he had just arrived in London.

"I have," he replied, perfectly unruffled. "My meeting with Lady Pamela took place elsewhere. But since it obviously made no impression upon her I shall not be so rude as to try to make her recall it."

At that moment, to Lady Pamela's intense relief, a magnificently stout woman in a pomona-green gown strode masterfully into the room and took up a position beside the great carved-leg leather-cased pianoforte. A small, depressed-looking man came behind her to play her accompaniments, and together they launched furiously into a very long aria by Handel, in which the cantatrice shook out such astonishing clusters of notes upon every syllable that it seemed possible she might burst with the effort, like a music box wound up too tight, and spill out her springs all over the room.

Lady Pamela sat listening, or rather pretending to listen, for some minutes. Finally, feeling that she would go mad if she did not find out without another instant's delay under what guise Carlin had got into Lady St. Abbs' house, she said to him in a fiercely sibilant whisper, without moving her lips or looking at him, "Who are you *this* time?"

"S-sh-h!" said Carlin reprovingly.

Lady St. Abbs and Lord Babcoke looked at them suspiciously; Carlin looked virtuous; and Lady Pamela, biting her lip, relapsed into seething silence.

Not until an interminable hour had passed and the company rose to repair to the supper-room, where such refreshments as Lady St. Abbs' frugality considered sufficient for them had been set out, was she able to satisfy her curiosity. And then it was not Carlin who imparted the information to her that she sought, but Lady St. Abbs.

"You may take me in to supper, Dalven," she said to him, reaching out to prod him imperiously with her fan, which was her way of gaining people's attention. "And mind you be quick and snabble a lobster patty for me. Told 'em only to make a dozen. Don't want people comin' here and stuffin' themselves at *my* expense."

Carlin said gravely how very wise, and if all hostesses followed her plan there would be very little dyspepsia in the *ton* and almost no gout, after which he gave the Countess his arm and she toddled out of the room beside him.

Lord Babcoke stood looking after them with a slight frown upon his face.

"Rum sort of thing to do, turning up here without being asked," he said dissatisfiedly. "Dalven—Scottish peerage, I gather, from what Great-aunt Augusta said. Never been on the town, as far as I can remember. What do *you* know about him?"

"I? Nothing at all!" Lady Pamela disclaimed hastily.

"Says he's met you—"

"Well, if he has, I'm sure I don't remember *him*," Lady Pamela said firmly, and, finding the puce pelerine still about her shoulders, cast it down upon the *canapé* with loathing and stood up. "Do come along, Adolphus, or we shall get nothing but ratafia and biscuits and I am quite famished after all that hideous music, if one can call it music!" she said crossly.

Lord Babcoke obediently led his betrothed into the supper-room, where they were rewarded by the sight of the supposed Lord Dalven and Lady St. Abbs eating lobster patties but had to be satisfied themselves with some very small aspic jellies. Lord Babcoke, who found he had taken an unaccountable dislike to Lord Dalven, perhaps because he felt there was something mysterious about Lady Pamela's not remembering him and of all things mysteries having to do with the beloved object are most displeasing to prospective husbands, looked for a place as far as possible from that gentleman for them to sit, but while he was looking Lady Pamela perversely sat down directly beside him. The fact was that she had recovered her poise by this time and was determined to give Carlin quite as bad a time as he had given her.

"You are from Scotland, Lord Dalven?" she enquired sweetly. "How totally incredible! Do you know, I should never have thought that anyone from north of the Tweed could tie a cravat like that. But perhaps you have an English valet?"

"Not at all," said Carlin amiably. "It is entirely my own creation. And now may I return the compliment, Lady Pamela, and tell you how much I admire your gown?"

"Well, it is horridly uncomfortable," said Lady Pamela frankly, forgetting momentarily to bait her opponent and ignoring Lord Babcoke's expression of disapproval over the turn the conversation was taking. "Like having been caught in a rainstorm and having no dry things to change into. I can't think why people like Caro Lamb go on in this fashion, but perhaps that is why they always look so far from robust."

Lady St. Abbs said that if Lady Pamela caught her death of a chill she would have no one but herself to blame, and added belligerently, "Why ain't you wearin' that shawl I sent Dalven to bring you?"

"Because I don't like it," said Lady Pamela unanswerably, and turned back to Carlin again. "Have you just come from Scotland, Lord Dalven?" she asked him, with one of her more angelic smiles. "I have been racking my brains to think where you can have met me, for I have never been in Scotland. But perhaps you have mistaken me for someone else?"

Carlin, looking into her limpidly enquiring eyes, said that on second thought he believed he might have done exactly that.

"Now that I think of it, her name was Maria, not Pamela," he said. "I must say, though, that she bore a remarkable resemblance to you."

Lord Babcoke, puzzling darkly over this interchange, said after a moment, with an air of triumph, "But you knew her name, Dalven! I mean you knew who she was. I mean," he went on painstakingly, as Carlin turned a politely interrogatory eye upon him, "Great-aunt Augusta said, 'Babcoke, where's that young woman of yours?' and told me to bring her the pelerine. And you took it to *Lady Pamela.* If you'd never met her, I mean if you'd met a girl whose name was Maria—"

"What *are* you talking about, Adolphus?" said Lady Pamela. "You *can't* be foxed on one glass of champagne."

"Of course I'm not foxed!" said Lord Babcoke indignantly. "I am merely pointing out that if Lord Dalven thought you were a girl named Maria, he couldn't have thought you were engaged to me."

Carlin said magnanimously that as far as he was concerned Lord Babcoke might be engaged to a girl named Maria if he liked, which did not help in the least to clarify matters and made Lady Pamela almost have the giggles. Lady St. Abbs, who was always impatient of conversations in which she was not playing the leading part, then took charge of the whole affair by remarking terrifyingly to Lord Babcoke that whatever was going on she was sure it was something havey-cavey, as that Frayne breed were all alike.

"*I* told you not to marry into that family," she said. "Unstable, all of 'em. Look at Wynstanley. And there was an uncle—can't remember his name, but he came to His Majesty's Coronation in a suit of armour—"

"A suit of *armour*? I think you are making that up, Great-aunt Augusta!" said Lord Babcoke, rising loyally to defend the honour of his betrothed's house.

"Well, I ain't!" snapped Lady St. Abbs. "I ain't in my dotage *yet*, Babcoke! I know what I'm sayin'! You remember that when you've a nursery full of brats all actin' as queer as Dick's hat-band. Frayne blood! Pah!"

Which final exclamation so impressed her hearers that they all fell silent and forgot what they had been quarrelling about, and then Carlin, recovering himself, said he was sure Lady St. Abbs and Lord Babcoke would prefer to discuss such matters alone and had Lady Pamela on her feet and out of the room before anyone well knew what was happening.

"You really are the most abominable man!" said Lady Pamela with feeling, when he had managed with great adroitness to steer the way unerringly to one of the small, dimly lit, secluded anterooms that always exist in great houses but are usually so difficult to find. "This is the second time you have almost driven me into strong hysterics by appearing where no one had the least right to expect you! It was bad enough at Whiston Castle, but this is a dozen times worse! What if you meet someone here who knows the real Lord Dalven?"

Carlin raised one black brow at her. "Oh, I think I am reasonably safe," he said easily. "Dalven must be quite unknown in England; when he is not in Scotland he is on the Continent."

"Well, there are people here and all over London who have been in Scotland and on the Continent, too!" said Lady Pamela. "You must be quite mad, I think! Why did you come here?" A sudden thought struck her and her face brightened. "*Don't* tell me you have found the memorandum!" she said.

"Nothing so fortunate. I wanted to talk to you, and they told me at your grandfather's house that you were here with

Babcoke. By the bye, you aren't really going to marry that poor fellow, are you?"

"Of course I am!" said Lady Pamela indignantly. "And he is *not* a poor fellow!"

"My dear girl, you will lead him a dog's life! I can't think what can have possessed him to offer for you."

"He is in love with me!"

"I daresay he is. We *do* have a habit of becoming enamoured of the most unsuitable females. I've done it myself."

"Oh, have you?" Lady Pamela, that model of social poise, looked for a moment as uncertain and sulky as any schoolroom miss suddenly confronted with the fact that she was not the centre of the universe, and then asked herself crossly what possible difference it could make to her with whom a coachman fell in love or how many times. "Well, I cannot see what that has to say to anything," she went on hastily. "What is important is the memorandum. Why have you come to London if you have not got it? Is it because Mr. Broadbank has come here, too?"

"Right the first time," said Carlin approvingly. "You *do* have a quick mind, my love."

"I am *not* your love!"

"Of course you are not," said Carlin. "How could you be? You are engaged to Babcoke. And by the way, if I know the look of suspicion in a man's eye, he will be down upon us as soon as he has contrived to rid himself of Lady St. Abbs. We had best arrange now to meet somewhere tomorrow, so that we can discuss this matter at our leisure. I am staying at the Pulteney, incidentally, if you should wish to reach me with a message."

Lady Pamela was about to say grandly that there was no possibility whatever that she would ever wish to send him a message, nor had she the least desire to meet him on the following day, when another thought suddenly struck her and she asked, "Isn't that horridly expensive?"

"Yes, it is, of course," acknowledged Carlin. "But then you will remember that you still owe me fifty guineas, so that I shall have no difficulty in paying my shot."

Lady Pamela, who had quite forgotten her debt in the press of other events, blushed, and was about to enter upon a confused explanation of her remissness when Lord Babcoke walked in with the air of a man who had been perseveringly looking into every room he came upon in search of her, and was prepared to go on looking, at any cost to himself, until he found her.

"Oh, here you are!" he said, looking at Carlin with an expression in his eye which Lady Pamela was obliged to acknowledge fully justified the description Carlin had given of it a few moments before. And it must regretfully be recorded of her that, far from feeling compunction at the thought that she was the cause of the unpleasant sensations within Lord Babcoke's breast that must be causing him to look like that, she felt nothing of the sort, and was perfectly willing to see two very handsome specimens of manhood prepared to make cakes of themselves over her. "I have been looking," Lord Babcoke went on to her, but gazing rather, in a somewhat challenging manner, at the supposed Lord Dalven, "everywhere for you."

But if he and Lady Pamela expected that Carlin would rise to the challenge and speak in defence of the lady or of himself, or attempt to keep on having her to himself any longer, they were disappointed.

"No, have you?" he said cheerfully. "What a dead bore! I expect you want to discuss the guest list for the wedding with her, or new furniture for the Green Saloon, or one of those serious subjects engaged couples seem to have to spend so much time talking about to each other. Don't let me discommode you; I'm off." He bowed to Lady Pamela. "Tomorrow, then, at eleven?" he concluded, with the air of a man confirming an engagement previously entered upon. "The weather appears to be moderating; a drive should be quite delightful. I shall look forward to it."

And he walked out of the room before Lady Pamela could open her mouth to protest that she neither knew anything about such an engagement nor had the slightest intention of honouring it.

This was unfortunate, for of course Lord Babcoke had no way of knowing that the engagement was a purely fictitious one which Carlin, with his usual devilish ingenuity, had invented upon the spur of the moment, and he at once stiffened perceptibly.

"Going for a drive, eh?" he said, in what he himself considered was a tone of remarkable forbearance, but which to

Lady Pamela sounded accusing, if not censorious. "Rather odd thing to do, isn't it? Fellow you scarcely know—"

Lady Pamela, who had had every intention the moment before of sending word down to Carlin, if he had the temerity to arrive in Berkeley Square on the morrow expecting her to be prepared to go for a drive with him, that she was otherwise engaged, immediately forgot this praiseworthy resolution and asked Lord Babcoke very unfairly if he intended to get up upon his high ropes every time she left the house in company with someone other than himself.

"No, of course not!" said Lord Babcoke, who had thus far, in his short life as an engaged man, contrived to avoid quarrelling with his betrothed by the simple expedient of closing his eyes in comfortable indolence to anything she did or said of which other people told him he ought to disapprove.

But now it was not other people telling him; it was himself. There was something havey-cavey, his clubman's instinct informed him quite as plainly as Lady St. Abbs had done, going on between his beloved and the tall Scottish peer who had suddenly erupted in Lady St. Abbs' house like the devil in an old morality play; and he would not have it. At least he would try not to have it, which, he was well aware, with Lady Pamela was the best one could do, the final outcome always depending upon her.

So he said manfully that naturally there could be no objection to her going for a drive with whomever she liked, only he thought she would find Lord Dalven not at all in her line.

"How do you know?" Lady Pamela demanded. "I thought you were not acquainted with him."

"I am not," acknowledged Lord Babcoke. "But Great-aunt Augusta—who you know manages to know everything about everyone without stirring from London—says he is rather the black sheep of the family. Low company in Scotland, and off to any odd part of the world that took his fancy as soon as he came of age. Then he joined the army, and his family had the very deuce of a time of it to get him out of the Peninsula and back to East Lothian when his father died and he came into the title. Sounds a queer sort of fish altogether. Not your style."

He looked hopefully at Lady Pamela, but that young lady, being completely uninterested in this history of a man she had never met, was only thinking that it was no wonder Carlin was well acquainted with Lord Dalven, if this was the sort of person he was. As for allowing Lord Babcoke to dictate to her what company she might keep, that, of course, was out of the question. And at any rate, she thought, it really was necessary for her to talk with Carlin about the memorandum, and what was to be done about Mr. Broadbank, and where the Honourable Cedric was.

So she said very firmly to Lord Babcoke that she thought a drive would do her good, cooped up so much as she had been in Kent with Peggy and the measles, and, having thus put the whole matter upon a purely therapeutic basis, said now he really must take her home, as they had quite done their duty by Lady St. Abbs and if she stayed a moment longer she would die of boredom or a chill, but probably of the former, she thought, so as to disappoint Lady St. Abbs.

Twelve

On the following morning Lady Pamela visited her grandfather's sickroom and then, having donned an altogether delightful moss-green pelisse and bonnet, the latter with the new and dashing jockey-front, was awaiting, on the stroke of eleven, the arrival of Carlin when to her mixed annoyance and gratification the door was opened by Hadsell to Lord Wynstanley instead.

"Wyn! What are *you* doing here?" she greeted him. "I thought you were in——" She suddenly became aware that Hadsell was still in the hall and motioned her brother into a small saloon that opened from it. "I thought you were in Wiltshire," she finished her sentence, once they were inside this sanctuary.

The Viscount, who was looking rather tired and more than a little cross, said no, he wasn't in Wiltshire and what was more he wasn't going back to Wiltshire, no matter if she got down on her knees and begged him to, because he had had enough of haring back and forth across the country on wildgoose chases.

"Well, I certainly shan't get down on my knees because I don't want you to go anywhere," said Lady Pamela, with some slight asperity upon her own part. "I only want to know what happened at Whiston, and what you are doing *here*."

"Well, where else was I to go?" demanded the Viscount in a very loud and exasperated voice that in a member of the Lower Orders would have been described as shouting, for though he was extremely fond of his sister he was also tired and frustrated and therefore not inclined to take kindly to questions the moment he stepped inside the house. "If you think I could have done the least bit of good by staying on at the Castle, with Broadbank and Ceddie both gone and nobody there but Sabrina and that female dragon and the old Earl—"

"Wyn!" interrupted Lady Pamela, between awe and amusement. "You didn't *go* to the Castle! I mean, you didn't just walk up to the door and—"

"Well, why shouldn't I?" said the Viscount belligerently. "I wanted to find out what was going on, didn't I?" A flush suddenly rose in his young, fresh-coloured face. "Only I dashed well wished I hadn't before I'd been there for a brace of snaps!" he confessed. "Do you know, that tottyheaded woman had taken the notion that I'd run off with you—I mean with Sabrina's abigail—oh, dash it, I mean she *thought* it was Sabrina's abigail and I couldn't tell her it was only you, of course—"

He paused, looking disgustedly at his sister as she broke into a peal of helpless laughter and collapsed into a chair.

"Oh, Wyn!" she gasped, when she could speak. "She *didn't!* I mean she didn't accuse you to your face—"

"Well, not quite," the Viscount admitted, a reluctant grin appearing upon his own countenance as the humour of the situation struck him. "But she pulled such a Friday-face at me when I walked in as you never saw, and started off hinting like mad about young men having no sense of propriety these days, and then she sent Sabrina out of the room and said she was going to talk to me like a mother, because she knew I hadn't one of my own—"

By this time Lady Pamela was quite helpless again.

"Well, it wasn't all that much of a joke to *me*," Lord Wynstanley said, regarding her with some slight bitterness. "She never stopped talking, I swear, for a full quarter of an hour, and there I sat like a gudgeon—"

"I know. She doesn't. Stop talking, I mean," said Lady Pamela, wiping her streaming eyes. "Isn't she *awful?* I don't know how poor Lord Whiston endures it. And she *won't* let him go off to Newmarket, or to London—"

"Well, she's letting him go off to London now," Lord Wynstanley said, "because she told me they're all coming up today"- –which was enough to make Lady Pamela stop laughing abruptly and turn a startled and suddenly sober face upon him.

"Are they? So soon?" she said, feeling more than a little taken aback, for though she had told her brother quite truthfully that she would enjoy facing Mr. Broadbank down were she to meet him in London, the thought of being obliged to cope in tonnish saloons with three members of the aristocracy, all believing her to be a lady's maid named Maria Clover who had decamped from Whiston Castle under highly suspicious circumstances, was a somewhat daunting one. But she recovered herself almost immediately and told herself that after all it was quite possible she might contrive to avoid the Whistons during the short period of time that they would be in London; and then Hadsell announced Lord Dalven.

The Viscount stared. "Dalven?" he repeated. "Dalven?" He looked at Lady Pamela as Hadsell departed. "Does he mean the real man or is it that coachman fellow again? What the devil does *he* want here?"

At that moment Carlin himself, looking extremely smart in a box-coat of white drab, with a few whip-points thrust through the buttonhole in place of a nosegay, in the fashion favoured by the out-and-outers of the *ton*, strolled into the room.

"Good morning," he said cheerfully. "Lady Pamela—" He bowed over her hand. "A really charming bonnet; pray accept my compliments upon it. Wynstanley, I hope I see you well."

"Well, you don't!" blurted out the Viscount, who had stiffened visibly at the sight of Carlin's easy intimacy with Lady Pamela. "In the first place, I'm dashed well burnt to the socket with running back and forth between here and Wiltshire, and in the second place, I want to know what the deuce you're doing here."

"Well, I am afraid, you know, that I can't do anything about the first of your troubles," Carlin said apologetically, "but I *can* relieve your mind in the second case. I am here to take Lady Pamela for a drive."

The Viscount's young, pleasant face darkened. "Not," he proclaimed, "while I am here to prevent it!"

"Oh, Wyn, don't be so utterly gothic!" Lady Pamela begged. "Why shouldn't I go for a drive with him? Everyone thinks he is Lord Dalven, so it is perfectly proper! Besides, I *must* talk to him and find out what is happening about the memorandum."

Carlin, addressing Lord Wynstanley, said politely that he was driving a curricle so that there would scarcely be comfortable room for the three of them, or he would be delighted to ask him to accompany them.

"To prove the purity of my intentions," he added helpfully,

which caused Lady Pamela to round upon him and say with great emphasis that if he spoke another word she would take off her bonnet and pelisse and not go for a drive with him at all.

This restriction naturally had a somewhat damping effect upon the conversation, and although the Viscount still looked as if he might have a few things to say, Lady Pamela managed to get herself out of the house and down the steps to the very smart curricle standing before the door without his having the opportunity to say them. To her surprise, the groom standing at the horses' heads turned out to be the Scotsman, Quinting, who had been the guard on the *Lightning*. He touched his hat to her, a slight grin lightening his dour face, as Carlin helped her up into the curricle.

"Quinting! What are *you* doing here?" she asked involuntarily, pausing upon the step. "Have you lost your employment, too?"

Quinting, instead of replying, cast a glance at Carlin as if inviting his help, but, seeing that none was forthcoming, he muttered something sheepishly about going wherever the Master went.

"The Master?" said Lady Pamela in a rather puzzled tone, recollecting that Quinting had also used this odd term in referring to Carlin at the time of her previous meeting with him; but she had been too much preoccupied then with other matters to pay a great deal of heed to it. "Do you mean Carlin?" she demanded. "But why do you call him that? You are not in *his* employ, surely!"

Quinting cast a second agonised glance at Carlin and, again seeing nothing but unhelpful amusement in that gentleman's face, blurted out in feeling tones and a strong Scots accent that he had been with the Master, man and boy, since he had been breeched and there was nothing that would keep him from his place, no matter how many silly rigs he chose to run.

Lady Pamela stared. And all at once, as she stood there in the pale March sunlight with one foot poised upon the step of the curricle, the whole sedate Square suddenly seemed to reel about her in an unseemly and very peculiar way, as if nothing were fixed firmly in its proper place and even the cobblestones would begin to waltz if she tried to walk upon them.

"Oh!" she gasped, and her eyes flew to Carlin. *"Oh!* You are not—You *are* Lord Dalven!"

Carlin, who appeared to consider that she had been standing there in this state of suspended animation quite long enough, gently but firmly urged her into the curricle and then came around and took his place beside her, while Quinting jumped up into the groom's seat between the springs behind.

"Well, yes, I am," he said amiably, as he gave his horses the office to start. "I was rather wondering, you know, how long it would take you to arrive at that conclusion. After all, even my well-known audacity should have failed me at the thought of pretending to be someone I was not among so many people who—as you very rightly pointed out last night—might have been expected to have come across the real Lord Dalven at some time in the course of his career."

"But you said your name was Carlin!" began Lady Pamela indignantly.

"And so it is. My Christian name, my dear."

"And you *were* employed as a coachman when I met you!" Lady Pamela went on, still overcome by a strong sense of ill usage. "How was I to imagine that a peer—?"

"My dear girl, only consider the advantages for a moment! As a peer, I am expected to attend *ton* parties of the very acme of dulness, such as the one we were both condemned to last evening, to sit in the House of Lords listening to interminable speeches, to be flattered by an invitation to join the Four-Horse Club and so be able to drive a yellow-bodied barouche at a strict trot to Salt Hill on the first and third Thursdays of the month, wearing a blue waistcoat with inch-wide yellow stripes and a revolting spotted cravat. While as a coachman—as you saw for yourself—life can be full of the most extraordinary adventures. I must confess I have followed the profession only for a few weeks, having been led into it by what my relations unkindly refer to as my propensity to take up any harebrained wager proposed to me, and that I can see certain disadvantages to adopting it as a permanent career, especially in view of the fact that it would confine my activities rather narrowly to the Bath Road."

Lady Pamela said, still in a distinctly injured tone, that she dared say he had not lost all his fortune, either.

"Well, not all of it," admitted Carlin—for so, she felt, she would always continue to think of him, however improper the use of what she now knew to be his Christian name must be. "But far more than my relations approve of. Does that sink me below reproach in your opinion?"

Lady Pamela said uncompromisingly, yes, it did, because he had certainly led her to believe otherwise, and then asked if it was also true that he had left the army not for a lack of ability to pay his debts of honour or an intrigue with the Colonel's wife, as she had had every reason to think, but merely because he had come into the title and had felt obliged to do so for family reasons.

"Alas, true again!" Carlin said, with an air of great regret. "A deuced handsome woman she was, too—the Colonel's wife, I mean. What a pity I never thought of that!"

Lady Pamela, losing the battle to maintain her sense of having been highly ill-used, gave up upon this and broke into her enchanting ripple of laughter.

"Oh, dear! What a villain you are! And what a fool I have been!" she gasped, when she was able to speak again. "But you really *are* abominable to have hoaxed me so! Don't you know I went in terror of your being unmasked and taken up by the authorities all the while we were at Whiston?"

"No, did you?" said Carlin, glancing down at her with interest as he featheredged a corner with great skill. "I wasn't aware—"

"You were perfectly aware," said Lady Pamela. "And, what is more, you were enjoying it immensely!"

"Well, perhaps I was," her companion admitted, a smile touching the corners of his mouth. "You were so damnably highhanded and sure of yourself, you know! You really needed taking down a peg."

"Well, you have taken me down nicely," said Lady Pamela, in the tone of one fairmindedly acknowledging a superior stroke in a game of skill. "But as for people needing taking down a peg, you know you were quite shockingly impertinent yourself—for a coachman! And even for a peer," she added, glancing at him darkly.

She was startled at this moment to hear a brief, unprofessional crack of laughter from Quinting, perched up behind them, and turned to see a remarkable expression upon his dour face, apparently indicative both of his exquisite inner enjoyment of the joke and his appalled consciousness of having demeaned himself by giving vent to it.

"Yes, and *you!*" she said to him severely. "*You* are quite as bad as he is, leaving me to imagine all sorts of horrid things about your master! And if you intend to boast of having followed him into every rash adventure he takes it into his head to engage upon, where were you, may I ask, when he was at Whiston Castle? You *might* have been of some use to us there."

"What," said Carlin, "and run the risk of his exposing you in your true character in the Servants' Hall by the same sort of injudicious remark with which he has just unmasked me? No, no; I put a stop to that notion! Besides, it would have been rather too hard on the proprietors of the *Lightning*, you know, to deprive them of both a coachman and a guard at one fell swoop."

Lady Pamela said fairly that she dared say there was something in that, but that all the same she still considered they had both behaved very badly to her, and she would overlook it only because she believed Carlin—or, rather, Lord Dalven—was really trying to help her.

"Which reminds me," she said, "that you had best tell me now what happened at the Castle after I left. You know I sent Wyn down there to consult with you as soon as he had brought me up to London, only he found you already gone, and Mr. Broadbank and Cedric, too, and he says Lord and Lady Whiston and Sabrina are coming to London today—"

"Are they? That ought to be amusing!" said Carlin.

"It won't be in the least amusing to *me;* I shall probably have to tell some shocking rappers if I meet them!" said Lady Pamela. "But if they discover that I am really Wyn's sister, they can't think the *worst* of me, at any rate—I mean, that I ran away with him for immoral purposes."

"Oh, no," Carlin agreed calmly. "They will probably think then, on the contrary, that your brother's arrival at the Castle was for the purpose of snatching you from your dalliance with *me*." Seeing the startled glance she gave him, he went on, "Well, you know our reprehensible behaviour—meeting in gardens and such goings-on—must have reached the ears of the Upper Orders as well as those of the Lower at Whiston. Droz knew; we can be sure of that. And if he did. so must Broadbank have done. And we certainly did not escape Lady Whiston's eagle eye, for I must tell you that Lord Whiston confided to me, after your disappearance had been discovered, that his wife had at first been of the opinion that you had gone off with *me,* and was much surprised to find me still in the house and the coachman telling tales of young Lord Wynstanley's clandestine enquiries for you."

"Good God!" exclaimed Lady Pamela, whose expression had been growing increasingly rueful as this conversation progressed. "And she will be certain to gossip about the matter, I should think, if she meets me somewhere and recognises me."

"Should you mind that so much?" enquired Carlin, looking faintly surprised.

"No, of course not! But Grandpapa would; he always flies up into the boughs when Wyn and I get ourselves bibble-babbled about by the tattlemongers. Fortunately he is in such queer stirrups now, poor lamb, that it isn't likely he will be going into society soon. But there is Adolphus—"

"Adolphus?"

"Lord Babcoke." Lady Pamela looked at him challengingly, as if defying him to deny that he knew who that gentleman was.

"I see," said Carlin. "You don't think he will like it."

"Of course he will not like it!" said Lady Pamela, rather flushed. "Would you like it if *your* betrothed ran off to Wiltshire and disguised herself as a lady's maid and went into gardens meeting other men?"

"Only one other man," Carlin pointed out soothingly. "And in answer to your question—as I have not got a betrothed, I really don't know, but I expect I should not. Like it, I mean. Had I best look out for a pair of duelling pistols, do you think?"

"No, of course not! Adolphus is not in the least that sort of man!" Lady Pamela looked suddenly rather harassed. "All the same, if I were you I should keep out of his way as far as possible," she said. "He is—he is an excellent shot, you know."

"Is he, indeed?" said Carlin with equanimity. "Well, it takes two to quarrel and I shan't quarrel with him, so you may set your mind to rest on that score. I have the greatest sympathy for him." Lady Pamela opened her mouth for indignant speech, but he went on without pausing, "By the way, I daresay we had best decide now what sort of story we are to give out about Whiston Castle. It won't do to tell the whole truth, of course, but I do think there may be certain advantages in our holding to the same story."

"I," said Lady Pamela firmly, "shall Deny Everything. I was in Kent with my cousin, Lady Ashlock, whose baby had the measles. And," she added, looking at him darkly, "as I told Lady St. Abbs, I never laid eyes on you until I met you last night at her house. So pray do not continue hinting otherwise."

"Very well," agreed Carlin. "But we shan't be believed, you know. People have nasty, suspicious minds, and with Lady Whiston spreading *her* tale to the contrary, and Babcoke already off and away after his own idea that we actually *have* known each other in some guilty past—"

"Yes, I know," said Lady Pamela. "I *do* wish to goodness I had never met you!"

"Well, I call *that* distinctly unfair," Carlin pointed out reasonably, "when it was you who embroiled me in your affairs in the first place. I was only trying to be helpful."

"You were trying to win a wager!" said Lady Pamela unkindly. "Which reminds me—"

And she opened her reticule and took out a roll of bank notes, which she endeavoured to hand to him.

"I see!" said Carlin, looking amused. *"Play or pay!* is your motto. But I assure you that I shall do very well at the Pulteney without your roll of soft. I am not exactly at Point Non-Plus, you know."

"No, I can see quite well that you are not," said Lady Pamela, looking at his very smart driving-coat, "but that does not signify. You won the wager, so you must take the money."

Carlin said that was her opinion, not his, and if she insisted upon his taking it he would only buy her a new dressing-case to replace the one she had had to bribe Maria Clover with, which it might embarrass her to accept, so she had as well keep it and buy the dressing-case for herself.

Lady Pamela, well aware that this was a specious argument, was about to attack it with some vigour when her attention was suddenly attracted by something that made her forget completely what she had been about to say. They had entered the Park by this time, where a rather thin group of vehicles and riders had put in an appearance to enjoy the brisk morning air, and the sight that had so riveted Lady

Pamela's interest was that of a very elegant yellow-winged phaeton with double perches of a swan-neck pattern, driven by an immensely stout gentleman in a fashionable driving-coat boasting such a number of capes that his bulk was multiplied to that of a veritable mountain. A high-crowned beaver surmounted this gigantic edifice, and a smile expressing the utmost benevolence towards the human race illumined the face beneath it.

"Mr. Broadbank!" gasped Lady Pamela. "Oh, do look, Carlin! In the yellow phaeton, just approaching us!"

Thirteen

Obviously Mr. Broadbank had observed them as well, for he was already engaged in bringing the very creditable pair of match-bays drawing the phaeton to a halt.

"My dear Lord Dalven—what a pleasure!" he exclaimed, in the rich voice that seemed to come rumbling up with some difficulty from the internal depths of his enormous bulk. "So we meet again! You did not remain long in Wiltshire, then, after my departure from Whiston." His beaming gaze fell upon Lady Pamela. "Will you make me known to your charming companion? But no—we have met before, I believe. Miss Clover, is it not?"

Lady Pamela returned his gaze with the hauteur of a long line of Fraynes.

"I fancy, sir, that you are under some misapprehension," she said coolly. She turned to Carlin, who was holding his own impatient team easily in check beside the phaeton. "Dalven, are you acquainted with this gentleman?" she enquired, with an air of such ineffable condescension that even Mr. Broadbank's monumental self-assurance was shaken for a moment and an irrepressible smile twitched at the corners of Carlin's lips.

Carlin asked if he might present Mr. Broadbank, who had been a fellow guest of his on a recent visit he had made to Whiston Castle. "Lady Pamela Frayne," he then said, with an aplomb that matched Lady Pamela's own, upon which Mr. Broadbank looked distinctly surprised and even chagrined for such a fleeting fraction of a second that one could scarcely have been certain that the expression had ever been present upon his benignly smiling face.

"Lady Pamela Frayne," he repeated, after that infinitesimal pause. "I see. A pleasure, ma'am. A very great pleasure indeed. And a thousand pardons for my error in believing that what I hope I may be forgiven for describing as your quite unique face could possibly belong to any other lady."

Lady Pamela looked bored. "You are, I believe," Mr. Broadbank went on perseveringly, his small eyes now revealing nothing but benevolent interest, "you must be, by your name, connected with the illustrious Lord Nevans?"

Lady Pamela, examining her swansdown muff as if enquiring of it why she must be subjected to the tedium of this conversation, said that she was.

"Ah!" said Mr. Broadbank. "I hope his lordship is enjoying good health at this present. I have not the pleasure of a personal acquaintance with him, but anyone who has the interests of the country at heart must hear with the greatest concern the reports that he has not been lately in plump currant."

Lady Pamela raised utterly uninterested eyes to Mr. Broadbank. "Thank you," she said. "He is much improved," and even Mr. Broadbank, who had successfully ignored all Lady Whiston's hints that it was time for him to cut short his visit to the Castle, realised that the conversation was at an end. Carlin nodded a brief farewell and gave his horses the office to start, and in a moment the two carriages had parted and were bowling along in opposite directions.

"I don't think," Carlin said, his eyes now alight with unrestrained amusement, "that I have properly appreciated you until this moment, Lady Pamela. To see you posing successfully as a lady's maid was one thing, but to observe you transform yourself just as readily into your own grandmother, if you have one, in a purple turban, with a *fraise* around your neck to hide the wrinkles, as you snubbed the pretensions of an encroaching mushroom—"

"I did do it rather well, didn't I?" said Lady Pamela complacently. "He won't try *that* again, I fancy. But I haven't got a grandmother."

"That doesn't surprise me," said Carlin, "since you have no doubt driven both those respectable ladies into their graves. By the bye, to grow more serious—what have you told your grandfather about your meddling in this affair?"

"Nothing at all," confessed Lady Pamela. "Actually, you see, he has been quite horridly ill ever since I have come home, and Mr. Underdown, his secretary, has been keeping people off, so that he isn't being worried with anything official just now. But I know he is fretting himself to flinders. He hasn't said anything directly about the possibility of Wyn's being involved in it, because I really don't think he could bear it if he were, but I am quite sure he is still afraid he is. It is all a dreadful muddle, and I really cannot imagine what we are to do next."

At this unwonted admission of inadequacy Carlin looked slightly surprised, and said if she had finally attained enough wisdom to realise that they were indeed at a stand he would tell her what to do.

"Go to your grandfather and tell him what you have done and everything you know about this business," he said. "If he is not well enough to attend to the matter personally, perhaps his secretary—Underdown, is it? Is he trustworthy?"

"Oh, completely!" said Lady Pamela, with a confidence that would have flattered Mr. Underdown so much had he heard it that he would no doubt have had to restrain himself forcibly from rushing out and finding something heroic to do to merit it. "But I can't worry Grandpapa now, and Mr. Underdown can't do anything himself except tell other people who can, and that would be *treason*. I mean to Grandpapa, because then everyone would *know* he hadn't taken proper care of the memorandum, and there would be official enquiries and—oh, I *couldn't!*"

Carlin pointed out that if the matter were allowed to go on much longer it would doubtless be beyond her power or anyone else's to prevent official enquiries from being made, and that at least if Lord Nevans or Mr. Underdown was made aware of the dealings between Mr. Broadbank and Cedric Mansell he would be able quietly and perhaps semiofficially to do something about bringing those gentlemen to book and getting the memorandum back.

"But we don't even know if either of them has it!" Lady Pamela objected. "Do look at the facts! Mr. Broadbank would certainly not have followed Wyn and me up to London if *he* had it, and if Cedric Mansell has it, his only object must be to sell it, and why not to Mr. Broadbank?"

"Won't meet his price," Carlin said promptly. "That must have been the cause of the hitch in the proceedings in the first place at Whiston Castle."

"Yes, I know that, but why, if he has the memorandum himself and still wishes to sell it, should he have insisted to Mr. Broadbank, when I heard them talking at Whiston, that he *didn't* have the memorandum and accuse Mr. Broadbank of having taken it? And if he had already sold it to someone else, he wouldn't have come back to the Castle and Mr. Broadbank, would he?"

Carlin said very well, her reasoning was entirely sound, but as far as he could see it still left them just as muddled as they had been before and it therefore appeared to him that the only sane thing to do was to put the matter into the hands of someone who knew a great deal more about it than they did.

To which Lady Pamela replied that she would think about it, and Carlin, who had learned that no matter how charmingly featherheaded his companion appeared she had a very sound understanding and considerable common sense when she chose to use it, felt that he had gained the victory and wisely did not press his advantage, enquiring instead if she would be at the Pelfreys' party that evening.

"Oh dear, I expect I shall have to be," she said. "I have known the Pelfreys forever and Adolphus is escorting me. Will *you* be there?" she asked, adding accusingly, "I don't mean have you got a card of invitation because of course you have not, but I can see, after last night, that *that* wouldn't stop you."

"As a matter of fact, I haven't and it won't," he acknowledged. "I shall get Lady St. Abbs to take me. She goes everywhere, I understand, and from what I have learned of her she will have absolutely no scruples about bringing uninvited guests to other people's houses."

Which was so true that Lady Pamela could not help laughing, but said he would regret it because she could see he was becoming a favourite of the terrifying old lady and that meant she would try to bullock him even more outrageously than she did the people she didn't like, which latter category included almost everyone she knew.

"Are you a favourite?" Carlin enquired, and Lady Pamela said no, and neither was Adolphus, which was a pity as it would be rather nice if she would leave him some of her money.

"Does he need it?" asked Carlin in a rather odd way.

Lady Pamela raised her brows. "Not really," she said, "if it's any concern of yours. But he is not a very rich man—"

"Then you aren't marrying him for that reason," Carlin stated, as if he were getting something clear in his own mind.

Lady Pamela grew pink with indignation. "Of course I am

not! What made you think such a horrid thing? As if Adolphus were the odious sort of man no one would marry except for his fortune!"

"Not at all!" said Carlin. "He is well-born, handsome, agreeable, a prime whip, I hear, an excellent shot, a bruising rider to hounds—but not your sort, my girl! Too conventional by half to suit *your* ideas."

"Adolphus," said Lady Pamela, setting her teeth together, "is *exactly* the sort of man to suit my ideas of the *ideal* husband, Lord Dalven! As a matter of fact—if you would like to know the truth—I have been in love with him since I was fifteen."

To her intense resentment, Carlin greeted this romantic piece of information with a shout of laughter.

"In love with him! No, no—you mean you made up your mind to have him when you were a schoolroom chit and hadn't any more idea of what you wanted in a man than what you read in novels. And I must say Babcoke could do Sir Charles Grandison very well if he had the least idea of what it was all about and didn't fall asleep in the middle of it."

At this point in the conversation—fortunately for the prospects of any future collaboration between the occupants of the curricle—that vehicle arrived in Berkeley Square, and Lady Pamela in high dudgeon descended from it.

"I shall see you this evening." Carlin said cheerfully, as he helped her to alight. "Don't look so vexed, love; you're not married to him yet. I'll see what I can do—and meanwhile, do *you* see what can be done about turning this whole matter of the memorandum over to your grandfather or Underdown. Did you say something?" he added, for Lady Pamela had turned the sort of look upon him that the leading lady usually puts on in the theatre when she is about to denounce the villain in ringing terms.

But Hadsell opened the door at that moment, and Lady Pamela, sailing into the house, took her revenge by saying nothing at all.

It had been her intention, upon entering the house, to go at once—in spite of the note of distinct disagreement on which she had parted with Carlin—to her grandfather's room and disclose to him the whole of her involvement in the affair of the memorandum. But unfortunately this praiseworthy resolution received a severe setback the moment she had stepped inside the door.

"The Honourable Mr. Cedric Mansell has called, my lady," said Hadsell, in a tone strongly indicative of disapproval, for, like all good servants, he knew quite as well as those who employed him the difference between a gentleman, Honourable or not, whom it was proper for a lady to receive and one whom it was not. "I informed him that Lord Wynstanley was gone out, but he has Seen Fit to Remain," he continued, with dark emphasis. "He says it is You he wishes to see, my lady."

He paused, with an unexpectedly hopeful air—for he was at least sixty and quite portly—of anticipating an order to evict the Honourable Cedric from the house, by force if necessary. But Lady Pamela, upon whose face a slight, thoughtful frown had appeared, did not direct him to do anything of the sort, being engaged at the moment in trying to imagine why the Honourable Cedric had come to see her and getting nowhere near an answer.

Of course, if Mr. Broadbank had been able to follow her to London by means of the Whistons' coachman's knowledge of the identity of the young gentleman with whom Maria Clover had fled from the Castle, so might the Honourable Cedric have done. But on the other hand, Cedric must by this time have learned who she really was or he would not have known to seek her out in Berkeley Square, and he must therefore realise that, if she had indeed found the memorandum at Whiston Castle, it would now be back in the hands of Lord Nevans. Which left her exactly where she had started, facing the question: Why did the Honourable Cedric wish to see her?

It seemed that the only person who could give her the answer to this riddle was the Honourable Cedric himself, so she took off her bonnet and pelisse and went at once, much to Hadsell's disapproval, into the little ground-floor saloon where he had meanly bestowed Mr. Mansell instead of ushering him upstairs to the apartment where more respectable callers were received.

"Good morning, Mr. Mansell. You wished to see me?" she said, coolly surveying the tall figure that had turned from the window upon her entrance. The Honourable Cedric was wearing, not the accepted town-dress of coat of blue superfine, pantaloons, and Hessians, but a russet riding-coat and boots, proclaiming that he had just arrived from the country, and upon this, her first really good view of him, she found that the dislike his voice, overheard from beneath the table in the east withdrawing room in Whiston Castle, had prepared her to lavish upon him was fully justified. This was in spite of the fact that his face and figure were undoubtedly handsome; but the face bore the unmistakable signs of dissipation, the eyes were too close-set and of a disagreeable pale blue, and the mouth, she decided, would be able to sneer even when it smiled. Which it at once proceeded to do.

"Lady Pamela?" said the Honourable Cedric, succeeding in insinuating into those two simple words the fact that he knew very well that she had not been using that name when they had been briefly under the same roof at Whiston Castle, although never actually meeting. "I must apologise to you for this intrusion, but the fact is that I believe we have a matter of considerable importance to discuss."

He came towards her as he spoke, scrutinising her with a careless arrogance that at once set her hackles up. But she knew very well that one never got any information out of men by being angry with them, so she immediately decided to be rather stupid instead and, opening her eyes a little wider, said innocently, oh, had they?

"Come, come, Lady Pamela!" said Cedric, his disagreeable eyes still fixed upon her face. "You know very well what I am referring to. Whiston Castle—Maria Clover—a certain document—"

Lady Pamela, faced with this direct attack, tried rapidly to imagine what a *really* stupid girl would do, thought of Cissie Pelfrey, and doubtfully said, "Oh!" and nothing more.

The Honourable Cedric began to look exasperated.

"My dear Lady Pamela," he said, "this is really getting us nowhere. If you were clever enough to disguise yourself as a lady's maid—as I have been assured by the real Maria Clover that you did—in order to gain entrance to Whiston Castle and pilfer a document—"

"To *what!*" said Lady Pamela, forgetting to be stupid in her wrath. "I did *not*—"

"We shan't quarrel over terminology," said Cedric. "To take possession, we shall say if you prefer, of a document—"

"I don't know what you are *talking* about," said Lady Pamela, rapidly becoming Cissie Pelfrey again and looking perturbed and much alarmed. "I wish you will *go*, Mr. Mansell. I am sure Grandpapa would not like—"

"Grandpapa will like it even less if your brother finds himself in the briars over this matter, Lady Pamela," said Cedric grimly. "Don't imagine you can fob me off with a pretence of innocence. You know a great deal about this matter—and would like to know a good deal more, I dare swear," he added, looking keenly into her face. "But I may warn you that it may be unwise for you to give way to your curiosity in this regard. Leave well enough alone, Lady Pamela. You have the document—"

"I *have?*" Lady Pamela could not restrain the exclamation, which broke from her quite involuntarily, and then immediately wished she had not been so idiotish. She saw the Honourable Cedric's eyes narrow suddenly.

"I see," he said slowly, after a short pause during which he had evidently been endeavouring to rearrange his thoughts just as Lady Pamela was frantically endeavouring to rearrange hers, for if both Mr. Broadbank and Cedric thought *she* had the memorandum, who in the world could have it, then? "You were *not* successful in finding the memorandum," he went on. "That alters matters a good deal—but the danger, my dear Lady Pamela, remains. In point of fact, one may say that it grows. For if it would have been unwise of you to have mentioned your suspicions that I was concerned in the memorandum's disappearance to Lord Nevans *after* it had been returned to him, when he might have been inclined to keep a still tongue about the whole affair in order to draw no attention to his own culpability in allowing it to be taken from his possession, it is doubly so now. You see, it will really be so very embarrassing for your brother if suspicion is cast in *my* direction."

"Embarrassing for—Wyn?" Lady Pamela's eyes involuntarily flew to the Honourable Cedric's face, and what she saw there did nothing to calm the sudden anxiety that had touched her heart at this unexpected and very disquieting statement. The Honourable Cedric looked—the word for it, she decided, could only be smug. Like a man who knew he held a winning hand at cards and was looking forward to playing it. "Why for Wyn, Mr. Mansell?" she went on, in a voice that, in spite of all she could do, sounded a little breathless.

Cedric smiled unpleasantly. "Why, because," he said, "if the document was indeed ever in my possession it could have got there by only one means, could it not? I am not an habitué of this house, you know. But your brother and I have been upon very close terms for some months now."

"But Wyn couldn't—He *didn't*—" Lady Pamela interrupted, indignation and loyalty suddenly getting the better of fear.

"Perhaps so," Cedric imperturbably agreed. "Perhaps he neither would nor did, but if I *say* he did, will his denial be believed, do you think? Unfortunately, it is widely known that your brother has had a most disastrously bad run of luck at the tables during these past few weeks, and when young men find themselves at Point Non-Plus they are so very likely—are they not?—to try to rescue themselves by any rash expedient that occurs to them."

He paused, and appeared to observe with satisfaction that his words had had the effect he had desired. Lady Pamela's face was flushed, and her manner, when she spoke, though determined, was far more disturbed than she liked.

"I don't believe that Wyn gave you that memorandum, Mr. Mansell," she said. "He says he did not, and I am sure that he is speaking the truth. If you care to hear it from his lips—"

"My dear Lady Pamela, he may swear on the Bible to me or to any magistrate in the land that he did not give it me," Cedric said with a shrug, "but as it will be his word against mine and it will appear that he has so very much to gain by denying the fact, it is scarcely likely that *his* story will be the one to carry the day. Now in spite of the show of milky innocence you put on for me just now, I am quite sure you are a young woman of sense, who has no desire to see her brother in serious trouble. Will you allow me to advise you, therefore, to say nothing at all to Lord Nevans or to anyone else that might result in my being obliged to resort to the unpleasant necessity of implicating your brother in this affair? It will really be so much more prudent of you, I assure you, not to meddle in it further."

Lady Pamela did not enjoy being threatened, even in a very veiled and civil way; but as it was quite impossible not to see that the Honourable Cedric would have all the advantages on his side if she were inclined to do any counter-threatening, she held her tongue. And at any rate Cedric now appeared to consider that, having made his point, he might bring the interview to an end, which he proceeded to do by leaving. Really a *most* disagreeable man, Lady Pamela thought, as she fulminatingly watched him walk out of the room, and though it was not her practice to interfere in Lord Wynstanley's affairs, she determined to let him know at the earliest opportunity exactly what sort of rogue he had been entertaining as a friend.

But upon this occasion Lord Wynstanley, returning home to face a severe lecture on this subject from his sister, had not a word to say in his own defence. He was, in fact, not only startled but alarmed to learn that his erstwhile friend and mentor had the dastardly intention of involving him in his own downfall, and, suddenly finding it impossible to maintain the veneer of a man of the town that he had been priding himself on during the past six months, abruptly looked not a whit older than his nineteen years and asked his sister rather desperately what they were to do.

"Nothing just now, I should think," said Lady Pamela, who had used the hour that had elapsed between the Honourable Cedric's departure from Berkeley Square and Lord Wynstanley's arrival there to ponder the situation. "He has not got the memorandum now, at any rate—I am sure of that—so what should we gain by telling anyone that he once had it? And Mr. Broadbank has not got it, either. Perhaps it is Droz—"

She looked thoughtful, and Lord Wynstanley, who had a sudden wild vision of his sister's discovering that Droz had left Mr. Broadbank's employ and disguising herself as an abigail once more to go in search of him, said in a harried voice, "No! I won't have it!"

"You won't have what?" enquired Lady Pamela, looking puzzled.

"Your mixing yourself up with fellows like that valet again. You let *me* handle it."

Which, since he had not the faintest idea what to do, was not a very sensible or helpful statement, but as Lady Pamela was quite as perplexed as was he, she forbore to argue the point with him, and in this unsatisfactory state the matter remained.

Fourteen

If neither Lord Wynstanley nor his sister knew what to do about the affair of the memorandum, however, the matter was quite clear in Lord Dalven's mind, and the result, when he learned at the Pelfreys' party that evening that Lady Pamela had neither told her grandfather what she knew of the document's disappearance nor had any present intention of doing so, was a quarrel that left them not quite on speaking terms, if these are the proper words to describe a state of affairs in which the gentleman is perfectly willing to speak but the lady not willing to be spoken to.

Of course all this was observed by Lady St. Abbs, and she told Lord Babcoke as soon as she could get hold of him that if she were a man she would not put up with it.

"Put up with what?" asked that noble peer, who had noticed that there was something going on between his betrothed and Lord Dalven, but hoped, as he usually did about difficulties, that if he paid it no heed it would go away.

"Quarrelin' with Dalven," said Lady St. Abbs, pounding her stick upon the floor in an ill-tempered way, which Lord Babcoke had never seen anyone do outside the theatre and which considerably alarmed him. "I won't have it! And if you had an ounce of rumgumption in you, Babcoke, you'd put a stop to it!"

"A stop to it?" said his lordship, looking bewildered.

"Yes! And don't keep repeatin' everything I say! *I* know what I've said! Say something of your own!"

If Lord Babcoke had said what he wished to say, he would have said, "Great-aunt Augusta, you are a very bad-tempered, rude old lady," and thereupon have walked off. But being noted for his excellent manners he did not, and instead said quite civilly that he believed she was refining too much upon the matter.

"No, I ain't!" said Lady St. Abbs. "You mark my words, Babcoke; when a woman comes to dagger-drawin' with a man every time she meets him, there's mischief in it! And *don't* come cryin' to me one day to say I didn't tell you so!" she added, already gloating with ghoulish satisfaction, it appeared, over some future scene in which Lord Babcoke would cast her negligence in this respect in her teeth, only to be reminded by her that he had had his warning.

Unfortunately, although Lord Babcoke was perfectly willing—nay, anxious—to stop his betrothed from acting in the very peculiar manner towards Lord Dalven that had attracted Lady St. Abbs' attention, he knew very well that he had never, in all the years he had been acquainted with her, succeeded in preventing her from doing anything she wished to do, and he was not very optimistic about his chances now. He was therefore not very surprised when a mild hint from him that the discussion of whatever disagreements she had with Lord Dalven might better be carried out in some less public place than Lady Pelfrey's saloon received a very tart reception, which discouraged him so much that he beat a hasty retreat and said in a cowardly fashion that he dared say it didn't matter, after all.

This was perhaps as well, because Lady Pamela, who was at her wit's end as to what to do, with Carlin pulling her one way and the Viscount the other, might have forgotten that he was the Ideal Husband with whom she was shortly going to begin to live in perfect felicity and have scratched his eyes out, metaphorically speaking.

But if Lady Pamela thought she had troubles then, they were as nothing compared to those that began for her that very evening—that is, the evening after the Pelfreys' party, for the above conversation between her and Lord Babcoke had taken place on the morning after that highly successful social event.

On that evening she accompanied her betrothed to view a performance at the handsome new Covent Garden Theatre Royal, which had recently been rebuilt at great expense after having been burnt to the ground a few years before. Their carriage, along with a stream of others—for the popular Kemble was playing that night—arrived in good time before the handsome Doric portico, thronged now with the entering crowd, the flower girls, and the lurking old women in duffle cloaks and black bonnets, surrounded by their young charges in trumped-up finery, who had come to ply their trade among the London dandies as their predecessors had done since the days of Charles II, and who were carefully ignored by the fashionable ladies of the *haut ton* as they descended from their elegant carriages and swept into the building.

Among these latter was Lady Pamela, looking very fetching indeed in a robe de Levantine of amber crape and quite determined to forget her difficulties for at least a few hours and enjoy the play. But her determination suffered an immediate setback when, upon entering the box that Lord Babcoke had procured for the evening, she found herself regarding the unwelcome sight of Lady Whiston, attired in a robe of sapphire-blue satin lavishly trimmed with lace, with a Spartan diadem on her masses of fair hair, just in the act of settling herself, her husband, and her daughter in the very next box.

Lady Pamela's initial impulse was to fall ill immediately, swoon, if necessary, and require Lord Babcoke to take her home at once. But it was too late. Lady Whiston's eyes, eagerly roaming the theatre, like Satan, in search of whom she might devour, had lit instantaneously upon Lord Babcoke. She had met Lord Babcoke—a number of years before, it was true, when he had visited her elder son, Lord Weare, at the Castle—and she pounced upon him now with all the enthusiasm of a lady who feels herself upon very uncertain footing in Society and is determined to do something about it.

"But it is—surely it *is* Lord Babcoke!" she exclaimed, leaning forward in her chair the better to fasten her victim with her large and rather protruding blue eyes. "You *do* remember don't you? But you *must!*" she went on, as Lord Babcoke, obviously searching his memory, bowed and smiled rather blankly. "Whiston Castle, '06—or could it have been '05?—the year you came down with Ferdy and spent a week with us, or perhaps not *quite* a week—"

"Lady Whiston! Of course!" said his lordship, enlightened by these hints. "How very nice to see you again."

"Yes, isn't it!" said Lady Whiston, who considered ten words quite enough for her to allow anyone else to speak before she was off again at a conversational gallop herself. "Here you see us, Babcoke, quite a set of country mice—for you must know that we find Whiston so *very* attractive, so perfectly suited to *all* our moods, that we are seldom able to tear ourselves away from it—What was I saying? Oh, yes—a set of country mice, come up to the metropolis for a little shopping—*quite* a necessity for you know I am to bring out my little Sabrina this Season. Oh, this *is* Sabrina. You will not remember her, of course, for she was in the nursery when you were at Whiston, but I—*Oh!*"

This last exclamation, and the sudden halt in the flow of her ladyship's conversation, considerably startled Lord Babcoke, but upon Lady Pamela they fell like the anticipated stroke of the guillotine upon its hapless victim's neck. She was quite aware of the reason for Lady Whiston's sharp ejaculation: her ladyship's protuberant blue eyes had just fallen upon her. An affronted surge of colour rushed into her ladyship's face, and she glared—there could be no other word for it—at Lady Pamela.

Lord Babcoke, looking quite madly bewildered by this time, followed that furious gaze to Lady Pamela's face.

"Oh! Do you two know each other?" he suggested helpfully.

Lady Whiston, like a devout church-goer to whom acquaintance with Beelzebub has been imputed, shuddered and transferred the glare to him.

"No?" said Lord Babcoke, more at sea than ever. "In that case, may I present Lady Pamela Frayne? Lady Whiston—Lord Whiston—Lady Sabrina Mansell—"

But if Lord Babcoke hoped by means of this introduction to calm the troubled social waters into which he appeared somehow to have fallen, he was much mistaken. True, Lady Whiston's glare faded, but it was replaced by an expression of such mingled incredulity and outrage that no one could have said the change was for the better, while Lord Whiston, who had been looking his usual diffident self, appeared to be searching miserably for a place to hide, his eyes, like a hunted rabbit's, selecting and regretfully rejecting the shelter of curtains and alcoves. As for Sabrina, she was gazing at Lady Pamela with a dawning expression of what could only be interpreted as heroine-worship upon her piquant little face.

Under these circumstances it was scarcely surprising that Lord Babcoke felt himself to be the only sane person in a world that had suddenly decided to go mad. Fortunately, at that moment the curtain went up, so that he was able to sit down quietly beside Lady Pamela and contemplate the unusual events that had just transpired. Not that his contemplation did him much good, for in the first place it was not so peaceful as he might have desired. It was true that Lady Whiston was not directing any more remarks at him, but she *was* directing a number of what could only be described as dagger-glances at Lady Pamela, interspersed with periods of furious whispering to her lord, who looked more than ever like a hunted rabbit with a terrier close upon its heels.

This kept up for a good five minutes, at the end of which time Lord Babcoke gave up trying to contemplate and did a little whispering of his own.

"Do you know Lady Whiston?" he hissed to Lady Pamela.

Lady Pamela, pretending to be virtuously intent upon the play, shook her head violently without looking at him.

"Then what the deuce is the matter with the woman?" Lord Babcoke persisted, in the same harassed whisper. "Dash it, she looks as if she'd enjoy seeing you drawn and quartered!"

"Case of mistaken identity, I expect," Lady Pamela whispered back, with a dismal attempt at airiness that became even more dismal when she saw, across the theatre, Carlin amiably gazing at her through his quizzing-glass from Lady St. Abbs' box, a smile of unalloyed amusement upon his dark face. If there was anything else needed to make this wretched evening complete, she thought bitterly, it was having Carlin grinning at her discomfiture from the superior vantage point of knowing that *he* really was who the Whistons thought he was, so that he was quite safe from any embarrassing discoveries. Also, it was very unsettling not knowing what he would say about her to the Whistons, for she could see that Lady Whiston, like herself, had already espied him across the theatre and was only biding her time until the first interval before she pounced upon him to confirm her suspicions that Maria Clover, the abigail, and Lady Pamela Frayne were really one and the same person.

And, in truth, even as the curtain descended upon the first act of the play she saw Lady Whiston beckoning imperatively to Carlin, while at the same time she ordered her husband out of the box, no doubt to bring Carlin to her himself should he not prove amenable to her signalled invitation.

Lady Pamela, though she was not wanting in courage, promptly and ignominiously decided to flee.

"We really *must* go and pay our respects to your great-aunt Augusta," she said hastily, surprising Lord Babcoke a good deal by this unexpected consideration for Lady St. Abbs; but on the whole he had already decided that this was going to be one of those occasions when it did a man no good to try to understand what women were up to and that the best thing to do was to give them their heads and take cover (in a rather muddled metaphor) if the firing grew too hot.

So he accompanied Lady Pamela with his usual docility to Lady St. Abbs' box, where his great-aunt at once demanded of him what that Whiston woman had been making such a to-do about.

"Shockin' mushroom she is—daughter of a Cit and has all the shabby-genteel airs you'd expect of her, to say nothin' of bein' the biggest gabblemonger you'll meet in a month of Sundays," she said. "Remember her when she came up to town with Whiston after he married her—must be thirty years ago—tryin' to walk out of the room before *me* with her airs and her graces! *I* set her down, you may believe!" Which her hearers did. "Haven't seen much of her lately," the old Countess continued. "Who's that with her? Her daughter? Well, she's a passable gal. Daresay she's after Dalven for her and he might do worse, if he don't mind havin' a brimstone for a mother-in-law and a rakeshame like Cedric Mansell for a brother-in-law. Whiston's no better than an old woman, but the family's a good one and that female is swimmin' in lard, they tell me. The gal should be well dowered."

It would have puzzled Lady Pamela to say why it was that, with all the other anxieties she had at the moment, she should have taken the time to feel scornful at the idea of Carlin's marrying Lady Sabrina, but so she did. No doubt, she told herself, it was because the notion of Carlin's settling down and marrying anyone, not to say a child like Sabrina, was quite ridiculous. And then she found herself wondering, with a sudden rather horrid little pang, if it was so very ridiculous after all, and looked at Lord Babcoke in a kind of panic, as if hoping he would remind her of the Ideal Life they were going to live together and of how she had lain awake one cold November night when she was fifteen, after a particularly good run with the hounds, thinking how handsome he was and how splendidly he had taken that regular rasper at the bottom of Downer's Hill and saying, "Adolphus, Adolphus," over and over again in a quite besotted way until she had at last fallen blissfully asleep.

But Lord Babcoke, who of course had no idea that she wanted him to remind her of those younger, foolish days (and why, she asked herself, in one of those flashes of insight that seem to come at the most peculiar moments, had it taken her almost six years to come to the point of getting engaged to him if she had really been in love with him all that while?) only went on patiently trying to explain to Lady St. Abbs what he did not understand himself, namely, why Lady Whiston had behaved so oddly when he had introduced Lady Pamela to her.

"Well, she's still at it, whatever it is," Lady St. Abbs declared, looking across the theatre to where Lady Whiston was to be seen talking sixteen to the dozen, in a most emphatic way, to Lord Dalven, meanwhile directing frequent meaningful glances at Lady Pamela. "What have you been up to?" she demanded of Lady Pamela. "Somethin' disgraceful, I'll be bound—and that woman's got hold of it somehow. You had as well tell me," she added grimly, "for I'll get it out of *her* if you don't."

Lady Pamela said desperately, she had been up to nothing at all.

"Very well," snapped the old Countess. "Have it your own way, miss! Babcoke, you tell that woman to come to my box during the next interval!"

"But, Great-aunt Augusta," protested Lord Babcoke, "I scarcely know her! I can't simply *order* her—"

"Yes, you can. Easiest thing in the world. Don't be such a looby, man! The woman's mad to be accepted in Society. She'll come like a shot."

Lord Babcoke looked as if for two pins he would say, "A plague on all women," and walk out of the theatre, but having been too well brought up to do that contented himself with looking somewhere between sulky and exasperated and took Lady Pamela away.

"I don't know what has come over Great-aunt Augusta," he said rather crossly, as they walked back to their own box. "Really, she is growing more eccentric every year! If Lady Whiston *has* taken some odd notion into her head about you, it is not Great-aunt Augusta's affair to try to set it to rights. Perhaps *I*—"

"No!" said Lady Pamela.

Lord Babcoke looked rather surprised at her vehemence. "But really, old girl," he said, "as your betrothed, if Lady Whiston *is* spreading some disagreeable story about you—"

"Adolphus, if you say a word to that woman, I—I shall never speak to you again!" said Lady Pamela; and then had to compose her countenance at once into a charming smile to greet the Countess Lieven, the Russian ambassador's wife, who, with her usual court about her, came up from the opposite end of the corridor and paused to greet them.

This meeting occurred just as they were passing the Whistons' box, and Lady Pamela, who was standing on the outskirts of the little group, not feeling much inclined for conversation, suddenly found herself addressed by Carlin, who had just emerged from the box behind her.

"Good evening, Lady Pamela," he said, with an impeccably correct tone and manner for a gentleman greeting a young lady with whom he was no more than formally acquainted; but there was a gleam in his dark eyes that did not escape Lady Pamela's observation. She quickly drew him a little aside.

"Carlin, don't you *dare* laugh at me!" she said threateningly. "Don't you know I am in the most dreadful pucker? What did that woman say to you? Or no, *don't* tell me that, for I am sure I already know! Tell me what *you* said to *her*."

"Do you mean about the most unusual likeness she has detected between a runaway abigail named Maria Clover and the Lady Pamela Frayne?" asked Carlin, his face perfectly grave but the gleam even more pronounced now in his dark eyes. "Never mind, love, I handled it beautifully, *I* thought. First I was quite unable to see the likeness at all, said I was sure Miss Clover had had a squint—"

"Carlin, you *didn't!* How *very* clever of you!"

"And then, when I found myself being forced out of that position by the combined weight of Whiston opinion against me, I changed my ground and dropped a few dark hints about your late father, to whom I very improperly attributed a weakness for the female sex that had resulted in the possibility that he had—er—littered the countryside with his butter-prints." Lady Pamela choked. "I hope you don't mind," Carlin continued apologetically. "It was really the only thing I could think of at the moment."

"Oh, no—no!" said Lady Pamela, controlling a gurgle of laughter. "It was a masterstroke. Only poor Papa! He was the soul of propriety, you know!"

"No, was he?" said Carlin, interested. "I can't think how he could have been, and still have produced such a pair as you and Wynstanley."

"Well, Grandpapa *does* say that we both resemble Mama in our characters more than we do him," Lady Pamela admitted fair-mindedly. "But that is neither here nor there. The point is, does Lady Whiston believe you? I mean, does she believe that Maria Clover might have been one of Papa's by-blows?"

"No," said Carlin. Lady Pamela looked disappointed. "Well, you see," Carlin went on, "I think I am almost as much in her black books as you are, which makes her rather unwilling to rely upon my word. I told you, you know, that she would suspect me of having carried on an intrigue with Maria Clover at Whiston Castle, and now that she also suspects that Maria Clover was really you in disguise she is not prepared to forgive me, I think, unless I Confess All and throw myself upon her mercy."

"In which case, no doubt," Lady Pamela said in a suddenly horrid, flippant voice that she could scarcely recognise as her own, "she will set Sabrina to reforming you. Are you quite sure the prospect doesn't appeal to you?"

But before Carlin could reply, Lord Babcoke, who had suddenly become aware that his betrothed had, so to speak, absconded from the general conversation and was carrying on a private dialogue with Lord Dalven, said, "Good evening," in a very cool, stiff way to that gentleman and suggested to Lady Pamela that they had best be returning to their own box. Carlin, looking amused, returned a careless greeting and went away, leaving Lord Babcoke to say in a rather nettled manner that he wondered what that fellow found to laugh about.

"You, I daresay," said Lady Pamela, still in the grip of that peculiar emotion, whatever it was, that made one behave quite horridly to people, while feeling inside as if one would like to go off to the nearest and darkest cellar and have a good cry. "*Must* you be so rude to him? Too, too ridiculous, my dear!"

Lord Babcoke, following her into the box, said stubbornly

that he didn't like the fellow, but then immediately forgot all about Lord Dalven as his eyes took in the rather terrifying sight of Lady Whiston, crouched and ready, so to speak, like a tigress in her box, waiting to pounce upon them.

"Lady Pamela," she began, in a loud, clear, determined voice—but at that precise moment, to the intense relief of both Lord Babcoke and his betrothed, Lord Wynstanley abruptly entered the box and claimed their attention.

Fifteen

Lord Wynstanley appeared to be quite as excited as if he were aware of all that had been going on in the theatre that evening, which he was not, for he had just arrived there.

"I want to talk to you," he said at once, sitting down beside his sister and fixing her with a harassed gaze. "Fellow I know—some relation of the Whistons—mentioned to me at White's just now that they'd arrived in town and were planning on attending the theatre this evening. He didn't know if it was Covent Garden or the Lane, but I thought I'd best warn you."

At this point Lady Pamela, who had been trying ever since the Whistons had been mentioned to communicate to her brother by means of a severe frown and slight gestures towards the next box that every word he spoke was being taken in by six avidly attentive ears, gave it up and, employing direct methods, said, "Sssh!"—which brought Lord Wynstanley to a sudden halt.

"What—?" he began, and then his eyes fell upon the Whistons and he flushed to the roots of his hair. "Oh, good evening, Lady Whiston! Good evening, sir!" he stammered, and was ever afterwards to believe that, as a result of some forgotten but noble action in his own short past, Providence at that moment elected to favour him by causing the curtain to go up.

It was a very uncomfortable trio who sat in Lord Babcoke's box watching the second act of what might have been a very entertaining play if anyone had been attending to it. Lord Wynstanley was wishing very much that he might consult his sister as to what the situation was in regard to the Whistons, but felt Lady Whiston's eye upon him like a basilisk's and so did not dare to speak. Lord Babcoke, who was also wishing, wished that Lord Wynstanley would go away so that he could make up his quarrel with Lady Pamela, but as he wished that Lord Dalven, the Whistons, Lady St. Abbs, and, indeed, everyone else in the theatre would go away, too, there was nothing personal about it. As for Lady Pamela, she was trying to decide whether a dramatic swoon or merely pleading a migraine would be the best way to get herself out of the theatre, but unfortunately the blood of the Fraynes came up in her and informed her sternly that retreat was the coward's way out. And at any rate she felt what was no doubt a somewhat morbid curiosity to see whether Sabrina would make any advances that evening to Carlin or vice versa.

So she stayed, and the act came to an end, and in spite of the fact that she felt a good deal like a Christian martyr in the arena waiting for the lions to devour her, she remained in her seat when the curtain came down.

But though one may be prepared to sacrifice oneself to one's duty, there is nothing in the rules of heroic conduct that says one cannot take an honourable way of postponing the evil hour, if possible. Lady Pamela thought she saw that way, so she said rapidly to Lord Babcoke, before Lady Whiston could say, "Lady Pamela!" again, that he must not forget that Lady St. Abbs had expressed a wish to see Lady Whiston in her box during the interval. This speech at once caught Lady Whiston's ear and distracted her from the purpose of Getting to the Bottom of Things that had been simmering inside her like a kettle on the boil all during the act. She looked expectantly at Lord Babcoke. Lady St. Abbs was no mean prey for a socially ambitious female, and if she was inclined to make overtures, Lady Pamela could wait. The play, after all, was in five acts.

Lord Babcoke, finding Lady Whiston's blue eyes fixed firmly upon him, said reluctantly, "Oh—er—yes, of course. My great-aunt Augusta, you know, Lady Whiston. If you'd care to—?"

Lady Whiston promptly said she would adore to and stood up, upon which Lord Babcoke, with a reproachful glance at his betrothed, stood up too and prepared to accompany Lady Whiston to Lady St. Abbs' box, from which Lady St. Abbs herself was already beckoning violently.

"Frederick," said Lady Whiston to her spouse, as she departed, "*you* may take Sabrina for a stroll in the corridor."

And she swept out of the box, bestowing as she did so a

severe nod upon Lord Wynstanley, which appeared to promise him that she would deal with *his* case later.

The Earl, who seemed only too anxious to remove himself from present company, got up at once and looked at his daughter.

"But I don't *want* to go for a stroll in the corridor, Papa!" said Sabrina in a very positive voice. "I want to stay here and talk to Wyn and—and to Lady Pamela," she finished, pronouncing the name with such a careful lack of emphasis that she had *Third Conspirator* written all over her and Lady Pamela wondered in sudden alarm what she had got hold of and how.

Lord Whiston, looking more hunted than ever, said she had heard what her mama had said. Sabrina shrugged.

"Oh, Mama!" she said. "She will be so busy talking that she won't even notice."

Which Lady Pamela could see was indeed true, for Lady Whiston, who must have sped through the corridor with the speed of the goddess Diana following the chase in her zeal to arrive at Lady St. Abbs' box, was already visible there, and apparently engaged in a contest with the old Countess as to which one could speak the most and the fastest, with Lord Babcoke as judge.

Lord Whiston then gave up and said he would go alone, probably feeling that half a loaf would be better than none when it came to reporting to his spouse how her orders had been carried out, and went away. Sabrina at once turned her eyes raptly upon Lady Pamela.

"Oh, Lady Pamela," she breathed, "I won't tell anybody, but I *do* think you are so brave!"

Lady Pamela blinked. "Brave?" she said.

"Oh, yes! I mean, pretending that you were Maria Clover, and searching for missing documents *just* like Cleonice in that absolutely *thrilling* novel where the Count is going to be beheaded if he can't find it—"

Lady Pamela, upon whom light had begun to dawn, looked severely at her brother.

"Wyn!" she said awfully. "You *didn't!*"

"Well, I couldn't help it!" said Lord Wynstanley, rather sulkily. "Dash it, how else was I to find out anything at the Castle, with Dalven gone and Lady Whiston doing nothing but ringing a peal over me for taking you—I mean she thought you were that abigail, of course—off? I *had* to talk to Sabrina. I didn't tell her any more than was absolutely necessary, and I made her understand I'd comb her hair with a joint-stool if she squeaked beef," he added hastily, seeing that his sister was looking as if the peal Lady Whiston had rung over him would be as nothing compared to the one she was preparing to let loose upon him. "And she didn't—did you, Sabrina?"

"Not a word! Honour of a Mansell!" said Sabrina proudly. "Oh, and you said Dalven, Wyn. Is he in it, too?"

"No!" said Lady Pamela, forestalling any answer the Viscount planned to make. "Wyn, this is really *too* bad of you! How *could* you?"

"Well, *you* told Dalven," Lord Wynstanley defended himself. "And you knew a deuced bit less about *him* than I know about Sabrina."

"That was different! I needed his help."

"Well, *I* needed Sabrina's," Lord Wynstanley said stubbornly.

"Yes, and I *will* help," Sabrina promised, her eyes glowing with the fervour of self-sacrificial devotion. "And you needn't worry, Lady Pamela, because I won't tell Mama, no matter *what* she says or does. Papa doesn't count. I've told him already."

"Good God!" said Lady Pamela, now quite aghast. "How many other people know about this?"

"Well, I should think Lady St. Abbs and Lord Babcoke know by this time that you came to Whiston Castle disguised as my abigail," Sabrina said judiciously, looking across the theatre to where Lady Whiston, who had evidently won the contest as far as doing all the talking was concerned, was to be seen moving her lips rapidly and nodding her head emphatically while Lady St. Abbs registered shock, disapproval, and eager curiosity in almost equal amounts. "I hope you don't mind—"

"But I *do* mind!" said Lady Pamela. "I—I am betrothed to Lord Babcoke!"

"Are you?" said Sabrina. She looked slightly disappointed. "Well, I daresay he is very handsome, but somehow I don't think he is *quite* the sort of man you ought to marry. I mean, he doesn't care much for adventures, does he?"

Lady Pamela, observing from across the theatre the dazed

look on Lord Babcoke's face as, sitting between Lady Whiston and Lady St. Abbs, he listened to the ceaseless flow of their conversation washing over him, said rather faintly that she dared say he did not.

"Well, it doesn't matter, I expect, at any rate," said Sabrina optimistically, "because in that novel I read Cleonice was betrothed, too, but he turned out to be the villain and had the papers all along himself, so of course she didn't marry him, after all."

And she looked at Lord Babcoke with sudden interest, as if casting him in her mind in the rôle of villain and deciding that he might do very well, which made Lady Pamela tell her rather sharply not to be silly.

At that moment a knock fell upon the door of the box and Carlin walked in.

"Carlin!" said Lady Pamela, falling upon him like a general upon much-needed reinforcements before he had time to open his lips. "*What* do you think that idiotish brother of mine has done? He has told Lady Sabrina Everything!"

"Good God, has he?" said Carlin, but looking amused rather than alarmed. "Lady Pamela, I ask your pardon. You told me once that your brother was much worse than you are, and I didn't believe you."

The Viscount, who had again flushed up scarlet, muttered rebelliously that if Dalven had stayed on at the Castle he would not have been obliged to take Sabrina into his confidence.

"Well, I think it is a very good thing you did," said Sabrina, springing at once to Lord Wynstanley's defence, "because how could I help you if I knew nothing about anything? And, after all, Ceddie is *my* brother, so I do think I should have been told—*not* that I know a great deal about him because I almost never see him and he never tells me anything, but something *might* turn up—"

"I have no doubt that it will," said Carlin, cutting her short but quite kindly. He turned to Lady Pamela. "What is more to the point," he observed, with a nod in the direction of Lady St. Abbs' box, "is that Babcoke seems to be experiencing Revelation at first hand for himself. Couldn't you contrive to keep him away from Lady Whiston?"

"I didn't try," Lady Pamela confessed. "In fact, I sent him off with her myself. I daresay it is cowardly, but I felt that anything was better than being obliged to face her myself before all these people!"

Carlin looked more amused. "Cowardly—you!" he said.

"But I am! I don't know *how* things have got into such a muddle, but they have, and I don't know what to say to anyone because I can't remember any more *who* knows how much about what, and—Oh, dear! There is Mr. Broadbank!" she broke off suddenly to exclaim. "In the pit, bowing to me. What can *he* be doing here?"

"Keeping an eye on you, I imagine," Carlin said calmly. "Things appear to be coming to a head. I just ran across the Honourable Cedric in the corridor and I rather think he has me set down now as his most likely suspect. We had a most improbable conversation, which seemed to revolve very discreetly about the subject of whether I was in need of money."

"Well, I think you would make a very good suspect," said Sabrina, who had been eavesdropping shamelessly, "only not quite so good as Lord Babcoke, because if he is the villain Lady Pamela couldn't marry him. I don't think they are suited," she added firmly, looking at Lady Pamela.

"And quite right you are," said Carlin approvingly. "Do you think *we* are?"

"You and I? Or you and Lady Pamela?" enquired Sabrina. "If it's you and I, I *did* think you were most frightfully interesting when you came to the Castle, but I rather believe now that I like Wyn better. *He* doesn't laugh at me."

Lord Wynstanley, who had been sunk in what seemed rather sulky self-reproach, looked up, alarmed.

"Now, see here!" he said.

"Oh, it's quite all right," said Sabrina kindly. "I don't intend to marry anyone until after I am out, and have made heaps of conquests. But when I *do* think about marrying someone, I shan't forget *you*, Wyn."

Lord Wynstanley looked as if he found this statement something less than reassuring, but Lady Pamela, who for some reason suddenly felt quite light-hearted, even in the midst of all her troubles, laughed.

"I don't see anything to laugh about!" said the Viscount. "Dash it, you don't know her! She's as bad as her mother when it comes to something she's set her mind on!"

Carlin said that she sounded to him exactly the sort of wife the Viscount ought to have, as he appeared to need someone to keep him out of mischief and look what Lady Whiston had done for Lord Whiston.

"Yes, poor Papa!" said Sabrina sympathetically. "He *never* gets away from Whiston; as a matter of fact, Mama wouldn't even have allowed him to come to London with us if he hadn't flown up into the boughs and insisted upon it in a way I have never seen him do before. He even made her set the journey forward by several days, which was very fortunate, or otherwise we shouldn't have been here tonight."

Lady Pamela looked rather as if that was a treat she could well have done without, but did not say anything, as at that moment her attention was distracted by the sight of Lord Babcoke and Lady Whiston departing from Lady St. Abbs' box. She turned to Carlin in alarm.

"Oh! They are coming back!" she said. "What shall I *do?*"

Carlin, considering gravely, said that in his military experience he had learned that it never served to stand and face insuperable odds, and advised retreat.

"But I can't retreat from Adolphus!" Lady Pamela said, "*He* will have to take me home."

"Well, at least you will have halved the number of your opponents," Carlin pointed out encouragingly, "and on a man-to-man footing against Babcoke I should certainly sport my blunt on *you*, love."

This last word caused Lord Wynstanley to bristle, but fortunately at that moment Lord Whiston came back, looking so harassed and guilty that the thought just passed through Lady Pamela's mind that, if she had been an unbiassed observer—say, a Bow Street Runner—looking for a really first-rate suspect in the case, she would at once have lit upon him. Whereas, as a matter of fact, she thought, he was doubtless merely wondering how to explain to Lady Whiston why he had not followed her directions and taken Sabrina with him for a stroll in the corridor.

Then Lord Babcoke and Lady Whiston entered their respective boxes, the former still looking dazed and the latter very flushed and triumphant, rather like an avenging Fury who has just done a really prime piece of avenging work. Lady Pamela, casting a despairing glance at Carlin, said hurriedly to her betrothed that she was dreadfully sorry but she had had the headache all evening and it was growing worse, and could he possibly take her home?

"Yes, she doesn't look at all the thing," Carlin said helpfully, as he rose to leave the box. "I should certainly advise you to take her home, Babcoke. Unless, of course," he added, with a show of punctiliousness that did not in the least deceive Lady Pamela, "you prefer to remain yourself and see the rest of the play, in which case I shall be happy to escort Lady Pamela."

"By no means! That is not at all necessary!" said Lord Babcoke, looking at Carlin in as unfriendly a way as if he had offered to ravish Lady Pamela rather than merely take her home. "I shall escort Lady Pamela myself!"

"Very well," said Carlin and, bestowing something uncommonly like a wink upon Lady Pamela, unfortunately intercepted by both Lady Whiston and Lord Babcoke, he lounged out of the box.

Lady Whiston, baulked of her prey, looked rather as if she would have liked to issue orders to Lord Babcoke to keep Lady Pamela in the box by force, if necessary, but Lady Pamela gave her no opportunity for this; in a trice she had herself and her betrothed outside in the corridor, and very shortly afterwards, having parted company with Lord Wynstanley, who had followed them out and said he was going to look in at Watiers', she and Lord Babcoke were seated together in the latter's carriage, on their way back to Berkeley Square.

Not until then did Lord Babcock, always the soul of propriety, introduce to his betrothed, in tones of subdued outrage, the subject of the remarkable story with which Lady Whiston had regaled him and Lady St. Abbs in the latter's box that evening.

"The woman must be out of her mind!" he said, with a severity quite foreign to his usual mild nature. "She spent the entire interval babbling the most extraordinary Banbury tale to Great-aunt Augusta about your having turned up at Whiston Castle a week or so ago posing as her daughter's abigail and then eloping from there in the dead of night with a young man who turned out to be Wyn. I never listened to such miff-maff in all my life! Why, I ask you, would Wyn want to elope with his own sister? It doesn't make sense! The truth of the matter is, I expect, that that young scoundrel has been carrying on one of his petticoat affairs and has tried to drag you into it to cover his tracks."

Lady Pamela, who had been of two minds up to this moment as to whether to confess the truth to her betrothed or not, now found the decision taken out of her hands. She could not abandon Wyn to Lord Babcoke's ill opinion, so she said in a rather small voice that it was not that way at all, and she could not explain, but she *had* gone to Whiston Castle as Lady Sabrina's abigail.

"It was—it was something that had to do with Grandpapa," she continued, as Lord Babcoke turned a face expressive of complete incredulity upon her. "Only you must *promise* not to say a word of this to him, Adolphus, because he is still not at all well and it would upset him dreadfully if he knew!"

Lord Babcoke, in a rather stunned voice, said, if he knew what?

"Anything!" said Lady Pamela, all-inclusively. "You *won't* speak to him, will you, Adolphus?"

Lord Babcoke, instead of answering her directly, sat for some moments in silence, with the look upon his face of a man struggling with some knotty mental problem.

"Now look here—" he said at last, and then stopped.

"Yes?" said Lady Pamela helpfully.

"Let me understand this," said Lord Babcoke doggedly. "You went to Whiston Castle—pretending to be an abigail—on business for Lord Nevans—that he knows nothing about. And then you eloped with Wyn—"

"I didn't elope with Wyn," Lady Pamela said indignantly. "He came to find me, and then Carlin—I mean Lord Dalven—insisted upon his taking me away, so he did. I know it all sounds rather peculiar—"

"Very peculiar," said Lord Babcoke, with an unusually grim note in his pleasant voice. "So Dalven was there, too, was he? I thought you told me you had never laid eyes on him before the other evening at Great-aunt Augusta's."

Lady Pamela, mentally damning her unwary tongue, said weakly that it was all very secret and something she couldn't talk about, even to him, and then wondered, looking apprehensively into her betrothed's face, if it would be pistols at twenty paces on Paddington Green the next morning.

"There really *isn't* anything for you to fly up into the

boughs about, Adolphus," she said rather anxiously. "It just *happened* that Lord Dalven was there—I mean that I met him—and I had to have *someone* to help me—"

Lord Babcoke said, in the voice of a man repressing strong feelings with great effort, that he must remember to thank Lord Dalven for his services to her.

"Oh no, *don't* do that!" said Lady Pamela hastily. "He is—he is such a very odd sort of man, you know; one never knows what he will say! I am sure it will be much, much better if you simply ignore him."

"And ignore as well Lady Whiston's hints that you and he were engaged in some sort of intrigue at Whiston Castle?" said Lord Babcoke, now provoked beyond either reason or courtesy; and received in reply, to his amazement, a stinging slap across his face that made his eyes water and quite upset his equilibrium for a moment, to the extent that he scarcely realised that the carriage had stopped and the footman had jumped down to let down the steps and open the door.

"And let *that* be a lesson to you not to listen to people like Lady Whiston when they tell you things they made up out of their own nasty little minds!" said Lady Pamela, unexpectedly very close to tears herself as she gathered her amber draperies about her and stepped out of the carriage. "No, *don't* come in with me; I have had quite enough of you and of *everyone* for one evening!"

With which violent words she walked into the house, surprising Hadsell, who had opened the door for her, very much by stalking past him without a word and with wet, flashing eyes, causing him to remark a little later to Lord Wynstanley's valet, Brill, that he had been having Feelings for some time now about the projected marriage between her ladyship and Lord Babcoke, and if he were Lord Babcoke he would not count upon anything, seeing as by the look of her ladyship it seemed there would shortly be the devil to pay and no pitch hot, and his lordship square in the middle of it.

Sixteen

To say the truth, had Lord Babcoke been unwise enough to have disregarded his betrothed's dictum and followed her inside at that particular moment, there is no saying that Hadsell's forebodings might not have become reality and his lordship have found himself with a broken engagement upon his hands.

But he did *not* follow her, not having attained the age of three-and-thirty without having discovered the valuable truth that it does a man no good to quarrel with an angry woman, and the wisdom of this decision was attested to on the following morning by Lady Pamela's coming down to breakfast in a very subdued mood, and much inclined to censure herself for having been extremely unreasonable the night before. Of course, she told herself, Adolphus had been upset by the revelations that had been made to him, and if he had taken some quite ridiculous maggot into his head about her and Carlin, one could scarcely blame him for that, either, in view of all the circumstances.

Only it *was* ridiculous for him to be jealous of Carlin, she thought, as she dawdled over her morning chocolate in the breakfast-parlour in a dispirited manner quite unusual with her, since Carlin had never, from the day she had first made his acquaintance, given the least indication that he considered the adventure in which he was engaged with her as anything more than a means of lightening the tedium of daily existence, as he had previously sought to lighten it by taking employment as a coachman.

It might have been considered that this conviction of her own and Carlin's praiseworthy innocence, as far as any intentions of amorous dalliance were concerned, would have raised Lady Pamela's spirits; but it did not. Neither did the sight of a bright March day outside the window, presaging spring, for it reminded her only of the fact that when the spring had fully come there would be a very fashionable wedding at St. George's, Hanover Square, in which the Lady Pamela Frayne would become the bride of Adolphus George Frederick Lashbrooke, Earl of Babcoke, and forthwith begin to lead the life of wedded felicity of which she had dreamed.

"But I don't *wish* to be married!" a panicky little devil whispered somewhere inside her. "Not to Adolphus—not to *anyone!*"

"Oh yes, you do!" said that stern, uncompromising Frayne conscience that never permitted one to enjoy telling oneself a comfortable falsehood. "And you know very well to whom!"

Which was so unanswerable that Lady Pamela merely said crossly, in this very peculiar interior dialogue, that she didn't know *what* her conscience was talking of, and at any rate one simply *couldn't* cry off from a betrothal when the announcement had been made and the wedding date set, and besides there was no one else who wished to marry her.

Fortunately, when the conversation had reached this uncomfortable point, an interruption occurred: Hadsell, entering the room, enquired if she was at home to callers, for Lady Sabrina Mansell had just arrived and was asking to see her.

"She seems a trifle Upset, my lady," he went on, with the carefully noncommittal air of an excellent butler, but communicating a great deal to Lady Pamela by means of his eyebrows. "If I may say so, even Distraught."

His words were immediately confirmed by the appearance in the doorway of Sabrina herself, with her bonnet-strings tied quite askew and a general appearance of having hurled on her clothes without regard for anything but haste.

"Oh, Lady Pamela!" she gasped, as soon as her eyes fell upon her seated at the table. "*Do* forgive me, but I could not wait! It is a matter of the greatest urgency!"

She halted, casting a glance at Hadsell that would have roused the curiosity of a statue, of which classical form of ornamentation he was now giving an excellent imitation, though inwardly speculating violently on what sort of May-game her ladyship had got herself mixed up in now.

Lady Pamela, however, showing no signs of the perturbation to which her guest was obviously a prey, merely said calmly, "That will be all, Hadsell," and, rising, came forward to Sabrina.

"Now do sit down and tell me what the matter is," she

said, as Hadsell left the room. "Would you like some chocolate, or coffee?"

"No, no—nothing!" Sabrina said, in a dramatic style that would have done credit to a Siddons. "Lady Pamela, you don't understand! I have come to you because I Know All!"

And she sat down, unfortunately knocking her bonnet even further askew as she did so, and looking so much like an earnest amateur participating in a melodramatic play that Lady Pamela could not help smiling.

"Yes, yes, but there is no need for you to fall into such a pucker," she said soothingly. "What is it that you Know All about?"

"About the paper! The document! The memorandum!" said Sabrina, growing more exalted with each exclamation. "Oh, Lady Pamela, how can I tell you? But I must! You see, it was Papa!"

Lady Pamela looked blank. "Papa? Do you mean Lord Whiston? But—but what has the memorandum to do with him?"

"He stole it! I mean, he found it in a book where Ceddie had hidden it, and this morning he has sold it to Mr. Broadbank! Oh, Lady Pamela, the disgrace!" said Sabrina, who had obviously taken *that* phrase whole from one of the romances she so much admired and enjoyed saying it immensely. "What are we to *do?*"

She looked hopefully at Lady Pamela, as to one who might well be expected to play up to her in a most satisfactory manner at this climactic moment; but Lady Pamela, who at bottom, as Carlin had obesrved, had a considerable store of strong common sense, disappointed her by at once becoming sharply and even rudely practical.

"Now listen to me, Sabrina!" she said, standing over her like a schoolmistress. "I don't want any more of your play-acting. Tell me *exactly* what has happened."

"But I *have* told you!" said Sabrina, looking injured. "Mr. Broadbank came to the house this morning—by appointment, I believe, for I am sure that Papa was expecting him—and of course I thought at once that it might have something to do with the document, so I listened at the door. Well, it's not wrong when there are secret papers involved," she argued, seeing Lady Pamela's disapproving look, "else how would one ever be able to find out where they were? And Papa gave Mr.

Broadbank the document and Mr. Broadbank paid him for it, I am quite positive, for I heard them discussing whether it was to be eight hundred or a thousand, and Papa said it would have to be a thousand or he would not give up the paper. He *does* need money so dreadfully, you know, because it is all Mama's and she will never let him have any of his own. And then he told Mr. Broadbank that he must leave the country at once, and Mr. Broadbank chuckled in that *odious* way he has and said he would certainly do so now, and that there was a boat waiting for him at Newhaven, and then he went away. So I put on my bonnet and came here to you at once without even telling Mama, because she would have been certain to try to stop me, and—oh, Lady Pamela, we *must* do something but I can't think what it is! Can you?"

It was at this inauspicious moment that Hadsell, returning to the room, announced, "Lord Babcoke!"

There was a pregnant silence while Lady Pamela and Sabrina stared at each other. Then Sabrina said urgently, "Oh, *do* say you won't see him, Lady Pamela! We *cannot* be interrupted now!"

But Lady Pamela, her brow wrinkled in thought, had suddenly come to a decision. She said to Hadsell, "Pray ask Lord Babcoke to join us here," and, to Sabrina, who had uttered a cry of protest as Hadsell left the room, "Don't be gooseish, Sabrina! Of course Adolphus is exactly the person we want! *He* can go after Mr. Broadbank and stop him from leaving the country with the memorandum, which we cannot do ourselves. I fancy he may not *quite* like it," she confessed, as Lord Babcoke's step was heard approaching the door, "but that cannot signify. He *must* go! I do hope he is driving those chestnuts of his!"

Lord Babcoke, entering the room upon these words, looked a trifle surprised, and looked even more surprised at finding a somewhat dishevelled Sabrina with his betrothed. But, recovering himself with his usual well-known aplomb, he trod across the room and greeted both ladies with great civility.

"I shouldn't have intruded upon you if I had known you were engaged, m'dear," he said to Lady Pamela, giving her a look that added very plainly, "Get rid of her," and, "I have come to apologise."

But his betrothed was in no case to attend to the niceties of sign language; instead, she launched at once into a terse exposition of the very tangled affair of the missing memorandum and the present necessity for preventing Mr. Broadbank from taking it out of the country. Lord Babcoke's understanding, though not powerful, was quite adequate to any normal demands made upon it, but, as Carlin could have informed him, the necessity of coping with Lady Pamela's explanations placed a strain upon one's faculties that could only be compared to that caused by the solving of a highly confusing puzzle. Lord Babcoke was not good at puzzles. It required a full quarter hour before he could take in the essential facts of Lady Pamela's narrative, and even then he did not believe it.

"Preposterous!" he summed it up at last. "My dear girl, I'm sure you must be exaggerating the matter! Perhaps if I could speak to Lord Nevans—"

"No!" said Lady Pamela, who was rapidly losing patience with him. "I have told you, Grandpapa knows nothing about the matter except that the memorandum is missing." She stood up, confronting him, and obliging him to stand up, too. "Now listen to me, Adolphus," she said ominously. "Either you will go off to Newhaven at once and stop Mr. Broadbank or I shall be obliged to ask Mr. Underdown to go in your stead. I am sure *he* will not sit here cavilling and objecting and saying, 'Preposterous!' when the whole fate of the country and of Lord Wellington's army may depend upon him!"

"But I don't know the fellow—Broadbank, I mean," Lord Babcoke, visibly weakening, objected. "Dash it all, Pam, how am I even to recognise him?"

"I have *told* you that he is enormously stout and—and benevolent-looking. Good heavens, he is a positive mountain; you could not possibly mistake him! And I am sure that *any* magistrate will act upon the information you will be able to give him, and see that he does not leave the country until enquiries can be made."

"A magistrate! Oh, no!" exclaimed Sabrina, suddenly flying back into the conversation in an alarmed way. "There mustn't be a magistrate. I mean, poor Papa—"

"Your poor papa should have thought of things like that before he sold the memorandum to Mr. Broadbank," Lady Pamela said firmly. "Now don't be a ninny, Sabrina," she went on impatiently, as her young visitor showed signs of being about to dissolve into tears. "You *can't* expect Adolphus simply to knock Mr. Broadbank down in the street and take the memorandum from him, can you? Not," she added, with a satisfied glance at her prospective bridegroom's athletic figure, "that I don't think he could do it. But we can't ask him to go so far as *that*."

Lord Babcoke, looking grateful for small favours, said he was glad to hear it, but all the same it was the very deuce of an errand she was sending him on.

"All the more reason for your leaving at once, then," said Lady Pamela, ruthlessly shepherding him out of the room. "Are you driving your chestnuts? Good! You should certainly be able to overtake him with them, for he cannot have had more than half an hour's start on you, and perhaps not even so much if he stopped at his hotel when he left the Whistons'. Now *do* make haste, Adolphus!" she went on, as Lord Babcoke, having received his driving-coat and high-crowned beaver from Hadsell, stood hesitating on the doorstep. "Goodness! If I were a man, I should be *happy* of an opportunity to be of so much service to my country!"

Lord Babcoke, who looked anything but happy, said mendaciously that indeed he was. He then looked miserably at his smart sporting curricle drawn up before the door and, turning in a last desperate appeal to Lady Pamela, said, "Are you *sure?*"

"Yes!" said Lady Pamela, pushing him out the door, and, having seen him mount dejectedly into the curricle and drive away, went back to the breakfast-parlour to find Sabrina choking and sniffing into her handkerchief.

"Now don't be a widgeon, Sabrina," she said to her, but quite kindly. "I am sure that Grandpapa will be able to hush the whole affair up, if only he gets the memorandum back— Yes, Hadsell? What is it now?" she enquired, as the butler once more appeared in the doorway.

"If you please, my lady," said Hadsell, who was burning with curiosity about all these odd goings-on, but still managing to maintain his professional aloofness, "Lord Dalven has called."

"Dalven!" said Lady Pamela. "Oh! What a pity he couldn't have come just a few moments earlier! Then I could have sent *him* along with Adolphus. But perhaps it isn't too late. Do ask him to come in, Hadsell," she said to the butler. And she went to Sabrina, as he left the room, "He can go after

Adolphus and help him, you see, if he falls into any difficulties. Carlin, you are exactly the person I most wanted to see!" she continued, greeting his lordship with enthusiasm as he walked into the room.

Without giving him the opportunity to speak a word, she described to him what had occurred that morning at the Whistons'.

"And luckily Adolphus turned up here exactly in the nick of time," she concluded, "so of course I sent him after Mr. Broadbank to stop him from leaving the country with the memorandum. And now that you are here, you may go, too, for I can well see that he may need some assistance. You *are* driving, of course? Your curricle?"

"Now draw bridle, my girl," said Carlin firmly. "You may have succeeded in sending Babcoke haring off on what may well be a wild-goose chase, but you are certainly not going to do the same with me."

"But it is *not* a wild-goose chase!" said Lady Pamela, almost dancing in her impatience. "Sabrina says—"

"Yes, you have told me what Sabrina says," said Carlin. "But as it seems that it is Lord Whiston, and not Sabrina, who can give us the best information as to what has actually occurred, it will be much better, I think, if we hear an account of it from his lips. What is more," he went on, seeing that Lady Pamela was about to break into impetuous remonstrance again, "your grandfather can't be kept out of this any longer. Is he well enough to see me?"

"Yes, but—but he doesn't *want* to see you!" Lady Pamela protested indignantly. "Carlin, now really—"

"You never know till you've asked," Carlin said imperturbably. He went across to the door and opened it, revealing Hadsell, in whom curiosity had so far overcome professional ethics as to keep him lingering where he had no business to be. Carlin turned to Lady Pamela. "Will you give the order or shall I?" he enquired. "After all, he is *your* butler."

Lady Pamela, admitting defeat with a fulminating glance, asked Hadsell if he would enquire of Lord Nevans whether he was able to see Lord Dalven.

"On urgent business," Carlin added amiably. "Oh, and will you send someone at once to present my compliments to Lord Whiston in—" He turned to Sabrina. "Where is your father's house in London?" he asked her.

Sabrina automatically gave an address in Mount Street.

"Mount Street. How very convenient," said Carlin, satisfied. "And ask," he continued, to Hadsell, "if he would be kind enough to step round to Lord Nevans's house at once. Also upon urgent business," he concluded.

Hadsell, looking gratified and eager, said, "Yes, my lord," and hurried off. Carlin closed the door.

"Carlin, your impudence passes all bounds!" Lady Pamela said wrathfully. "What can you mean by it, sending such a message to Lord Whiston? He will think you have run mad!"

"Oh no, he won't!" said Carlin cheerfully. "If I know him, he will be as relieved as anything to get it off his chest and let someone else take over. Only I hope he won't feel obliged to bring Lady Whiston with him—with all due respect, Sabrina, to your revered mama."

Sabrina said frankly that if her mama heard about it she would undoubtedly come, whether Lord Whiston felt obliged to bring her or not, and then fell into a slight panic, enquiring of Lady Pamela what she could say to her mama if she found her there.

"Never mind about that. Lord Dalven will no doubt be happy to do all the explaining, since *he* seems to have taken charge of everything," said Lady Pamela witheringly, at which point Hadsell, re-entering the room in so spirited a way that it might have been called bursting in in anyone less dignified, announced rather breathlessly that Lord Nevans would see Lord Dalven and was coming downstairs from his bedchamber at that moment to instal himself in his study.

"Oh, dear! But ought he to leave his room?" Lady Pamela asked, looking rather anxious.

"Well, my lady, as to that I can't say," said Hadsell judiciously, "but you know when his lordship makes up his mind to do something, wild horses, so to speak, will not begin to stop him, much less I or Mr. Underdown."

Having uttered which opinion, he became aware of having overstepped propriety, and, freezing himself into butlerlike rigidity once more, took himself sedately out of the room.

A series of sounds now made themselves heard from above, consisting of heavy footsteps, occasional explosions of wrathful expletives, and an undercurrent of hurried, soothing murmurs, all of which was rightly interpreted by Lady Pamela as being Lord Nevans coming downstairs, attended by his valet and Mr. Underdown. She went out into the hall, followed by Carlin and Sabrina. Lord Nevans, who, wearing a handsome brocade dressing gown, had just attained the last step of the staircase, halted at sight of them, his bushy white brows drawn together in a frown.

"Ha!" he ejaculated, thereby much impressing his hearers. "There you are, Pamela! Now what the deuce is the meaning of all this? House in an uproar—fellow named Dalven demanding to see me—knew his grandfather—at least I expect it was his grandfather—damned high-nosed interfering fellow—"

Whether these last words were meant to apply to Lord Dalven's grandfather or to the present bearer of the title, upon whom Lord Nevans's glance was fixed unfavourably at the moment, was unclear. Lady Pamela, however, stepped into the breach by remarking, with calming intent, "If the house is in an uproar, Grandpapa, it is you who are causing it. Now *do* stop fretting and let me help you into your study. Really, all this is *quite* unnecessary, you know! Carlin—that is to say, Lord Dalven—could just as well have come up to your bedchamber."

Lord Nevans, casting a penetrating glance at her, said, "Oh, so it's *Carlin*, is it?"—in a tone of daunting grimness, but permitted himself to be led into the study and installed in a very comfortable winged armchair, with his gouty foot propped upon a stool before him. He then dismissed his valet and secretary with a word and, gazing at Sabrina, demanded, "Who's this?"

"It is Lady Sabrina Mansell, Lord Whiston's daughter," Lady Pamela began, as Sabrina, quite terrified before Lord Nevans's wrathful blue glare, looked around as if for something or someone to hide behind.

"Well, what's *she* doing here?" Lord Nevans enquired, not illogically. "If that fellow Dalven has business with me, well and good, but where's the sense in bringing a schoolroom chit into it? *I* ain't her guardian, if he wants to marry her."

"Of course he doesn't wish to marry her, Grandpapa!" Lady Pamela said indignantly.

But at this point Carlin, again taking matters in hand, said authoritatively that either she and Sabrina would sit quietly while he told Lord Nevans the gist of the affair or he would send them both out of the room, upon which Lord Nevans, though evidently against his will, looked impressed.

"Think you could do it, eh?" he demanded skeptically.

"Yes, sir," said Carlin, quite matter-of-factly.

"We'll see that," said Lord Nevans, looking as if he rather relished the prospect of a clash of wills between his strong-minded granddaughter and Lord Dalven; but Lady Pamela said with some asperity that he wouldn't, because Lord Dalven had begun all this and she had no intention of helping him out by speaking a single word.

Quelled by a glance from Carlin, she then relapsed into a prim and vengeful silence, sitting with her hands folded in her lap while Carlin rapidly described to Lord Nevans the remarkable series of events that had led to his requesting the present interview with him. Several times, indeed, as Carlin referred to certain of her activities in something less than complimentary terms, she went pink and showed every sign of being about to enter the conversation, but as neither Carlin nor her grandfather so much as glanced in her direction she was obliged to seethe in silence, except for a few pointed mutterings, among which "Overbearing!"—"Abominable!"— and "Rude!" could be distinguished.

"And that's where the situation stands now, sir," Carlin concluded at last. "I daresay we'll have made a proper mull of it between us if Broadbank really has the memorandum and succeeds in getting out of the country with it, but there's no use in fretting over what's past. The question is, what would you wish to do at this point? I've sent round to ask Lord Whiston to come to Berkeley Square and give you his story in person, by the bye. Obviously you can't rely on a schoolroom miss's tale of an overheard conversation in a matter of this moment, and I rather think you'll find that Whiston gives a different account of the matter. He doesn't strike me as the sort of man to involve himself in a treasonous affair. Are you acquainted with him yourself?"

Lord Nevans, across whose face conflicting emotions of incredulity, anxiety, relief (this last when it was made clear to him that Lord Wynstanley had certainly had nothing to do with the purloining of the memorandum), and grim determination had passed as Carlin's story was in progress, said that he was.

"Nervy little fellow, starts at his own shadow, but *not* a

commoner," he said. "You're right there." He then added, with a fine disregard for Sabrina's presence, "Never liked that female he married above half, though, and that son of his, Cedric, is an out-and-out wrong 'un. Do you say you've sent for him to come here?"

But Carlin's answer was forestalled by the reappearance of Hadsell, who announced, "Lord Whiston," in a portentous voice, and then stood aside to allow the Earl, closely followed by Lord Wynstanley, who had just come downstairs from his bedchamber and had met Lord Whiston in the hall, to enter the study.

Seventeen

⚲

Lord Whiston came into the room with his usual nervously deprecatory air strongly modified by an appearance of what might have been desperation, or triumph, or both. He checked for a moment upon the threshold, however, on seeing the company assembled to greet him, and a look of positive bewilderment crossed his face as he took in the presence of his daughter Sabrina.

"Sabrina! What are *you* doing here?" he ejaculated. "Your mama has been turning the house upside down looking for you!"

To his obvious astonishment and discomfiture, Sabrina's reply to this was to hurl herself upon his chest in a fit of uncontrollable sobbing.

"Oh, Papa, I am so very *sorry!*" came in muffled accents from the folds of the Earl's coat of Bath superfine as she tightened her arms about his neck in complete disregard of his embarrassed attempts to free himself. "I should never, never have done it if I had known Lady Pamela would be so b-beastly as to tell Lord Babcoke he must call in a magistrate! Oh, *pray* don't let her do it, Papa! And now she wishes to send Lord Dalven after Mr. Broadbank, too."

"Send Lord Dalven after Mr. Broadbank?" Lord Whiston's face, which had been unwontedly flushed when he had come into the room, suddenly became pale with alarm. "No, no! Good God, mustn't do that!" he ejaculated, redoubling his efforts to free himself from the stranglehold his daughter maintained about his neck. "Wouldn't do at all!"

"Allow me," said Carlin, stepping forward and firmly detaching Sabrina from Lord Whiston. "Now go and sit down, like a good girl," he admonished her. "And be quiet!" he added, in a tone that made her jump and caused Lord Whiston to regard him gratefully. "Now, sir," he went on, addressing the Earl, "I must offer you my apologies for bringing you here in this unceremonious way, but, as I believe you apprehend, the matter is of some urgency. You know Lord Nevans, I understand?"

Lord Whiston, with an agonised glance at Lord Nevans, who had been a grimly silent observer of the scene that had just taken place, acknowledged that he did.

"I was—as a matter of fact, I was coming to call upon you later today," he said, suddenly beginning to search feverishly through his pockets. "I—it seems I have come into possession of something that—Now, where *did* I put it?" he enquired, in mingled irritation and perplexity. "—that belongs to you," he continued, still actively searching. "Here it—No, that's not it!" As the others watched in fascinated silence he tucked a folded paper back into one coat pocket and then, abruptly diving his hand into another, drew from it, with the triumphant air of a magician who has at last succeeded in producing the rabbit from his hat, a second paper, which he regarded proudly. "I *knew* I must have it," he explained. "Put it there myself only this morning."

And he proceeded to hand the paper to Lord Nevans, who took it from him, unfolded it, and, after regarding it briefly, said explosively, "Good Lord! *You* had this all the while? But why wait until now—?"

"Is it the memorandum?" Lady Pamela, unable to contain herself any longer, asked eagerly. "Oh, Grandpapa, how splendid! Lord Whiston, how in the *world* did you—?"

"The questions," Carlin interrupted her equably, "will come from your grandfather, my girl." He turned to Lord Nevans. "Pray continue, sir."

Lord Nevans, again giving him and Lady Pamela, who had smoulderingly subsided, a penetrating glance from under his craggy brows, addressed himself once more to Lord Whiston.

"Perhaps you can explain to me, my lord," he said, "how you came into possession of this document?"

Lord Whiston looked unhappy. "Well, I *can* explain," he admitted, "but I would really much rather not, you know. Couldn't you simply say," he enquired with sudden inspiration, "that it comes from unknown sources?"

"No, I could not," said Lord Nevans roundly. "Good God, man, this document, as you must know, was filched from a Foreign Office box in this house under circumstances that *must* be explained. *You* did not do it—"

"No, no! Certainly not!" said Lord Whiston, managing to

look miserable and indignant at the same time. "Never had occasion to call upon you here. Wouldn't have taken anything from your despatch-box if I had."

"Exactly," said Lord Nevans. "Then who—?"

"With your permission, sir," said Carlin, once more entering upon the task of resolving an impasse. He addressed himself to Lord Whiston. "It was Cedric, wasn't it?" he enquired. "I understand your reluctance to involve him in this, but I must tell you that there is so much evidence pointing towards him that your confirmation of the fact is scarcely necessary."

Lord Whiston, who suddenly looked as if he might be about to cry, was heard to say in a quite despairing voice that if they already knew about Cedric there seemed little use in his denying it.

"But you won't feel obliged to *do* anything, will you?" he appealed to Lord Nevans. "I mean, now that you've got the memorandum back? And I've sent Cedric off, you know. To America. Sent him off this morning and told him not to come back. 'I'll see that your mother makes you an allowance,' I said, because that she *will* do, you know. Very fond of Ceddie. Always was. 'But you can't come back,' I said. 'Not after this—' "

"Papa, you *didn't!*" breathed Sabrina. "How did you dare? What did Mama say?"

"Doesn't know it yet," confessed Lord Whiston, beginning to look hunted again. "Didn't tell her."

"Yes, but why did Cedric give the memorandum to *you?*" Lady Pamela, impatient of these family details, demanded.

The Earl looked startled. "Give it to me?" he repeated. "Oh, but he didn't! Wouldn't have done such a thing for the world, I fancy. Very put out when he discovered I'd found it in Mr. Gibbon's history."

"In *what?*"

"Mr. Gibbon's *Decline and Fall of the Roman Empire*," Lord Whiston explained rather nervously. "Amelia—Lady Whiston, that is—said I ought to read it. And I *did* begin it, several—I daresay it must be several *years* ago now. Always meant to go on with it; kept it lying on the table in my dressing room. But there it is; I never did, until one night a week or so ago I picked it up—"

"Good Lord!" said Carlin, unable to restrain his amusement. "Then all the while Broadbank and that man of his were turning the house upside down searching for it, it was lying there, practically in full view?"

"Oh, were they?" said the Earl innocently. "I didn't know that. Only thought it was the deuce of a queer thing to find in a book. I saw straight off that it must be important, of course," he said with some pride, to Lord Nevans. "My old father was in the Government when I was a young fellow, you see. Always had one of those red Foreign Office boxes lying on the table in the library. But it was quite a while before I thought of Ceddie. Not till he came prying around with questions, saying he'd left an important paper in Volume One and had anyone picked it up by chance—Mr. Broadbank, for example, or that new abigail of Sabrina's. I beg your pardon, Lady Pamela," he added, suddenly growing quite pink with dismay at the thought of having referred to her in this manner.

"Never mind that," said Lady Pamela. "What I should like to know is, what did you do next, after you told Cedric you hadn't found the memorandum. You *did* tell him that, I expect?"

"Well, yes," said the Earl apologetically. "Could see there was something dashed havey-cavey going on, of course. Thought it might be best to take a little time to think matters over."

"Well, you *should* have turned it over to the authorities at once," said Lady Pamela with some severity, and then relented when the Earl, looking miserable, said that after all Ceddie *was* his son, even if he *had* gone beyond the line, and he couldn't seem to bring himself to the point of crying rope on him.

"No, of course you could not," said Lady Pamela more sympathetically, thinking of her own and Lord Nevans's dilemma when they had suspected that Lord Wynstanley had been involved in the matter. "So what *did* you do?"

Lord Whiston said that for a time he had done nothing at all.

"Then Sabrina told me about what young Lord Wynstanley had told *her* about the memorandum's having been taken from Lord Nevans's despatch-box, and that *was* a really dreadful moment," he confessed. "Knocked the wind quite out of me. Realised something must be done. Told Amelia I was going up to town with her and Sabrina. Thought I could manage some way to get the memorandum back to Lord Nevans without involving Cedric—"

"But how did Mr. Broadbank come into it?" enquired Lady Pamela, lighting upon this puzzling point and noting with some pride that neither Carlin nor Lord Nevans was now interrupting her inquisition of Lord Whiston as being irrelevant or inept. "Sabrina has told us, you know, that you sold the memorandum to *him* this morning."

"Oh, that!" said Lord Whiston, and suddenly blushed. "Inspiration, my dear Lady Pamela. Pure inspiration. You see, when I went for a stroll in the corridor at the theatre last evening, I ran across him, and we fell into conversation. First time I'd seen him since Sabrina had told me he'd been trying to purchase the memorandum from Cedric, and I suddenly saw that he had been sent by Providence—"

"By—Providence?" said Lady Pamela, looking quite blank.

"Why, yes," said Lord Whiston happily. "A method of killing two birds with one stone. Foiling the enemies of our country on the one hand, and on the other, providing myself with a small sum of ready cash for—for emergency purposes. I daresay," he said, looking rather wistfully at his spellbound audience, "that none of you knows what it is like to find yourself without a feather to fly with when you have a sudden urge to make a bolt to the village?"

This dashing manner of referring to a desire to visit the metropolis appeared to impress his assembled hearers to the point that none of them found a ready response. Lord Whiston continued, answering his own question.

"No, I expect not. All the same, it's a deuced uncomfortable sort of feeling, you know. And now here was this fellow Broadbank, panting to hand over practically any amount for that bit of paper. And you can see for yourselves, can't you?" he added rather anxiously, "that I really *had* to take it. He'd have seen the game in a minute if I'd offered to *give* it to him."

"But you gave the paper to Grandpapa!" Lady Pamela interrupted. "Do you mean you made a copy?"

"Not a copy. No, indeed!" Lord Whiston looked indignant. "My dear Lady Pamela, how can you think such a thing of me? But I *did* feel that, since Providence had also provided me with my old father's writing-desk, still quite well stocked with everything he had left behind him when he was taken from us very suddenly one morning while still in office—apoplexy, you know—always a very choleric sort of man—"

"Lord Whiston, if you do not explain all this at once, I shall go mad!" said Lady Pamela, with conviction. "You made a copy—"

"*Not* a copy," Lord Whiston insisted. "Made up my own memorandum. Very similar in language but quite, quite different in detail. Ought to confuse those Frenchies nicely, I fancy."

He looked happily at Lord Nevans, who said in a stunned voice, forestalling Lady Pamela, "You wrote an entirely false memorandum, using Foreign Office stationery of your father's?"

"That's right," said Lord Whiston. "Broadbank paid me a thousand pounds for it this morning. Fancy I bubbled him splendidly. He's off to Newhaven with it at this very moment. Which is why," he went on, turning to Carlin, "I must insist, my dear fellow, that you don't go after him and try to stop him. Ruin everything, you know."

"Yes, but I have already sent Adolphus after him!" Lady Pamela interrupted in an anguished voice. Lord Whiston looked at her reproachfully. "Well, how was I to know that it was not the real memorandum Mr. Broadbank had got?" she defended herself. "Sabrina *told* me—"

"And *I* told you that it might be something less than the height of wisdom to rely implicitly upon Sabrina," Carlin reminded her. She gave him a darkling glance. "I know, I know—odious of me to say, 'I told you so!' " he continued, with a grin. "But never mind; I shall engage to go after Babcoke and do my possible to stop *him* from stopping Broadbank from leaving the country."

"I'll go with you," said Lord Wynstanley, who had been taking no part whatever in the conversation, being too much overcome with relief and astonishment at its content to wish to contribute to it.

Carlin said, "No, you won't," but quite kindly, upon which Lord Wynstanley began to look mulish and opened his mouth to protest, only to be forestalled by the appearance of Hadsell, now perfectly demented with curiosity and excitement and showing it in a most unprofessional way.

"Lady Whiston!" he announced, in a voice actually trembling with joyful anticipation of the sensation his words would cause.

The Earl and Sabrina looked at each other in mutual terror; Lord Nevans looked annoyed; and Carlin, who was looking at Lady Pamela, who herself looked slightly apprehensive, looked amused.

Upon this tableau entered Lady Whiston. She wore sables, an extremely fashionable pelisse of Sardinian blue velvet, and a bonnet trimmed with ostrich plumes, so that she gave something of the appearance of a galleon prepared for battle, with all sails flying, if one could imagine sails made of sables and ostrich plumes.

"So! I find you here, Sabrina! And you, Frederick!" she went on, her eyes lighting upon her husband as upon lesser prey. "And what, pray tell me," she demanded awfully, "is the meaning of this?"

Lord Nevans, as has previously been noted, was not a patient man. He was still suffering painfully from the gout; he had had a most disturbing morning; and now, upon finding his study invaded by a female he cordially disliked, apparently bent upon causing as much unpleasantness as possible beneath his roof, he allowed his exasperation to take the upper hand.

"Madam," he said to Lady Whiston, in the voice that still had the power to cause opposition members of the House of Lords to wish fervently that they had decided to remain at home that day, "I do not know why you have come here, but if it was to find your daughter, you have my full permission to take her away. At once," he added, as Lady Whiston, staring at him in affronted astonishment, showed no sign of being about to avail herself of this privilege.

Lord Whiston, who, having found no suitable place to hide, had decided to be brave, here said in a determinedly offhand way that he thought that an excellent idea, whereupon Lady Whiston turned the full blast of her displeasure upon him.

"It is a thoroughly idiotish idea, Frederick," she said, annihilating him with a glance. "I have come here to Get to the Bottom of this Matter, and Get to the Bottom of it I shall. What, I must ask you, Lord Nevans," she went on, addressing that fuming peer with a courage that few men would have possessed, "are the wiles that your unfortunate granddaughter—*if*, as I understand, this young woman actually is your granddaughter and not an abigail named Clover, under which name, I may inform you, she insinuated herself into Whiston Castle—what, I repeat, were the wiles used by her to induce my daughter to leave her home clandestinely, without a word to her mama as to her destination—"

"Mama, for heaven's sake, you are behaving as if I had *eloped* with someone!" Sabrina, her initial fright having evaporated, remarked sensibly.

Lady Whiston, looking darkly at Carlin, said *that* would not surprise her, either, but that was neither here nor there, and not a step would she stir out of that house until she was informed why her daughter and her husband had each stolen separately—as she had finally been able, after exhaustive questioning of the servants, to learn—out of their home to go to Berkeley Square.

"Well, you *won't* be informed, Amelia," said Lord Whiston, apparently quite above himself now with excitement and the sensation his successful bubbling of Mr. Broadbank had occasioned, "because no one will tell you. *I* shan't, and neither will Sabrina. Wouldn't be at all proper. Highly confidential matter, you see."

Lady Whiston looked at him, her bosom swelling.

"Very well, Frederick! *Very* well!" she said, with an air that seemed to add, *And just wait until I have you alone!*" "We shall say no more about it at present! But if you think I do not know that it has something to do with this abandoned young woman, whose conduct in my house in connexion with a gentleman I see standing before me in this room at this very moment"—here her baleful blue gaze turned upon Carlin—"I should blush to describe—"

"One moment, Lady Whiston!" Carlin's voice cut through her words, with an edge upon it so sharp that it made Lady Pamela stare. Lord Nevans and Lord Wynstanley, who had each begun to rise hotly to the defence of their respective granddaughter and sister, fell abruptly silent, as recognising a more able champion. "If you have any comments to make upon the conduct of Lady Pamela, under your roof or elsewhere," Carlin went on, in that same chill voice, "may I suggest that you make them exclusively to me? In that case, it will be most convenient for me to explain to you how very strongly I shall feel myself obliged to resent slurs cast from any source upon the young lady who is to be my wife."

"Who is to be your *what!*" exclaimed Lady Whiston, her blue eyes almost starting out of her head. "But—but she is betrothed to Lord Babcoke! Lady St. Abbs told me so only last evening!"

"Unfortunately," said Carlin, his cool manner now tempered by the gleam of amusement in his dark eyes as they rested upon Lady Pamela's perfectly bewildered face, "Lady St. Abbs' information is somewhat outdated, Lady Whiston. Lady Pamela *was* engaged to Lord Babcoke—true. But as it is obvious that they will not suit, Lady Pamela will marry me, instead. I hope we may count upon your felicitations; if not, I fear we must resign ourselves to doing without them."

He glanced again, that glinting smile in his eyes, at Lady Pamela, who, well aware that he was very accurately reading the explosive state of amazement, indignation, and some obscure and even more discomfiting third emotion into which his extraordinary statement had tumbled her, felt quite incapable of saying anything at all. She saw that Lord Nevans and Lord Wynstanley were both looking accusingly at her, as at a fiend in female form who would so far forget her duty as to break off one engagement and enter into another without troubling even to mention the matter to them. Lord Whiston, however, rising nobly to the occasion, shook Carlin warmly by the hand and assured him that he had his most sincere felicitations.

"Unusual way to carry on a courtship," he said affably. "I mean that business down at the Castle and all that, but young people nowadays have their own ways of going about things. Well, well! I often feel I am getting to be too much of an old fogey, rusticating in Wiltshire all year long. In the future I shall make a point of it to come to London more often."

"If this," said Lady Whiston terribly, "is an example of London mores, I feel we should both be far better advised, Frederick, to remain permanently at Whiston Castle! May I ask if you intend to stand idly by while Lord Dalven threatens—yes, *threatens* me? If Cedric were here, I am sure *he* would resent such a tone's being used to his mother!"

"Well, he ain't here, and what's more, he ain't going to be," said the Earl informatively. "Gone to America. Left this morning."

"To America! Cedric! But why?" Lady Whiston tottered to a chair. "I can bear no more of this!" she announced, "I am sure I feel one of my spasms coming on!"

Lord Nevans, regarding her with loathing, rang the bell violently for Hadsell, who appeared instantly, bearing a tray containing a decanter and glasses.

"If you please, my lord," he said, casting a professional glance upon Lady Whiston's drooping form, "I apprehended there might be a need for restoratives. Allow me—"

And he poured a generous amount of brandy from the decanter into one of the glasses and proffered it respectfully to Lady Whiston, who rejected it with a shudder.

"Oh, Mama, *don't* fly into the twitters! Drink it," said Sabrina, taking the glass from Hadsell and holding it to her mother's lips. "You can't have the vapours here, you know; Lord Nevans wouldn't like it above half."

Carlin, who was regarding quite imperturbably the emotional havoc his announcement had wreaked upon the company, at this point remarked that he regretted being unable to remain any longer, but if Babcoke was to be prevented from preventing Mr. Broadbank from leaving the country, it behooved him to be on his way.

"I'll come with you," Lord Wynstanley said again, evincing a cowardly but understandable desire to remove himself from this highly charged scene, and looking at Carlin with such man-to-man appeal to help him out of it that Carlin laughed and said, "Oh, very well. Come along."

He then bestowed a sort of mocking half-salute upon Lady Pamela, who was regarding him as if she would cheerfully have watched him being boiled in oil, bowed to the rest of the company, and strode from the room, with Lord Wynstanley at his heels. Lady Whiston, still choking over the brandy that Sabrina had poured down her throat, at this point announced a desire to be taken away from what she could only describe as a den of lunatics or worse.

"Quite right, my dear," said her husband approvingly. "Take you home. Far better for you to lie down quietly with some burnt feathers or hartshorn or whatever it is you females take." He looked apologetically at Lord Nevans. "Frightfully sorry to have caused such a dust-up," he said. "Afraid I bungled matters a bit. Still, you have the memorandum back, and if Broadbank manages to get out of the country with his—"

"One moment," said Lord Nevans, as Lord Whiston and Sabrina, assisting Lady Whiston from her chair, prepared to depart. "There is one point that still remains unclear to me," he said. "How did Cedric manage to get hold of the paper in the first place? I understand he has never come to this house."

Lord Whiston, struck by the question, abandoned Lady Whiston momentarily and confessed that he had never thought to ask. A discreet cough from Hadsell, who had lingered in the room with the ostensible purpose of seeing if anything further was required for Lady Whiston, here interrupted him.

"I beg your pardon, my lord," said Hadsell.

"Yes? Eh?" said Lord Whiston, starting. "What is it?"

"I beg your pardon, my lord," Hadsell said again, still more apologetically. "I was addressing Lord Nevans. You remarked, my lord," he went on to his master, "that the Honourable Mr. Cedric Mansell had never visited this house. That, to my knowledge, is an erroneous statement."

"It is, eh?" Lord Nevans stared at him from under his bushy brows. "He *did* come here?"

"Well, of course he did—to see me about the memorandum, only two days ago," Lady Pamela, now slightly recovered from the shock Carlin's statement had produced, interrupted impatiently. "But that can have nothing to say to the matter!"

"I beg your pardon, my lady," said Hadsell perseveringly, "but Mr. Mansell also came to the house upon another occasion. If I recall correctly, it was the evening before your ladyship left London—"

"The evening *before?*" said Lord Nevans sharply.

Hadsell, visibly gratified at having provided a new sensation in this sensation-filled morning, nodded demurely.

"Yes, my lord. I recall the matter particularly because Lord Wynstanley had expressed a good deal of annoyance to Brill that evening about having missed seeing Mr. Mansell earlier, and we both—Brill and I—understood that he strongly desired a meeting with him. So when Mr. Mansell himself called shortly afterwards, I thought it best to ascertain personally whether Lord Wynstanley was still in the house, leaving Mr. Mansell for a rather extended period of time alone in the hall."

"*With* the despatch-box!" said Lord Nevans grimly.

"Yes, my lord. I fancied at the time that it was not in the precise position in which I had left it when I returned, and that Mr. Mansell, far from being disappointed when I was obliged to tell him that Lord Wynstanley was gone out, appeared quite indifferent to this news and anxious to get away."

"Yes, I can well believe *that!*" said Lord Nevans wrathfully. "But why have you waited until now to tell me this? If I'd realised at the start that that fellow was in the house—"

"If by the term 'that fellow,' Lord Nevans," said Lady Whiston, suddenly halting her tottering progress towards the door and undergoing an instantaneous transformation from a drooping violet to a tigress responding to an attack upon its young, "you mean my son Cedric, I demand to know what charge you are insinuating against him! If it is *you* who are responsible for my poor boy's sudden departure for America—"

"Madam," said Lord Nevans—and if he did not say, "Woman!" the effect was the same, for he was quite out of patience with Lady Whiston by this time and capable, as his fond granddaughter well knew, of saying anything to anyone in this mood—"Madam, if you will make use of the little sense God gave you, you will cease from meddling in affairs that are much better left to your husband and go home!"

Which speech had such a powerful effect upon Lord Whiston that for the first time in his life he felt the wine of mastery flow through his veins and, taking his wife's arm, said firmly, "Come along, Amelia!" and led her from the room.

"And now," said Lord Nevans wrathfully to his granddaughter when their visitors, followed by Hadsell, had departed, "I'll thank you to tell me, miss, what the devil that fellow Dalven was talking about when he said you had broken off with Babcoke and were to marry him! Have you taken leave of your senses, girl?"

"No—*he* has! There has never been the least hint of such a thing! He is—he must be quite mad, I think!" said Lady Pamela, looking so flushed that her grandfather, who missed very little even when suffering from the gout, demanded sharply if she was in love with the fellow.

"In love—in love with *Carlin!*" said Lady Pamela incredulously. "I mean *Dalven!* Certainly *not!*"

Upon which she beat a hasty retreat to her own bedchamber to avoid further questioning; but she could not avoid the questions in her own mind, and wondered how she might ever be able to get through the hours that must elapse before Lord Babcoke and Carlin would return and the confusion surrounding her betrothal—not that there was the slightest confusion, really, because she was engaged to Adolphus and that was that!—could be cleared up once and for all.

Eighteen

❧

She was, it developed, to have a tediously long time to wait. An unusually fine March London day waxed and waned; fashionable people went shopping in Bond Street, drove in the Park at the hour of five, flirted, dined, made engagements, ordered their carriages and went off to the opera or an evening-party; but Lady Pamela Frayne, that ornament of the *ton*, took no part in all these activities. Instead, she continued to sit at home in Berkeley Square, pretending to write letters, all of which she tore up before they were finished, and to read a novel, which might have been written in Sanskrit for all she understood of it.

At various times throughout the day she determined, first, not to see Carlin at all when he returned, second, to demand with icy dignity an explanation from him of his statement concerning her, third, to ignore his statement completely, as beneath her notice, and fourth, to give him the trimming of his life as soon as she saw him. But when she actually heard the sound of carriage wheels below her bedchamber windows, and looked out to behold three very familiar male figures jumping down from a curricle before the door, she forgot every one of these resolutions and ran downstairs with quite undignified haste, almost colliding with Hadsell in her dash towards the front door.

"I beg your pardon, my lady," said Hadsell reprovingly, and moved with his usual magisterial calm to the door.

Lady Pamela, recollecting herself, went into her grandfather's study, where Lord Nevans had installed himself after dinner to await, with an impatience almost rivalling his granddaughter's, news of Lord Babcoke's pursuit of Mr. Broadbank and Carlin's pursuit of Lord Babcoke.

"They've come," she announced to him, a trifle breathlessly. "I mean Dalven and Wyn *and* Adolphus. All three of them, in Dalven's curricle."

The words had no sooner left her lips when the three

gentlemen themselves walked into the room. Lady Pamela and Lord Nevans, both bursting with questions, opened their mouths simultaneously to speak, but, though their mouths remained open, no words came. Amazement, so to speak, had seized them. And indeed this was not surprising, considering the sight that met their eyes.

The first to enter the room was Lord Babcoke, apparently in a state of violent indignation. He was also in a state of dishevelment such as it was unlikely he had publicly appeared in since, at the age of twelve, he had engaged in a no-holds-barred wrestling match at Eton with young Sir Ronald Edgerton over the matter of a gooseberry tart filched from his quarters. His coat of blue superfine, one of Weston's triumphs, was torn and mud-stained; his once snowy cravat, arranged by the hand of a master in the Mathematical style, was horridly crumpled; and, to crown it all, he sported what would undoubtedly blossom by the morrow into a splendidly refulgent black eye.

Carlin, entering behind him, also showed signs, though to a considerably lesser degree, of having been engaged in hand-to-hand combat, his coat, like Lord Babcoke's, being in a condition to cause any self-respecting valet to blench, and a slightly cut lip adding a somewhat raffish touch to his remarkably cheerful countenance. Only Lord Wynstanley, of the three, appeared to have returned to Berkeley Square in the same condition in which he had left it, and he began at once to account for this fact.

"I say!" he began, in a high state of excitement and satisfaction, as soon as he had caught sight of his grandfather. "I do wish you could have come with us, sir! You never saw such a grand turn-up! I didn't like it above half when Dalven told me to keep out of it, because there was always the chance Adolphus would have the best of it and be off again after Broadbank—well, I've *seen* him sparring at Jackson's, you know, and even Jackson says he's the best of *his* lot! But Dalven—oh, you should have seen him, Grandfather! I thought they had been evenly matched at first, but then he popped in a flush hit over Adolphus's guard—"

"What *are* you talking about, Wyn?" exclaimed Lady Pamela, unable to restrain her impatience and attend quietly any longer to these pugilistic raptures. "Do you mean to tell us that Adolphus and Carlin have been—have been engaging in a public brawl? I don't believe it!"

"Well, it wasn't a mere *brawl*, I can tell you!" Lord Wynstanley said, quite indignant, it appeared, at hearing what he obviously considered as a Homeric encounter so denigrated. "Prettiest exhibition of science I ever saw! And I wasn't the only one who thought so! Very knowing fellow in a Polish greatcoat who'd just got down from the Brighton stage said he'd been at Grinsted Green when Mendoza beat Harry Lee, and he'd sooner have missed that than *this* turn-up—"

"Are you telling me," demanded Lady Pamela, regarding her betrothed with awe, "are you actually telling me that they fought in an inn-yard? Adolphus, you *didn't!*"

"Well, he did!" declared Lord Wynstanley. "Wouldn't hear of our stopping him from going after Broadbank when we finally came up with him at the Chequers at Horley; we might as well have gone rabbit-hunting with a dead ferret as try to get him to hear reason! Said he was going on, no matter what, and planted Dalven as pretty a facer as you ever saw when he tried to stop him. That was when his curricle was overturned—"

"His curricle?" said Lady Pamela faintly.

"Why, yes! He was just mounting up into it, you see, and Dalven laid hold on him and then Adolphus jumped down and planted him that facer and the horses got frightened by the commotion and tried to bolt. Silly gudgeon of an ostler was gaping at the proceedings and let them go. That's why Adolphus had to come back with us, when they'd brought him round after that last dandy Dalven landed on him."

Carlin's hand fell upon his shoulder. "Enough, halfling!" he said, with an amused glance at Lady Pamela's stunned face. "You have already destroyed what little credit I had left with your sister, I fear. Sir," he went on to Lord Nevans, "I must crave your forgiveness for bursting in upon you like this, but I thought you would wish to know at once—"

"And *I* think you will wish to know, Lord Nevans," said Lord Babcoke, who had apparently been containing himself thus far only by the exercise of the most violent restraint upon his feelings, "that, owing to the interference of Lord Dalven and your grandson, that scoundrel Broadbank has no doubt by this time got clean out of the country with the memorandum!"

"Has he? Oh, famous!" exclaimed Lady Pamela, looking much relieved.

Lord Babcoke's one good eye (for the other was rapidly closing) surveyed her with an extremely jaundiced expression in it.

"Famous!" he repeated incredulously. *"Famous!* But *you* were the one who sent me—"

"Yes, I know, Adolphus," said Lady Pamela apologetically. "But, you see, I did not quite understand how matters stood then. I am so dreadfully sorry, but, as you see, everything has turned out for the best, so you must sit down now and Grandpapa will have Hadsell bring you some brandy."

"I don't want any brandy!" said Lord Babcoke, whose ordinarily equable disposition seemed to have been tried beyond its limits by the events of the day. "It may interest you to know, Pamela, that I have not dined!"

"Haven't you? Oh, very well; then Hadsell shall see about getting you something to eat. I'm afraid it will be cold, though."

To her extreme surprise, Lord Babcoke at this point swore quite violently and stated in a very unappreciative voice that he was not interested in either food or drink until he had Got to the Bottom of this.

"Oh, dear!" sighed Lady Pamela. "We had Lady Whiston here this morning, being quite tiresome about Getting to the Bottom of things, too, and now you, Adolphus! Really, it is all quite simple. You see, I didn't know when I sent you after Mr. Broadbank that Lord Whiston had given him the wrong memorandum."

Carlin flung up a hand. "No, my sweet!" he said firmly. "You are *not* going to embark upon another of your famous explanations and befuddle what wits Babcoke has left after this extremely fatiguing day. Perhaps Lord Nevans—"

He looked enquiringly at his host, who said bluntly to Lord Babcoke that he much regretted his having been sent off on a wild-goose chase, but the fact of the matter was that Lord Whiston had very cleverly managed to substitute a forged memorandum containing false information for the real one he had pretended to give Mr. Broadbank, so that it was not only unnecessary but inadvisable to stop him from taking it out of the country.

"You see!" Lord Wynstanley said, looking triumphantly at Lord Babcoke. "It's exactly as we tried to tell you! Only the muttonhead wouldn't listen to us," he went on, turning explanatorily to his grandfather. "Seemed to think we were in league with Broadbank and Ceddie—said Pam had charged him with seeing the memorandum didn't get out of the country and he dashed well wasn't going to let her down."

Lady Pamela blushed. "Oh, Adolphus, how chivalrous of you!" she said. "And I truly am grateful, and so *very* sorry to have got you into such a muddle."

"It was my own fault," said Lord Babcoke with bitter magnanimity. "Entirely my own fault, for listening to you! I *know* what you are—"

"You know what I am!" Lady Pamela's eyebrows rose and the apologetic look suddenly disappeared from her face. "That sounds ominous, Adolphus! And what, pray, am I?"

"A curst meddling shatter-brained little minx!" said Lord Babcoke roundly, and appeared to find great satisfaction in pronouncing the words.

Carlin said, shaking his head, "Yes, I fear you have nicked the nick this time, Babcoke. That is precisely what she is. You will have to beat her to keep her out of mischief if you marry her, you know, and somehow I can't think you are equal to the task."

"Oh! And I daresay you think *you* are!" said Lady Pamela, rounding on him, her cheeks now flaming.

"No, no, you flatter me!" Carlin said soothingly. "But then I shouldn't feel the necessity of doing so, being quite as prone as you are, my dear delight, to falling into harebrained scrapes. Which is one of the reasons why I am so sure we should suit—"

It is difficult for a man with a burgeoning black eye to assume an air of cold dignity, but to the best of his ability Lord Babcoke accomplished this feat.

"I have told you before, Lord Dalven," he remarked, "that I find such pleasantries in extremely poor taste. Lady Pamela is betrothed to *me*."

"Yes, I know. We all make mistakes," Carlin said sympathetically. "But when they are not irrevocable, there is no reason why we must live with them for the rest of our lives.

A quiet announcement to your friends, you know, to the effect that the engagement between the Earl of Babcoke and the Lady Pamela Frayne has been terminated by mutual consent—"

"Now see here, Dalven," interrupted Lord Nevans, "I have had quite enough of this talk about you and Pamela. What I want now is an explanation from you, young man. *You* say you're going to marry her; *she* says there ain't a word of truth in it; and Babcoke says she's still engaged to him—"

"Strictly speaking, yes," agreed Carlin. "But I appeal to you, sir, did you ever see two people so badly matched? Only look at poor Babcoke now: he is positively livid over the bumblebath in which she has landed him. And you know as well as I do that this isn't a patch on what she will do to him after they're married, if they're fools enough to stick to their bargain!"

An involuntary bark of laughter escaped Lord Nevans. "Yes, yes, you are right there!" he admitted. "Never knew such a little jade for falling into the briars, and dragging her entire family along with her! But she wanted Babcoke, and she has got him, and as far as I can see they are both satisfied with the match."

"But are they?" asked Carlin. "Perhaps we should put it to them, sir." He turned to Lord Babcoke. "Are *you* satisfied, Babcoke?"

"Yes!" said Lord Babcoke, but with such a baleful glance at his beloved that Carlin grinned.

"Scarcely as fervent a response as one might expect from an ardent lover—but let that go for the moment," he said. "And you, Lady Pamela?" he asked, turning to her. "Are *you* satisfied?"

Lady Pamela, looking at him with extreme hauteur, said she could not conceive how her feelings on the matter were in any way the affair of Lord Dalven.

"You see, sir—evasion," said Carlin, addressing Lord Nevans. "She knows she is a very poor liar—in point of fact, I have told her as much—and so she is unwilling to risk a direct reply."

"I am *not* unwilling," said Lady Pamela hotly. "I—I wish very much to marry Adolphus!"

"As you see, sir, a *very* poor liar," Carlin said, shaking his head. "I put it to you, does *that* answer carry conviction?"

Lord Nevans said he was bound to say that it did not.

"I'll tell you what, Dalven," he went on, with a rather dissatisfied glance at his granddaughter, "you may be right, you know. I gave my consent when she wanted to marry Babcoke—well, I thought she might have that Spanish fellow if I didn't, the Marqués de Barrera, and I don't fancy Spanish great-grandchildren, if it *is* the bluest blood in Europe, as he takes care to remind you. But I've had it in my mind for some time now that Babcoke can't manage her. Too hot at hand for him by half. And it's the devil of a thing for a man when he finds himself leg-shackled to a female who's bound on pulling him in a direction he don't want to go. Look at poor Whiston, now. Shocking exhibition that wife of his put on here today."

"I am *not* like Lady Whiston!" Lady Pamela interjected indignantly.

"No," her grandfather said candidly. "But you might very well turn out that way, my dear, if you married Babcoke. Not at all sure he can keep you in hand. Now Dalven is another matter. He don't mind pulling you up short when you need to be—saw that today. And the title's a respectable one. Never cared for his grandfather above half, but that's neither here nor there."

"It most certainly is not," said Lady Pamela, "since I am not going to marry either Lord Dalven *or* his grandfather! Grandpapa, how *can* you?"

"Am I to understand, Lord Nevans," Lord Babcoke interrupted with an outraged air, "that you have withdrawn your consent to my marrying Pamela?"

"No, I haven't," said Lord Nevans. "You can marry her if you want to, and if she wants you to. But, good God, man, if you *don't* want to—if you're going to make a piece of work over it every time she lands you in a scrape like this—now is the time to say so, and no niffy-naffy speech-making about honour or obligation to go along with it!"

Lord Babcoke, his one good eye looking quite despairing, said that perhaps if he could talk to Pamela alone—

"Talk to me alone!" Lady Pamela jumped up from her chair, her eyes alight with indignation. "Adolphus, tell me the truth this instant! You *don't* wish to marry me, do you? *Do* you?"

Lord Babcoke attempted a denial, but he was basically a

simple, straightforward man, unskilled in deception. He sought in vain for an elegant way to express his feelings, gave it up, and said truthfully, "No. Not," he added hastily and palliatingly, "if you don't want to."

Epics have been written about the wrath of a woman scorned. Lady Pamela, though a poor subject for an epic, being far too prone to laugh at herself—inexcusable behaviour in a goddess or a queen—did her best to uphold the traditions of her sex at this point by directing a look towards Lord Babcoke that caused him cravenly to turn cat in pan and stammer that he didn't mean—he hadn't meant to say—

"Never mind, Adolphus," said Lady Pamela, with awful forbearance. "We all heard what you said, and I can assure you that I, for one, am happy—very happy, indeed!—to be released from my engagement to you."

In proof of which she proceeded to burst into tears, which greatly alarmed and discomfited Lord Babcoke, though expressing pure rage, as her old nurse, who had suffered through more than one such incident in nursery days, could have told him. And had she been present upon this occasion she would doubtless have dealt with the matter by remarking reprovingly to Lady Pamela that young ladies who lost their tempers never got husbands, and why didn't she sit down now like a good girl and mind her manners?

Lady Pamela, however, being provided with an exclusively male audience, had the satisfaction of seeing her tears produce as devastating an effect as she could have desired, for her grandfather, her brother, and her betrothed—or ex-betrothed—all looked excessively guilty and uncomfortable and began trying in various ineffective but flattering ways to cause her to desist.

Into this agreeable tumult came Carlin's voice. "Now that's quite enough, my girl," it said, with detestable calm. "You know as well as I do that it's only your vanity that's wounded, and it's quite unfair of you to make Babcoke feel like the greatest rogue unhung when you are as happy to be quit of him as he is to be quit of you."

Lady Pamela, with a vengeful hiccup, but drying her eyes with her handkerchief, informed him tersely that he was a monster, who had no feelings of his own nor any conception of anyone else's.

"Oh, I have plenty of feelings," Carlin said, with an odd

glint in his dark eyes, "as I'll let you see at the proper time and in the proper place. At present, though, I think we have all had quite enough high drama for one day, and if you are a sensible girl you will cry friends with Babcoke and let him go home in peace and have his dinner, without enacting him any more Cheltenham tragedies."

Lady Pamela, her wrath now directed entirely away from Lord Babcoke in Carlin's direction, said with great dignity that as far as she was concerned she wished Adolphus very well, and added that, men being what they were, she would doubtless be far better off never to marry at all, which was now her firm intention.

"Oh, yes—for four-and-twenty hours!" Carlin said cheerfully. "I daresay you will have changed your mind by the end of that time."

"Well, if I have, it won't be *you* who has changed it!" said Lady Pamela, with crushing effect. She turned to her grandfather. "I am sure you will understand, Grandpapa, if I go to my chamber now," she continued. "It has been an excessively tiring day, and I believe I shall retire at once."

And with a slight inclination of her head in Lord Babcoke's direction and not so much as a glance in Carlin's she walked out of the room, leaving behind her a pregnant silence, broken at last by Lord Babcoke.

"Well, she's a wonderful girl, but I'd as soon live with a box full of fireworks!" he said with feeling. "Never know when she'll go up with a burst and a shower of sparks! I wouldn't for the world," he said to Lord Nevans, "let her see it, sir, but I really am deuced grateful to you! Had a feeling for some time I'd made the wrong move on the board, but hadn't a notion how to mend matters." He added anxiously, as a sudden thought struck him, "But, good God, it's just occurred to me! You *don't* think, sir, that I've broken her heart?"

Lord Nevans and Lord Wynstanley, who knew—or thought they knew—their Pamela very well, attempted to reassure him, but in spite of themselves sudden horrid and improbable visions of her sitting like patience on a monument, smiling at grief, abruptly assailed them, and even Carlin was conscious of a hollow feeling in the pit of his stomach, which might have come because, like Lord Babcoke, he had not dined; but somehow he did not think that that was it.

Fortunately, at that moment Hadsell, who had been lurking in a quite unbutlerlike way in the hall with a view towards filling in, by fair means, or foul, the gaps of his knowledge about the events of the day, and who had seen Lady Pamela leave the study and go upstairs like an offended Diana, came in unbidden with a decanter of brandy, and the libations that followed made all the gentlemen feel somewhat more cheerful, although inwardly not a great deal less apprehensive of what might happen in the days to come.

Nineteen

The news that Lady Pamela's engagement to Lord Babcoke had been broken off circulated with amazing rapidity through *ton* circles. Lady St. Abbs, who heard of it first of all, was of the opinion—despite her great-nephew's strenuous denial of the authenticity of this version of the event—that he had at last come to his senses as to the inadvisability of marrying Lady Pamela because of his having discovered that she had been behaving in a sinister and peculiar fashion indicating the mental instability Lady St. Abbs had always perceived in the family, and forthwith, as a reward, made a new will in which she named him as the heir to her immense fortune. Lady Whiston, who would have liked to be even more explicit as to Lady Pamela's unusual and reprehensible behaviour, did not dare, having had it impressed upon her by her husband and daughter that it all had something to do with the mysterious necessity for Cedric's making his sudden trip to America, and that if she spoke about it Cedric would be disgraced forever.

As for the unattached male members of the *ton*, they greeted the news with unalloyed satisfaction, and a good many of them, who had been obliged to drown their grief at Lord Babcoke's carrying off the most enchanting girl in London by paying court to less attractive young ladies, basely deserted these lesser beauties to bombard Lord Nevans's house with bouquets and invitations, much to the chagrin of the lesser beauties, some of whom were rather spiteful about the whole affair.

Lady Pamela herself spent almost two whole days, following the evening upon which she and Lord Babcoke had broken off their engagement, in rehearsing the cutting remarks with which she would repulse Carlin when he called in Berkeley Square to make his own offer of marriage to her. Unfortunately for the fruition of these delightful plans, Carlin did not call in Berkeley Square, either to make her an offer of marriage or merely to see her. This naturally made her even angrier with him than she had been before, and on the afternoon of the second day she not only accepted a pressing invitation from the most importunate of her former suitors, the Marqués de Barrera, to drive in the Park in his high-perch phaeton, but also waltzed three times with him that evening at a *ton* party, thus immediately causing rumours to circulate that he had been the reason for her breaking off with Lord Babcoke, and that a marriage would follow as surely as the night the day.

These rumours might have been harmless enough if they had concerned a high-ranking member of the English peerage, most of whom had known Lady Pamela all their lives and were quite aware of how much—or how little—importance was to be placed upon that dashing young lady's manifesting a sudden preference for their company. It was otherwise, however, with the Marqués de Barrera. That gentleman, whose acquaintance with English manners dated only from the period, some six months before, when he had become convinced that England offered the most agreeable place of refuge from the troubles at present afflicting his native land, was not yet sufficiently accustomed to the far freer behaviour of English young ladies not to leap to conclusions that might have been justified in Spain, but were considered quite gothic in these enlightened modern days in London.

Two days after the drive in the Park and the intoxicating series of waltzes, therefore, having been further encouraged by a tête-à-tête in a box at the Opera and two country-dances and the boulanger at Lady Wethered's evening-party, he determined to put his fate to the touch. Lady Pamela had granted him the privilege of escorting her to Lady Maytham's ball that evening, and he was confident that when he returned with her to Berkeley Square he would have the future Marquesa de Barrera on his arm.

How much Lady Pamela knew of these intentions is debatable, but the thought had indubitably crossed her mind, which was for some reason in a most unwonted state of turmoil and depression during this time, that if one married a handsome Spaniard who was deeply devoted to one, one might go to live on the Continent, accept his devotion with the sad complaisance of a heart that would never be touched again, and be free forever from the disagreeable necessity of meeting by chance Scottish peers whom one detested at *ton* parties or in the Park.

Chance, incidentally, had been kind to her thus far: neither in the Park nor at the *ton* parties she had attended had she had the least glimpse of Lord Dalven. Perhaps, she thought—unaccountably not with all the satisfaction this reflection should have caused her—he had gone back to Scotland, or resumed his position as coachman on the *Lightning*.

But that neither of these possibilities accorded with fact she was made aware the instant she stepped inside Lady Maytham's spacious saloon on the evening of that lady's ball, for the first person her eyes fell upon there was Carlin.

He was engaged in conversation at the moment with Lady St. Abbs, which compounded the misfortune in Lady Pamela's eyes. For Lady St. Abbs, with a reputation for being the most disagreeable woman in London, could do and say things that no one else could, and she at once proceeded to do and say them.

"Hah! Pamela!" she said. "Come here, gel. Haven't seen you since you broke off with my great-nevvy Babcoke. I say, come here, gel!" she reiterated, pounding her stick upon the floor as Lady Pamela did not move. "I want to hear your version of the affair. Was it you cried off or was it he?"

"It was both of us," said Lady Pamela, advancing reluctantly and bestowing a cool nod upon Carlin, who returned a very civil bow but with a look of amusement upon his dark face that at once set her hackles up. "We mutually agreed that we should not suit," she continued grandly, to Lady St. Abbs, and would have moved off, had not Lady St. Abbs said to her sharply, "I ain't through yet, miss. You can't play ducks and drakes with *my* great-nevvy and walk off with your nose in the air before I Get to the Bottom of this!"

Lady Pamela, rashly meeting Carlin's eyes as this phrase was uttered, almost had the giggles, but she withdrew her own eyes quickly from this dangerous contact and the Marqués leapt into the breach by saying in a severe voice that he imagined the subject must be painful to Lady Pamela and might best be dropped. He was a tall, spare man with an excellent though slightly overdignified carriage, perhaps befitting the ribbons of the awe-inspiring orders he wore; but Lady St. Abbs, who never submitted to being condescended to and had had several notable passages at arms with the Prince Regent himself, at once went on the attack.

"Painful!" she said, with her cackling laugh. "For her! You're a fool if you believe that, Marqués, is all I can say. Wait till your own turn comes, and then tell me who it's painful for—him or her! And I must say," she added, looking up spitefully at the Marqués's face, now rigid with disapproval, "that if I'm to credit what I hear, you're next in line for the honour. I thought it might be Dalven, but it seems he's shabbed off. Don't fancy bein' made a bobbing-block of like my great-nevvy, I daresay. Showed more sense than I'd have expected of him. If you're wise, you'll take a leaf from his book, my lad."

The Marqués, drawing upon his accumulated heritage of Castilian courtesy, restrained himself with a superhuman effort from audibly resenting this speech, made a very stiff bow to Lady St. Abbs, and marched off with Lady Pamela on his arm.

As soon as they were out of hearing, Lady Pamela, to whose face Lady St. Abbs' words had brought a distinct flush, said warmly, "What a detestable woman she is!"

"*Odiosa!*" agreed the Marqués, whose thin cheeks were also wearing a slight red colour. "Insupportable to me to hear you so maligned, Lady Pamela! It makes—how do you express it?—the blood to boil!"

And he gazed down at her with such a hungry glare of protective indignation that Lady Pamela, hastily mastering her own resentment, said soothingly, "Yes, yes, but it does not really signify, you know. Had we not better join the set? That is, if you meant what you said about our having this first dance together."

The Marqués said fervently not only the first, but also the second and third and as many more as she would grant him, but following this effusion was obliged to content himself with more conventionally expressed gallantries, as it was difficult to make ardent love to a lady while engaging in the pleasant intricacies of a country-dance—a fact that Lady Pamela had counted on in reminding him of his request to be allowed to stand up with her. However, her prejudice against this form of activity on the Marqués's part suffered a marked diminution when she observed that Carlin had also joined the set with one of the season's debutantes, a very pretty blonde in a white crape gown trimmed with velvet ribbons, with whom he appeared to be carrying on a quite agreeable flirtation.

"In *my* country," she awoke to hear the Marqués pronouncing, "a lady of beauty and high birth is cherished like an exquisite flower. *Como una flor exquisita,*" he added for emphasis, causing Lady Pamela, upon whom a feeling of depression had suddenly and unaccountably descended, to wonder whether if one lived in Spain and heard only Spanish one might not perhaps learn to consider speeches like that not quite so silly. Certainly being called *"una flor exquisita"* for some reason sounded much more sensible than being called "an exquisite flower" when one rode to hounds and enjoyed a robust appetite. And she lost herself so thoroughly in a rather gloomy vision of a future in which she would live in Spain, wear black velvet and a ruff like a Velasquez noblewoman, and daily enjoy being called *"una flor exquisita"* by the Marqués, that she absentmindedly agreed to stand up for a second set of country-dances with him.

Carlin promptly joined the set with a second debutante, this one Titian-haired, in blue gauze over satin. What was more, when Lady Pamela went down the dance he remarked to her, "Doing it much too brown, my girl!"—and had the effrontery to grin at her.

This was too much, and when the Marqués suggested meaningly, at the end of the set, "You are fatigued, *querida!* Come! We shall repose ourselves!"—"We shall indeed!" said Lady Pamela. And with a defiant glance at Carlin she walked off with the Marqués into one of the anterooms, conveniently dimly lighted—for Lady Maytham was very broad-minded—for the convenience of couples seeking respite from the brilliant bustle of the ball.

To the Marqués, opportunity suggested action, immediate action. Lady Pamela, turning from the frivolous gilded mirror over the fashionable two-storeyed mantelpiece where she had paused to push a vagrant black curl into place, found him already upon his knees before her.

"Querida! Amor!" he exclaimed. "Say it is true—what I have hoped, what I have dreamed! You will be mine! You will be my wife, my bride!"

Without waiting for a reply, he leapt to his feet and fervently clasped her in his arms.

"Say you are mine! I do not leave this room until you do!

Without you, life is nothing! With you—ah, with you, what bliss, what joy!"

He kissed her with an unexpected heartiness, the grandee suddenly quite forgotten. *Oh, dear! What shall I do now?* thought Lady Pamela in despair. *I can't go about refusing people all my life! And that odious Carlin obviously has no intention—*

"Very well! I'll be yours!" she said determinedly, as clearly as she could, what with being kissed violently every few seconds. And at that precise moment Carlin walked into the room.

"Here! What's this?" he enquired pleasantly.

The Marqués spun around, releasing Lady Pamela.

"Lord Dalven!" he said reproachfully. "A thousand pardons, but—but you interrupt! Do you not see that we are engaged?"

"Do you mean by that," said Carlin, ignoring the hint and crossing the little room in a few long strides to the mantelpiece, against which he comfortably leaned his big shoulders, "that you are merely occupied, or that you are engaged in the matrimonial sense? Because if it is the latter—"

"Yes, yes! It is, as you say, the latter," replied the Marqués, turning a proud, beaming gaze upon Lady Pamela. "Lady Pamela has this moment consented to be my wife!"

Carlin too looked at Lady Pamela, who looked back at him pertinaciously.

"Yes, I have!" she said. "I shall go to Spain to live, and never come back to England again!"

Carlin received this piece of news with the greatest equanimity. "What a tiresome girl you are, my love!" he merely remarked. "Obviously it is time I took you in hand, for it is quite apparent that someone must break you of this unfortunate habit you seem to have of getting engaged to men you don't really wish to marry." He turned to the Marqués and spoke a few words to him in Spanish.

"But no!" exclaimed the Marqués, also in Spanish. He turned a thunderstruck gaze upon Lady Pamela. "I do not believe it!"

"Unfortunate, since it is the truth!" said Carlin politely.

A torrent of Spanish interrupted him. The Marqués first spoke scornfully; then, as the civil expression upon Carlin's face remained unmoved, he began to storm up and down the room, loosing such a flood of impassioned language upon

Carlin's head that Lady Pamela, who understood not a word of what was being said, finally could bear it no longer and demanded of Carlin, "What did you *say* to him?"

"Only that you are going to marry me," said Carlin calmly.

The Marqués, hearing the odious words repeated, stopped storming and looked at Carlin with a proud, contemptuous gaze.

"*Una mentira!* A lie!" he said, and snapped his fingers.

"Is it?" said Carlin. He looked at Lady Pamela and there was a light in his eyes—not quite mocking, not quite tender—that she had never seen there before, a light that made her pulses suddenly leap. "Is it, my love?"

"N-no," said Lady Pamela, her own eyes held, as if hypnotised, by that light.

She might have said more, but the thunder of the Marqués's voice cut her short.

"*No!* You tell me—*you!*—that you are betrothed to this man?"

Lady Pamela looked at him contritely. "I am dreadfully sorry," she said, "but I—I really rather think I am. That is, if he—"

"Yes, I do!" said Carlin hastily. "I have! I am!—or whatever the affirmative answer is to what you were about to say. Good God, don't start him off again!"

"But I wasn't—"

"Yes, you were! Tell him in unequivocal terms that you are going to marry me and put him out of his misery! And he is the *last* man you are to get engaged to, do you understand? Didn't I have enough trouble getting you *un*engaged from Babcoke without your going and doing it again the moment my back was turned,"

"It wasn't a moment!" said Lady Pamela indignantly. "It was four whole days! You never came near me—"

"If I had, you would have snapped my nose off and you know it!" said Carlin. "I had to give you a *little* time to cool off!"

The Marqués, a bewildered auditor to this unloverlike exchange, looked at Lady Pamela as if she had been a female apparition in a peculiarly incomprehensible nightmare.

"Englishwomen!" he ejaculated, flinging out both his hands in a despairing gesture. "I do not understand—"

"No, of course you don't," said Lady Pamela soothingly.

"We are all quite, quite mad! And now, dear Marqués, don't you think you would like to go and have an ice, or a glass of champagne, or—or a lobster patty, for I think Lord Dalven has something of *particular* importance to say to me."

The Marqués, still muttering in Spanish, gave her a dark glance, bowed formally, and stalked forbiddingly out of the room. Lady Pamela demurely raised her eyes to Carlin's.

"And now—?" she said expectantly.

Carlin grinned at her amiably. "My love," he said, "I told you once that at the proper time and place I should let you see what my feelings were. This, however, is neither."

"The Marqués didn't appear to think so," said Lady Pamela, pensively playing with her fan. "And I am sure that *his* ideas of propriety are much nicer than yours."

"Ah, but then the Marqués fancied himself in love," Carlin reminded her calmly, a gleam in his dark eyes beneath the indifferently dropped lids.

Lady Pamela's own eyes involuntarily flew to his. "Oh!" she said. "And you don't—?"

"No," said Carlin. The indifferent lids lifted abruptly and she saw the dark eyes with the light in them that had so disturbed her while the Marqués had still been in the room. "I don't *fancy* myself in love," he said, and suddenly jerked her so roughly into his arms that she gasped, the fan dropping from her hand. "I *am* in love, you enchanting, maddening little termagant!" he said, kissing her in a way that could leave small doubt of this fact in her mind. "I've been in love with you—God help me!—ever since I first clapped eyes on you in the inn-yard at Hungerford and you looked down your disdainful, delightful nose at me!"

Conversation was once more interrupted at this moment, but when Lady Pamela could speak again she asked reasonably, "Then why didn't you tell me so before?"

A laugh shook Carlin. "Before! When I've known you for less than two weeks as it is, and for a good part of that time you thought me a penniless fellow who had come down in the world to the point of being obliged to drive a coach for a living!"

"You were a very good coachman," said Lady Pamela firmly, which compliment so unmanned its recipient that he felt constrained to respond to it in a manner that left his beloved not only breathless but also a trifle bruised and with her head in a bewildering whirl.

Upon this scene in toddled Lady St. Abbs.

"Well!" she exclaimed, her eyes snapping with malignant delight at the interesting sight of Lady Pamela Frayne being ruthlessly and ardently kissed by the ordinarily coolly composed Lord Dalven. "So this is what you are up to! I thought to myself, when I saw the poor Marqués come stumblin' out of here lookin' as mad as Bedlam, *That girl is up to something'—*"

"How very right you are, Lady St. Abbs," said Carlin, rapidly resuming his normal appearance, though there was still a most unusual light in his eyes. "As a matter of fact, she has been. Up to something, that is. If you can call getting engaged to me something—"

"*I* call it scandalous," said Lady St. Abbs, thumping her stick for emphasis upon the floor. "She's only just got herself *un*engaged from Babcoke. How d'ye think this will make *him* feel?"

"Grateful, I should imagine," said Carlin equably, which caused Lady St. Abbs to utter her cackling laugh.

"Well, he ought to be, if he ain't!" she agreed. "Had a very narrow escape, that boy. And so, I gather, had the Marqués." She looked at Carlin almost sympathetically. "But you, Dalven," she said, "you're for it now, ain't you? I wonder if you know what you're lettin' yourself in for!"

"I do," said Carlin, with something oddly vibrant in his voice, his hand seeking and finding Lady Pamela's. "And now, Lady St. Abbs," he went on, "if you don't mind—You *did* interrupt us, you know, and I am very much afraid that I hadn't quite finished—"

"Pshaw!" said Lady St. Abbs, scornfully. "I've seen kissin' before, Dalven! But I'll go! I'll go!"

And she turned and toddled out of the room, leaning on her stick, like a malignant fairy who had suddenly decided to be kind—at which point the interrupted proceedings went on quite as satisfactorily as before, so that it was a long while indeed before Lady Pamela and Lord Dalven rejoined the ball, where, inevitably, they conducted themselves in such a manner that everyone present came to the astounding conclusion that, for once, Lady St. Abbs had been speaking nothing but the truth when she had announced that there were wedding bells in the air.